MARRY MERRY MARY CHRISTMAS?

MARRY MERRY MARY CHRISTMAS?

P. G. WHEATLEY

Gourd Head & Grant Publishing

CONTENTS

To Sandy, Grace, and Mary who made my time at Fort Lewis so magical, and to my wife
who made the rest of my life so wonderful

GREETINGS

Hi There,

Thanks for joining me. You can blame this story on Nina Lincoln Searcy of Jacksonville, Florida. She wrote a highly accurate and well researched book about all the Wheatleys who lived from the beginning of time until 1938. I was born in 1939. How unfair is life? I missed the cut by three years.

However, it got me to thinking about the phrase, "WHAT AM I, CHOPPED LIVER?" which means, "Don't I count?"

(PSST! This particular paragraph is what's called an "aside") Don't tell anybody, but I hate chopped liver, even though I do feel sorry for it. I don't like un-chopped liver either, and I don't have to feel sorry for that one. I haven't **ever** cared for liver in **any** form. My first encounter with the horrible stuff was at the tender age of six. My parents made me stay at the table until I finished every bit of my dinner. It took a while, but I managed to get it all down. I was seven when I got up from the table. Can you imagine the cruelty of parents who would make their child sit at the table for three years?

WHAT AM I? I AM BACON! I want the world to know that I walked, skipped, square danced and sizzled across this planet wearing red socks and tasting good. No little kid had to ever sit at the table for four years because he didn't like bacon.

As things are now, my great great grandchildren and those that follow them will never have the joy of knowing me or my wonderful wife personally. And that bothers me. To quote that great English philosopher of the Hundred Acre Wood, Edwin E. Pooh, "Oh Bother."

I am not claiming this report is as accurate as Nina's, but that is her fault. She should have inspired me before my Alzheimer's kicked in. I believe you can learn as much about a person by palling around with them as by studying them in a text book.

HEY! I heard that snicker when I wrote **pal-ling around**. Well how would you spell it? I tried several ways and they all looked wrong: paling around, palling around. HOWEVER I would like to think you can learn as much or more about me by reading what I think and what I write about what I **see**...uh...what I **saw**. (sigh) My life has been a **teeter totter** with many **ups** and **downs**. Just think of this as a happy visit with a fun, but not too bright, guy who wants to be your friend.

My life changed for the better one Christmas long ago, and I would like to share that experience with you. This not only a FAMILY HISTORY, but a LOVE STORY, A CHRISTMAS STORY, and a jolly good visit.

Yours (71%) truly,

Pete

P.S. Please struggle through the "Ward" which comes next. It's not CHOPPED LIVER, or BACON, but it will help you keep the players straight and give you a place to come back to if confused. Plus, it will give us the opportunity to get to know each other better.

'WARD

This is my first attempt at writing a book, and I have a question about one of the first parts of a book. I'm talking about the part that comes before the main story kicks into gear. Is it spelled "forward" of "foreward"? I'll wait while you write down your answer.

I was tempted to call the "Forward" the "Backward" because this happened to me at Christmas almost 60 years ago. What If I just call it the "Ward" and let you decide Ward's first of last name? (Hint: the answer is not "Cleaver," "den," "Awk" or "Cow," although a case could be made for the last one.)

I forgot to ask. Did you spell it correctly?

I bet you think I don't know that the correct spelling is "foreword." Well, I didn't know it half an hour ago, but I do know now. However, changing it now would ruin my hints, so I'm not going to. Beaver's dad was not "Word" Cleaver. The boss of the prison is not the "worden" I have never heard anything referred to as "awkword" unless it is the cry of some birds of prey. And I am afraid there is no such thing as "cow-word." I guess a case might be made for "moo."

What you are witnessing here right now, is history in the making: the formation of a book part called the "ward." In the "ward" the writers can jolly well write anything they ding dong please which they think will help the reader.

The story is fictionally true: probably **71%**. (Can a story be 71% true and call itself non-fiction?) I have been told that is a "no no." I say it is a "yes yes." They argue it is like being a little bit pregnant. They say even if you are just a little bit (itzy-bitzy spermsywormzy) pregnant, YOU - ARE - PREGNANT. By the way, I am not pregnant, just a little over weight, and thank you so much for noticing... and commenting. I hope you know you just blew it. There will be no Christmas present under the tree with your name on it from me for you this year.

The remaining **79%** has been fictionally tweaked to make it more interesting and fun for you the reader.

("What a nice guy," says you.)

("Ah shucks," says I modestly.)

The story has been written from the perspective of Pete. Why? Because I am Pete, (Peter Grant - Not Pregnant- Wheatley, at your service.) and I am telling my story.

You will have to forgive me for jumping back and forth from third person to first person. As I am telling the story, I recall some of the events as they actually happened, and suddenly I find myself in the first parson living it again.

After seeing how great I am with numbers, I am sure you will be shocked to learn that I was not a math major at Fort Lewis College... or for that matter at Colorado State University, University of Alaska, Glendale Junior College, Glendale High School, Clark Jr. High School, La Crescenta Elementary School, Edison Elementary School, Romper Room, OR Harvard had they accepted me instead of laughing themselves silly when I applied. I am still harboring a grudge about that. BOO HARVARD! YOU'RE CHOPPED LIVER.

I have been told that several of these august earlier centers of my learning have taken out restraining orders to keep me from returning, or even so much as putting my big toe on their property.

My first grade teacher, Mrs. Reardon, told my mother at a teacher conference for my little brother three years after I had been in her class, "When I learned I had another Wheatley, I went home and cried." I think the tears were caused as much by the thought of butting heads with my dad again as anything else. It was early enough in my educational experience that he was still blaming the teacher and not the student. (By the time I reached the third grade, that misconception was ancient history.) Then Mrs. Reardon told Mom, Alan may be my favorite student **ever**." And that was saying something because she had had Gordon Hess as a student. I know because he was in the same class I was in.

Gordon Hess was one of the kindest, nicest persons I ever knew. He was a great athlete (the star of our high school football team). He was a top student. He held many elected offices in school. He was a fine singer and a Rotary Club's Student of the Month. He was also a member of the school patrol that enforced the rules and stood up to the bad guys. My brother Alan was a trouble making, sneaky, tattle-telling, undignified, little critter, so pay no attention to what Mrs. Reardon said. Do you know that Alan's first complete sentence was "Pete hit me."? (This was a lie. I was three miles away at a homeless shelter helping to feed the poor.) The use of a complete sentence earned him undo praise and me a warm, glowing feeling in a lower posterior part of my body.

BUTT it was really quite nice and took a lot of pressure off me to have Alan following and restoring the Wheatley good name.

I love math. I'm great at math. I just don't get the same answers that everybody else does. Albert Einstein used to come to me when he was having math problems with some of his formulas. (This paragraph is part of the 79% I told you about 10 paragraphs ago.) I really hated it when Al would come around because he would not only expect me to solve his math problems and help him with his homework, he'd want to borrow my comb. It never came back in the same shape as when he borrowed it.

The names in my story have been changed, not just to protect the innocent, but out of fear because some of the people are still alive, and all that are can probably whip me. I suspect a few might even be members of the Mafia, or are rich and influential dudes and dudettes who could afford to hire...uh...a hit person. (Did you catch that use of "person" instead of "man"? I am both politically correct and a 'fraidy cat.)

Mary Louise Christmas is a made up name and sounds much more descriptive of the once young lady than did her maiden name, Gertrude Matilda Plushbottom of the Chicago Plushbottoms. (Just kidding, Gert.) It gives me the opportunity to create such a clever title. I don't believer the title "Have a Hurdy Gurdy Christmas" (though) musical) is in the same class as "Marry Merry Mary Christmas?"

MaDonna Grace Cousins is a partially made up name. She doesn't deserve to be depicted as a saint or a sinner. But I imagine she is much more likely to have found someone who is a teacher than someone who is a preacher. And if that lucky guy is still living, I know he loves her with all his heart.

A third made-up name is **Sandy Anita Fay Sullivan.** I made up that name because she reminds me of a famous thoroughbred's greatest triumph. Whereas Mary was short, blond and outgoing and Grace was tall, quiet, dark haired, and shy, Sandy was right in the middle in all of those categories. She had light brown hair that almost looked red when the sun hit it just right. She was average height and liked by nearly everybody, even though not striving to be popular or part of the in crowd.

My first trimester I boarded in town and only went on campus to study or attend classes. Sandy was a good student, and we had several of the same classes, because good friends and often studied together, especially for tests. I would have to say she became my only real on-campus friend that first trimester. In a playful moment, she nicknamed me Petey-Pie, which got shortened to "Pie." I retaliated by calling her "Silky," which got shortened to "Silk." I chose this nickname because of another famous Sullivan: the race horse known for coming from last place to first. Silky Sullivan never seemed interested in the race until it was half over. Then he would decide he was Man O' War.

I only saw him race once. It was the 1958 Santa Anita Derby. It might have been the greatest horse racing come back in history. When the other horses left the starting gate, Silky was still there. He reminded me of my wife admiring her hooves (AKA fingernails) after a manicure. Then he decided to join some of his horsey friends who were merrily galloping along at the rear of the pack. His jockey, a Mr. William Lee Shoemaker, better known as Willie, shouted/whispered something in his ear. The horse shouter/whisperer/jockey never revealed what he said, but I can read lips. It was either "glue factory" or "dog food." I recommend you go to YouTube and watch the 1958 Santa Anita Derby.

Another made-up name is a student who came from Massachusetts: **William Bradford Bentley the Third** claimed his ancestors came to America on the Mayflower, in 1620, traveling in first class. It was he who introduced me to Mary, in a manner of speaking. Tom and I just called him Boston Billy or Boston Belly. (To my best recollection, although he came to Fort Lewis thinking he would be the starting quarterback all four years, I don't remember William Bradford Bentley the third ever getting into a game.)

Then there's the Colorado bully: **Eric "The Derrick" Meany**. He is no longer with us, Bless His Heart. So, I am no longer afraid of him. "Hey Eric Your mom wears combat boots." (Back in the 40's when I started school that was a biggie in the insult department.) "Hey Eric, NA NA NAH NA NA NAH." (That was pretty devastating too.)

During that time and earlier, before television when games were mainly broadcast on the radio, many of the good players had nicknames like Red "The Galloping Ghost" Grange (halfback); Lou "The Toe" Groza (placekicker); Elroy "Crazy Legs" Hirsch (end); David "Deacon" Jones (defensive end); Eric "The Derrick" Meany (linebacker); and Tom "Old 98" Harmon (halfback).

Gravel Gertie was a crazy old widow who lived alone in a gravel pit. She married a seedy looking character named B. O.

Plenty. They were friends of Dick Tracy a detective in newspaper comics.

Molly Malone was a fish monger in the 1800's in Dublin, Ireland. She would push her cart through the streets broad and narrow crying, "Cockles and mussels, alive, alive oh!" By night she would sell her beauty to strangers to make enough to survive. A ballad was written about her. My favorite rendition is by Burl Ives.

Granny Clampett was the feisty old mother-in-law of Jed in the television hit show, "The Beverly Hillbillies." She looked to be in her late 80's.

Tugboat Annie was the scruffy looking skipper of a tugboat in Puget Sound. She looked to be in her 60's and was a big woman.

Post Toasties: a breakfast cereal made by the Post Company. It was their version of cornflakes. Discontinued in 2016.

Wheaties: the breakfast of Champions. Whole grain cereal. Still going.

My brother and I were taught to respect our elders and use their titles such as "Mr.", "Mrs.", "Sargent," "Sir," "Mam," etc. My wife's family let the kids address the adult's using first names like Tom, Dick and Mary. That is why, as an example, you might see the same person referred to in different ways, e.g., Grant, Pete, General, Alpha Male, God's Gift, etc.

Before leaving the subject of names, I want to complete it by saying most of the names are the real names of real people who could be doing what I said they did...or didn't. If I couldn't remember the real name, I picked one out of the list of people I have met and admired over my lifetime. The real Dr. H. was a professor and a close friend of mine at the University of Alaska. If you happen to come across your name doing something you couldn't possibly have done, shoot me a note (NOTE, not a bullet) or a text saying, "I CAUGHT-CHA & GOT-CHA---on page_____ I never _____."

I know. That is as clear as mud. I think that needs an example: I CAUGHT-CHA & GOT-CHA---On page 71 you said I was killed at the Alamo. That is a lie. --Elton John (I'm sorry, Elton. Nobody is perfect. By any chance were you ever on the Lusitania? --Pete)

The name of the Fort Lewis College yearbook is "Katzima." I was told that this is an Acoma Indian word meaning "Enchanted Mesa." During my two years at Fort Lewis, I found it to be an enchanted mesa, and I imagine and hope it still is. The white man's word for the mesa was Reservoir Hill: informative, but (Yawn) BORING! I like the sound of Katzima much better, even if it turns out to mean "the cat sees ma or seize ma."

In case you're interested, the answer to the crossword puzzle, **#36 across** is "colonoscopy." Every good Christmas story should have at least one, don't you think? This reference at one time could be found on Page 178 in Chapter 21.

Before we start, I would like to apologize for the whole male gender. At a certain age, we sometimes find our language, motivation and actions a little rougher and hormone generated than what would seem appropriate, and we aren't nearly as holy or proper as when we reach our 70's, a milestone in my rearview mirror.

I hope you enjoy my story. Please, don't speed-read through it. You'll miss so many of the fun little nuances and hints I put in to keep you on your toes, e.g. the different meanings and spellings of the sound "MARE'EE" in the title. I have been told that reading what I write out loud adds to the enjoyment. AND please don't be mad at me for moving things around timewise, so I could fit them into this particular two week period.

I have always wanted to start a story with the words: "Once upon a time." This may be my last chance, so here comes a Christmas fairy tale hopping down the funny trail. ALL ABOARD! (I just threw that in because I love train.)

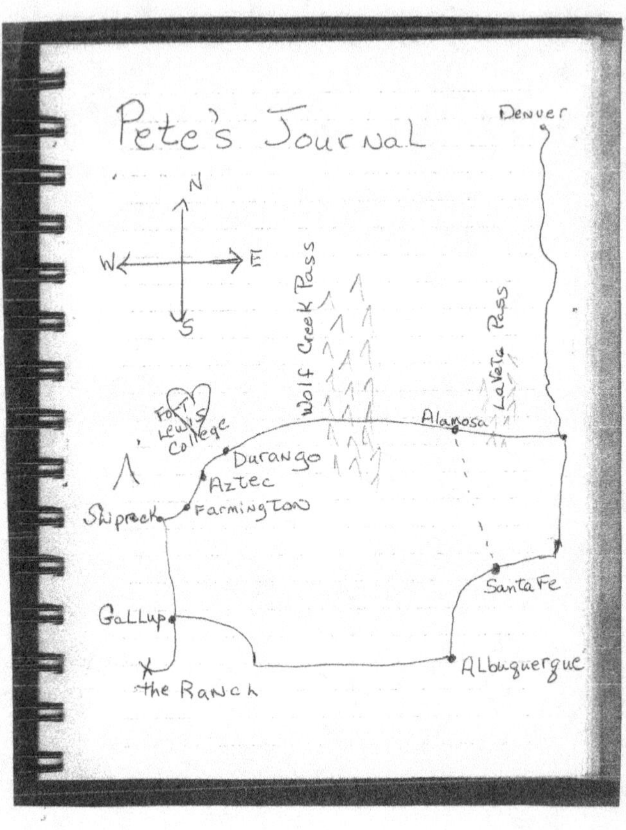

Pete's Journal
N
W
E
S
Denver
Wolf Creek Pass
LaVeta Pass
Fort Lewis College
Durango
Aztec
Farmington
Shiprock
Alamosa
Santa Fe
Gallup
Albuquerque
the Ranch

CHAPTER 1

It began in the enchanted land.

Once upon a time, long long ago, in a faraway land called Durango, there was a wonderful little college called Fort Lewis.

The snow fell silently upon the mesa that the Indians call Katzima. Katzima means enchanted. Large snowflakes the size of half dollars were gently floating down and altering the landscape on the little college campus and town below, changing them from winter brown to winter white. Fort Lewis College is perched on the edge of the enchanted mesa overlooking the small western community of Durango, Colorado. One more day of finals and the last of the students will rush home to spend Christmas with their family and friends.

The time is somewhere between two and four in the morning. Only a solitary single light shines from the second floor of a boy's dorm. In this room, at a desk, sits a sleepy eyed student trying to force his brain to think and his eyes to focus. It is obvious to him he is losing the battle and falling asleep. Suddenly, in desperation, he jumps up from his desk and rushes out into the cold night. He stands alone under the falling snow breathing in the freezing night air until he is shaking uncontrollably. His teeth are chattering as he returns to his desk. A movement from the other side of the room and a soft moan draws his attention.

"I hope I didn't disturb you," he apologizes.

There is no response. He goes back to his books, but it is not long before he starts losing his battle with sleep again. He lays his head on the desk and his eyes close. Then another moan from across the room wakens him, he forces his eyes open and looks into the face of the prettiest girl on campus. She smiles at him seductively, but does not speak.

"Good morning, Mary. I promise, just two more chapters and I'll turn out the light. By the way, did I mention you look particularly beautiful tonight?"

Her expression never wavered, but she continued to smile temptingly and invitingly from across the room. Sometimes, not speaking is a more effective way of communicating.

"This is a boy's dorm. What would your mother think if she knew you were here?"

His little speech had no effect on her because . . .

Well, because Pete was talking to a photograph taped on his roommate's wall. Benny fancied himself as a great photographer and when Pete first met him, Benny introduced himself as the "Photographer Laureate" of Colorado. Benny had dedicated the wall on his side of the room to pictures he had taken of the most beautiful girls on campus. The pictures were displayed in the shape of a pyramid, and the one on the top, the apex, the place of honor, was held by Mary Louise Christmas. Pete's friend Sandy was in the center of the pyramid and Grace was absent only because Benny didn't allow any freshmen to be part of his Pyramid of Beauty.

"Mary," Pete scolded the picture affectionately, "I am trying to study and I can't do it with you looking at me like that." He wondered how Benny coaxed Mary to look at the camera so seductively. He got up from his desk and walked over to the wall. He reached up for the picture that was in the Number One position, took it down, and set it gently on Benny's desk. None of the other pictures, though all beauties, had proved a distraction, or conjured up memories of last summer, so they were allowed to stay.

He glanced enviously at his roommate snoring soundly. Benny had promised to stay up with him all night studying for the test. That is, after he got back from his date with Patricia. When he got back, he fell asleep after 15 minutes. He was always making glorious plans to study and not following through with them. Benny was smart enough, but not motivated enough, and it would be a miracle if he did not flunk out.

Pete was bordering between an "A" and a "B" in this class and the final exam would determine which. He had a shot at straight "A's," a feat he had never accomplished in his whole academic career. His younger brother always got them. Well, not always. Once in the 8th grade Alan got two "B's" and was so upset, Pete set up a suicide watch and warned his parents not to let Alan get too close to any sharp objects. Alan was quite disappointed that his parent's hadn't taken up Pete's suggestion to sue the school district and the two teachers. Pete was joking. Alan wasn't. Maybe that was the root of Pete's trouble. His brother was so gifted that Pete had never been able to measure up. For a long time he had given up even trying. He told himself that he was competing against himself and the other students, but deep down, he knew better.

The pages blurred before his eyes and he was making silly mistakes. But for some reason he could not stop this useless attempt to cram more facts into his tired brain. Learning had never come easy to him, but he vowed to study until it was time to leave for the test. Five minutes later he was fast asleep with his head on the desk, and it looked like once again the fickle finger of fate had intervened to thwart him at the last moment.

His next conscious thought was Benny shaking him and saying some nonsense about Pete needed to take a cold shower to wake up. Pete got up from the desk and managed to make it as far as the bed before collapsing. The next thing he remembered was Benny shaking him again and saying something about going for breakfast. Pete said, "Go ahead, I'll meet you at the cafeteria."

Benny returned from the cafeteria to see his roomie fast asleep, on his back, in the bed, and snoring loudly. Benny had set the wind-up alarm to go off at seven before leaving for breakfast. He could tell it had gone off because the windup key for the alarm was unwound. The alarm had not been turned off. Pete must have slept through it.

Benny muttered something about desperate times call for desperate measures. He turned and went back outside, scooped up a handful of the fresh snow, returned, crept up to the bed, pulled back the waistbands of Pete's sweatpants and jockey shorts, then slammed the snow home. If God had been listening for the next 15 seconds he would have heard the snap of the waist bands, the screams and howls of the sleeper, then running footsteps and slamming of the door by the persistent roommate. Mission accomplished: Pete was awake.

There is no doubt that if Benny hadn't been so persistent, Pete would have missed and flunked the test that was supposed to be a third of the grade. If a student was late, Dr. H. would tear up his test and give him a zero or set up a time for the student to take a makeup test with different and usually harder set of questions. Doc had served in two wars and had no sympathy for those who didn't make the effort to be on time and do their best.

CHAPTER 2

Test Tickles

The walk over to the class was bitterly cold. The December north wind seemed intent on freezing the marrow in the bones of those foolish enough to be out and about. For Pete's sake (usually an expression of annoyance) this was a blessing. He was now awake and staying awake. He walked funny because of a handful of snow which had been slammed into his mid region with twice the force necessary. With the exception of his puffy eyes, he thought he was ready. In fact, he was confident, verging on being over confident. With each step this feeling grew stronger. He had put in the hours, more hours than anybody, and he knew this professor graded on the curve.

The professor was watching the room as the proctors passed out the papers. There was a message scribbled on the chalkboard. It instructed them to take every other seat in every other row. They were to write their names on the first page of the test and then turn it face down until instructed to start. The test consisted of several full pages stapled together.

Pete chose a seat in the front row as close to where the professor was sitting as possible. He did not wish to be drawn into any cheating conspiracies or the appearance of such. This professor had a reputation for ripping up the tests of anyone caught cheating, giving them an "F" and recommending expulsion. Pete knew there would be no whispered requests for help or cheating down in Row One.

Row One was where the "A" students would choose to sit. He looked down the row to check out his competition. Each position had an empty seat on each side. One position away sat his friend Sandy Sullivan, the first good friend he made on campus. She waved at him as he sat down. And on the other side of Sandy sat the dreaded S. C. (Susan Smith) from Southern California, looking down her nose at the mere mortals in the room.

So far, no surprises . . . until . . . No . . . it couldn't be . . . But it was . . . Benny. *Oh Gawd, what is he doing here in the front row,* Pete thought. Benny's only hope of even getting a "D" on this quiz would be divine intervention, that would be right up there with Moses parting the Red Sea and conversations with burning bushes. God might even have to add a chapter to the Bible if Benny passed the test.

Involuntarily, he cried out. "OH NO." Heads turned in his direction. He giggled. ***That** was embarrassing. What was happening to him? He had never giggled in his life. Girls giggled, not men.* It had to be the lack of sleep. "Sorry," he said. "I thought I . . . I . . . I (He struggled for a reason.) . . . saw a spider on the seat." He pointed at the empty seat between him and Sandy.

Sandy jumped up and started looking around her seat. Apparently she did not like spiders.

"Was it a big spider?" asked the professor trying to be funny. He was in a jolly mood. "Would you like one of my proctors to smash it for you?"

"No Sir." Quite a few laughed.

"Would you like to sit somewhere else?"

"Yes Sir."

"Where, Sir?" said the professor imitating Pete's voice. That got quite a few good chuckles.

"Honolulu, Sir." That got a bigger laugh than his, so the professor decided to call a halt to the interplay. He looked at his watch, "Five minutes to go. No more talking."

At three minutes to go Sandy jumped up and slammed her overshoe on the desk between her and Pete. It made a loud BANG startling nearly everyone in the now quiet room, including the professor. "WHAT THE . . . !" he shouted, catching himself in time not to swear.

"Got him, Sir." Sandy called out. "That spider didn't know who he was messing with."

"Thank you Miss Sullivan."

She smiled and winked at Pete as she put her overshoe back on.

Pete winked back. He loved this girl. She always had his back. Looking past Sandy he could see Denny calmly sitting there with a smile on his face like the Cheshire cat from Alice in Wonderland. *I bet he's found some way to pass this test,* Pete thought.

The seat behind Benny was empty, as was that whole row because of the instructions on the board. Two rows behind Benny stood Mary. She had just come into the room and was taking off her coat. It was the coat with the fur around the hood which framed her face so beautifully. Her face was pink from the cold outside, and she looked lovely beyond words. Underneath her coat, she was wearing a big fluffy, soft-looking, pink sweater.

Pete felt his heart skip a beat, then rush to catch up, then skip another couple of beats and rush to catch up. He was afraid everyone in the auditorium could hear it. *"Beat still my foolish heart,"* he quoted from he knew not whom in his brain. He thought she was easily the prettiest girl on campus; had the best personality, was the most popular, and most dated and most desired by the BMOCS (BIG MEN ON CAMPUS). In his mind, eighty percent of the men on campus were in love with her, and the other thirty percent would have jumped through hoops for her had she turned her charms on them. (I did tell you that math was not my best subject. Didn't I?) He himself had fallen into that category last summer. He had seen her turn that charm on one man after another to get whatever she wanted. With the girls on campus her popularity was not so unanimously favorable. Pete continued to watch her out of the corner of his eye while pretending to look straight ahead.

Her coat was on the seat next to her, and she was wearing a long skirt that buttoned up the side. He forced himself to look away but the image was firmly imbedded in his brain. She was dressed warmly and well covered, but he was remembering how she had looked last summer in shorts and a form hugging sleeveless blouse.

He couldn't help himself. The temptation was too great. He decided to sneak another peek. Everything was the same except she was sitting and showing more leg. He could see she was probably wearing pantyhose and the skirt was higher than mid-calf, just below the knee. Her legs were crossed and the top one flicking up and down at a pretty good pace. Although she was facing forward, he got the feeling she was looking at him.

His thoughts were interrupted by the sound of the bell to start the class. The professor told the proctors to secure the doors and let no one else in unless it were a man and his pregnant wife, three kings, or a group of shepherds. Then he explained a few questions the mimeograph machine had blurred, one his secretary had copied incorrectly, and instructed them to raise their hand if they needed some assistance. Then with a wave of his hand he bid them start.

Pete read the first question and was stumped, he looked at the next, and was not sure of the answer. *What was happening?* His memory seemed to be deserting him.

He'd heard the best way to study for a test, was to learn the material and then not study the day before the test. He looked down the row at his roommate. Benny was rapidly writing and filling in answers with a confident air. *I have really blown it,* Pete thought. I *should have gone to sleep when Benny did.* He started looking down the long line of questions searching for one he definitely, 100%, knew the answer to. He reached Number 13 before he started.

The first time through the test he only answered a third of the questions. But like doing a crossword puzzle, one answer led to another in his brain and he was forging ahead getting closer and closer to an "A". As he worked, he was vaguely aware of the room slowly emptying, but it wasn't until the professor came over and told him time was up that he became aware he was the last student still writing: in fact the last student in the lecture hall.

He panicked. Not because he did not have an answer for every question, but because there was still doubt about many of them in his mind. Some of the multiple choices seemed to have more than one correct answer, and others had no choice that was completely correct. On some of the True or False questions, he felt he could adequately make a case for either side. And on the essay questions, there were a few more points he wished to include to justify his answer.

"Did you do well?" the professor asked kindly.

"I have no idea, Sir. Would you correct my paper first?"

Dr. H laughed. "That's impossible, young man. I have already, with the help of my proctors, graded a third of them. They are doing the multiple choice and true or false questions, and I am doing the essay questions. Most of the students did not require the full three hours, and one, in fact, a Mr. Benjamin F. finished in twenty-five minutes. I think that must be a record. I don't remember anyone ever finishing one of my tests in under an hour. He even beat Susan Smith by 30 minutes." *I bet that pissed her off,* Pete thought.

"May I ask how he did?"

The professor gave him a stern look which seemed to say, "Son, I am disappointed in you asking a question like that."

"I'm sorry, Sir. I shouldn't have asked, but Benjamin is my roommate, and we are very close."

The professor's expression softened. It was Christmas, and he had always liked this student. "Your friend has quite an imagination. I don't recall ever reading a more . . . entertaining test paper. However, I fear, he did not have an adequate grasp of the material covered on the test. I'll have the grades posted on the door to my office by 3:00 p.m."

Pete said he would come and check. He had to wait around for Bryan who was taking an afternoon final. Pete and two others were carpooling with Bryan to Denver to save money.

Pete had no idea how he had done on the test and was extremely nervous. Then he started smiling as he realized Bibles would not have to be adding any chapters covering Benjamin passing Dr. H.'s class.

CHAPTER 3

Good-byes

Grace was taking a final, so Pete strolled over to the coffee shop to see if anyone wanted to talk about the test and discuss answers to certain questions. No one seemed interested in discussing the test, so he sat down at a table by himself. It was a small table, against a wall, only able to accommodate two chairs.

He watched the various cliques having a last visit before departing. The jukebox was playing Elvis' "Blue Christmas." His friend Sandy was in the center of the largest group along with her current boyfriend Eugene Jones. Pete took a text book out of his briefcase and started searching for the answer to the second essay question, but a large part of his brain was thinking about Sandy and hoping she'd notice him and come over.

Her name was Sandra Anita Fay Sullivan and she was from Santa Fe, New Mexico where her parents were teachers. Her father's ancestors were Irish and her mother's Spanish. Why the extra-long name? Two grandmothers and a mom wanted this precious baby named after them. She was mostly called Sandy giving the mother a partial victory.

Pete and Sandy tied for the second highest score on tests in both an education class taught by Mr. Phillips and Mr. Perriman's class on American Literature during his first trimester at the school. They might have been enemies if one or the other had earned the highest grade or they had tied for the highest grade. But that honor went to Susan Smith. And their scores weren't even close to hers. Susan had beaten them in both classes by approximately 10%. She had not missed any questions on either test.

Pete smiled as he recalled when he first met Sandy. It was during the five o'clock hour on a cloudy day near the first of the trimester the year before. The library was practically empty. Only three of the 30 tables were occupied. Most of the students were eating their evening meal in the cafeteria or at their homes if they lived in town. A girl of average height with light brown hair got up from her table, walked across the large room, and sat down across from him.

He looked up from his book into the determined face of a girl he recognized from two of his classes. She was the one who had tied him for second place in these classes. He didn't remember her name. Just that she said she was from New Mexico when the American Literature professor had them introduce themselves the first day. She seemed intense, even a little scary, like a cat preparing to spring.

The girl must not have remembered his name either because when she spoke she said, "Colorado," (Then she paused for the better part of a minute until she was sure she had his full attention.) (No problem, she had it.) "The California witch is going down!" she said with intensity and simultaneously lifting a fist with the thumb up and turned it forcibly so the thumb was facing down. (She might not have said "witch.")

"What?" He was shocked. He wasn't experienced enough with girls to know that girls swore. Especially pretty ones like this one sitting across from him. Her intensity was scary. His mind ran to a line from the movie "Casa Blanca," and he thought, *Of all the tables, in all the schools, in all the libraries, why did she have to sit down at mine?*

"It's a terrible state, full of **w**itches. (He emphasized the "w.") I hate California," he said. "I hate it and everybody from there. I can hardly wait for the earthquake that will break it off and send it out into the Pacific Ocean."

A look of concern crossed the girl's face. "I'm sorry. I guess I came across too strong. I just meant if we work together, we can beat Susan." Pete breathed a sigh of relief, and so did she.

"If it's all right with you," she continued, "we can leave California attached a little while longer." They both laughed and a friendship was born.

They studied together and played together and became best friends. Sandy had many friends but for Pete it was mostly just her. At first he just called her Sandy like everyone else did, but then when he learned her middle name was Fay, he started calling her Sandy Fay from Santa Fe, which got shortened to Fay. The rest of her friends stayed with the name Sandy and he alternated between it and Fay.

Most of the time they were "Pete" and "Sandy." But if it was something serious, they used "Silk" and "Pie." The "Silk" came from a play on words because her last name was the same as a famous race horse: Silky Sullivan. The "Pie" came from Mother Goose's Peter Peter pumpkin eater, plus pumpkins being associated with pies. Neither one liked sharing either one of these nicknames, so "Pie" and "Silk" were only used to clue the other about something serious. It was like their own special code.

Their collaboration was great for both of them. It raised their scores ten points and provided a beneficial relationship for both of them. It did not allow them to beat the student from California, but they did tie her a couple of times. (How do you beat someone who never makes a mistake?)

Then at the end of the first trimester Pete was called into the dean's office and told that the people he was staying with did not want to rent the room next trimester. The dean gave him a list of people in town who were interested in renting to college students, but he chose to move on to campus. It was a good move. It had been lonely living off campus and soon his circle of friends increased.

Suddenly, Pete's memories were interrupted and he noticed someone standing next to his table. It was Sandy. "Hey Fay, how long have you been standing there?"

"About two minutes. You were deep in thought and I didn't want to disturb you. What were you thinking about?"

"You . . . and the test."

She smiled nervously.

Pete couldn't help but think she had something on her mind, but then dismissed it. "Got a minute?" he said.

"Always for you, Pie. I wan . . ."

"How did you answer the second essay question?" Pete asked interrupting her.

Sandy let out a sigh, like a tire losing air. Her resolve seemed to wilt and then was gone. Whatever she had come over to say or ask, got moved to the back of the bus and would have to wait. Pete was instantly sorry he had asked about the test. The question was out of his mouth before he could stop it. "What is it, Silk? What were you going to say?" He had asked about the test before he realized she had called him Pie.

"Later," she told him. "Okay Buddy, you get two questions about the test." She sat down. It was like she was planning on and getting up the nerve to say something else, a game changer, but lost her nerve.

He was going to pursue what was on her mind, but she cut him off with the question. "How did **you** answer the second essay question?" They discussed a couple of the questions but were mostly enjoying each other's company and remembering the Christmas before, when she was his only real friend on campus and they spent so much time together. They had even remembered talking about teaching in the same school in some neat place one day.

He was just getting ready to demand she tell him what had been on her mind, when suddenly she reached out across the table and took his right hand with both of hers and said, "I've got to go. They're waiting for me." She wished him a very Merry Christmas then hurried back to rejoin the group she had been with which was breaking up. She left with her current boyfriend Eugene Jones who was frowning at Pete. He had been frowning at him ever since Sandy had come over to Pete's table. As they were leaving, she hesitated a moment at the door, turned back and waved slowly at the lone figure sitting by himself. It was like she was waving good-bye forever. He started to get up, but she was gone. He sat back down and reopened the book and pretended to read. But he was thinking, w*hat was she going to tell me?*

This same time last year he felt like he and she could possibly end up married and teaching somewhere. Then during the summer while Sandy was in Santa Fe he met Mary and fell under her spell. In the fall, Grace entered the picture for him and Eugene Jones for her.

The room was still about half full of jolly groups. Pete felt like a sore thumb, or an outcast sitting there by himself waiting for his coffee to cool. He was on the tall side of average at 6' 1" and weighed 185. At 25 he felt removed from the average students just out of high school, away from home for the first time, and financed by their parents. (Freshman years could be hard on grade point averages.) He took a sip of coffee. STILL PIPING HOT! He wished it would cool faster so he could drink it quickly and go back to the privacy of his room and take a nap.

Suddenly a pair of hands covered his eyes and he smelled the faint aroma of a familiar perfume. He had not seen her enter, or creep up behind him.

“Hey good-looking, guess who?” she whispered in his ear.

“Someone with 20/20 vision and a true appreciation for perfection,” he answered.

The hands were soft but firm. The voice was suggestive but perky. The perfume’s aroma was there but not boldly stated. There was just a hint of lavender.

“Gravel Gertie or possibly Tugboat Annie or maybe Granny Clampett.” Then using his best Sherlock Holmes voice he said, “Watson, I base this deduction by judging on the excessive use of cheap perfume, probably trying to cover up lack of bathing. Whew, the overpowering stench leads me to believe this person last bathed in October . . . on the 26th . . . at seven p.m. Then there is the rough hands and gravelly voice of a dock worker, fish monger or scrub woman. I tend to go with fish monger. Alive, Alive Oh. Is your name Molly Malone?”

The hands flew from his eyes and he turned to see a vision, 5’ 3”, blond hair and the cutest fake pout imaginable. Such was the magic of her charm, that had she been the ugliest girl on campus, she still would have been one of the most popular, he thought. For some reason, known only to her, she had taken an interest in this quiet, moody person last summer when there were very few men on campus. And because of this interest, Pete was becoming a total basket case, a candidate for the loony bin. Hours he could have spent studying were spent at his desk staring at an open book or the wall in his dorm room thinking about her.

“Well Jackson,” she never used his real name, “may I sit down?”

“No, GO AWAY. SCAT!”

“Thank you, I’d love to.” She sat down across from him in the seat Sandy had vacated and reached for his coffee. He didn’t notice.

One look at that face so close had caused his heart rate and blood pressure to go into fight or flight mode. He was concentrating on trying to calm down.

"OOH WEE, That's hot! Bet I burned my tongue."

"Serves you right, . . . thief."

"Well Jackson, I saw you through the window and said to myself, that poor dunce, sitting by himself, and crying into his coffee has flunked another final exam. So I thought in the spirit of the season it would be nice for me to come in and cheer you up."

Pete didn't say anything.

"By the way, I caught you ogling me out of the corner of your eyes during the test. Looked like you were checking out my legs. Were you admiring them or did you think I had the answers to the quiz written on them? Either way, shame on you, old man."

Pete's face turned an embarrassed red. She had nailed him. That's exactly what he had been doing. He had not realized she had caught him checking her out.

"It w-w-was before the test, not d-d-during, and I was only trying to see if you knew which end of the pencil to use," he stuttered. He thought about asking her if she rode a lot of horses to get so bow-legged, but didn't because they both knew those legs were perfect and that would be admitting her charge was correct.

"Hmph. So much for my good deed. I've got to hurry," she said jumping up. "You've made me late, but they'll wait. I'm riding to Albuquerque with Betty, George, and Robert. I will spend the night at Betty's parent's house and catch my flight to Chicago tomorrow." She bent over and gave him a kiss on the forehead. "You are fun. Merry Christmas, Sourpuss." Then she turned and bounced out of the room without looking back.

Mary Christmas had left the building. For him it was like the life or oxygen had been sucked out of the room with her, leaving only the faint scent of lavender.

While she had been in the coffee shop their table had been the center of attention and comments. When she bent over and kissed him on the forehead, to the others it was like watching the princess kiss the frog in a fairytale. This guy was a nothing. He never participated in any social activities. All he was interested in was grades. Yet within the space of five minutes he had been joined by both Mary and Sandy: two very hot and popular chicks.

Pete started mentally going through the mantra he used when trying to resist Mary and get her out of his mind. "(a) She is like a butterfly flitting from one flower to another; (b) She uses people; (c) The way she eats she is going to be one fat old lady someday when her metabolism slows down; (d) She is too short for me. I have to bend over to hug or kiss her; (e) Her parents are divorced, and statistics show that children of broken families are more likely to end up divorced; (f) She only keeps after me because I have not fallen into her harem; (g) She looks on me more as a challenge than anything else, etc., etc." The list was only about 10% effective, but it gave him something to do and he identified with the country song called Heartaches By the Number. The singer gave a number to each heartache and sang that when he stopped counting, he was toast. Or something like that. He used letters instead of numbers but it was the same principle.

One of the items in the mantra triggered a memory which triggered another memory and his mind drifted back to the first time he had heard her name and then the first time he had met her.

The first time he even heard the name "Mary Christmas" had been in January the year before. Boston Billy, said he would crawl a mile on his belly over rusty razorblades just to smell where Mary Christmas had peed. Her name stuck in his mind for its uniqueness, but it wasn't until the middle of the summer that he actually met her.

Pete's first month of the summer of '64 was spent at Camp Pendleton on the 105 howitzers as a member of Hotel Battery. Pete was within striking distance of graduating the next April, and this prompted him to look into summer school rather than get a job. He took out a loan which combined with the money he had earned working in Alaska and his miserly ways, left him in a comfortable position to concentrate on his studies.

The college offered what they called concentrated sessions during the summer. It made the classes fit in an eight week period by doing such things as meeting more days a week and more hours per day. One of the classes Pete needed ran through the lunch hour, so he signed up for sack lunches which he picked up at breakfast.

Only about a third of the students took advantage of the summer trimester or the concentrated classes. Therefore, with so few students, everyone soon knew almost everyone. It was like going to a party with a hundred people, you might learn 20 names or break off into little groups, but if you go to a party with just a few, you might learn everyone's name.

Pete had just arrived back at school that day and was sitting in the campus coffee shop getting to know Lyle his roommate for the summer. Lyle had mustered out of the Airforce in the spring. He was a wheeler dealer type but it looked like they would get along. Into the room bounced one of the most striking blonds Pete had ever seen. In fact, it was his first actual memory of seeing her. He heard they were filming a movie in town and wondered if she was one of the stars.

"Who who who is that?" he asked. Lyle, who had the benefit of being there the whole summer, looked at him like Pete had just asked what two plus two were.

"Her name is Mary Christmas," Lyle said.

The memory came back of William Bradford Bentley the third rushing into Tom's room and describing the two new girls who had transferred in. He shared the disgusting comment by Boston Billy with Lyle.

Mary was going from table to table and talking to everyone. It was obvious she intended to hit every table in the room. She still had about three tables to go to when she stopped at their table and gave her little sales pitch. She was promoting some student activity. Lyle was great: he matched her witticism for witticism and discussed intelligently what she was promoting. He seemed immune to her charms. Pete had no idea what they were talking about. Besides, his eyes had pulled rank on his hearing and directed all available energy to sight. When she turned to him and said something, he couldn't hear or speak, just look. Silence reigned. "Is your friend all right?" she asked Lyle.

"He's a mute," Lyle said, "He's deaf and dumb . . . and not very bright." Lyle smiled at his own witticism. "He is part of an experiment we are doing in the psychology department for the state this summer while there are fewer students on campus to be in danger. It has to do with rehabilitating the criminally insane. I am getting my room and board free by rooming with him this summer and spending some time away from the room with him. This is his first time out in public without restraints. Say something to the nice lady, Igor." Pete had no trouble hearing Lyle.

Pete wiggled his fingers and moved his hands and arms around in wild gyrations while making different expressions with his face like he had seen real deaf people do. The girl took a step back and looked nervous.

Lyle decided to join in and help. "Igor says you are the most beautiful girl in the world and he is so excited to make your acquaintance, and he would crawl on his belly over razor blades just to . . . " At that moment the "A" hand in the deaf alphabet which resembles a fist arrived at Lyle's solar plexus rendering him temporarily speechless and gasping for air. The girl must have thought the criminally insane Igor was attacking his handler.

"Gotta go! Thanks for listening, Igor." and in the blink of an eye, she was out the door leaving some disappointed tables in her wake that were to be next. When he got his breath back, Lyle said to Pete, "I don't think you made a very good impression on her. I hope you didn't injure your hand when it came in contact with my abs of steel." Pete made some disparaging comment comparing his abs of steel to bowls of Jell-O. "I think we are going to get along just fine," Lyle said and Pete agreed.

The next morning when he went back to pick up his sack lunch after finishing his breakfast, he was told to see the girl at the start of the serving line. "She'll check your name off the list and give you your lunch."

The girl was Mary. She looked at the list. "I don't see your name, Igor. Let me check with my boss." She was thinking perhaps he was getting a special lunch with some kind of medication in it. She returned. "There is nothing here for you and your name is not on the list. Please don't get mad."

"Would you look and see if they have reserved it under the name Wheatley."

"Yes. There is a Wheatley. First name, Please."

"Pete or Peter." She handed him the lunch.

"Thank you for being so patient. HEY!!! YOU CAN TALK! YOU'RE NOT IGOR, YOU'RE PETER WHEATLEY!" She grabbed some cinnamon rolls and started throwing them at him. She was not used to having someone get the best of her.

"Mary Mary quite contrary, how does your garden grow." he taunted. This was fun. Just like dodgeball. It could be called "Dodge Roll." Then while he was trying to remember the next line, one hit him in the forehead.

"With Silver Bells and Cockle Shells," she said with a smile.

"Exit, stage left," he said imitating Snagglepuss and he was gone.

The next day she seemed to have forgiven him and was as sweet and flirty as could be. However, when he went to eat his lunch at 2:00 p.m. after class, the sandwich was soggy as though someone might have poured water on it and there was catsup on his red jello.

They exchanged good natured insults every morning when he went to pick up his lunch, and the sack never said "Pete"; it said "Igor." By the end of the 2nd week they were both looking forward to that part of the day. She called him "Igor," and he called her "Gullible."

Then one afternoon he was in his dorm room studying how to teach modern math. It was a warm summer day, so he had both the window and the hall door open to catch any breeze available. The desk was next to the window, facing in, with just enough space between it and the outside wall to allow access and for the drawers to open.

He nearly jumped out of his skin when a voice from just outside, about two feet away said, "I have to walk down to the bakery and pick up a cake. It's Helen's birthday and we are going to have a surprise party for her. I volunteered to get the cake because I knew I could borrow Ken's car. I got the surprise party. The surprise was Ken's car has a dead battery that won't take a charge or a jump and he isn't going to fix it until the end of the month."

"Tsk, tsk," Pete sympathized insincerely.

"Do you want to come? I could certainly use someone who is criminally insane to carry it for me."

"What kind is it?"

"German Chocolate."

"Never heard of it. Sounds un-American." (The only cakes his mother had ever made were brown or white with icing to match.)

"If you go, I'll save you a piece."

"Sold," he said. He had had his fill of Modern Math.

They hiked down and back and really had a good time. That night when he got back from studying in the library, he found a large slice of cake on his desk and a fork from the cafeteria. He had no idea how it got there. The room was locked when he left the room, the window was closed, and Lyle was on a date with some girl named Gwen.

For the rest of the summer she would surprise him by showing up at the window with "Let's go swimming down at the river; Let's go hike to the top of the mountain behind the school; Let's go over to Frank's and ride horses," etc., etc. . But there were just as many days when she didn't come by. It was a summer of highs and lows.

Someone at a nearby table shouted MERRY CHRISTMAS SEE YOU NEXT YEAR. That brought Pete back from Memory Land to the present. He reached down for his coffee, took a swallow. He nearly spit it out. It was cold. He looked at his watch; half an hour had gone by since Mary had gone. It seemed like just a couple of minutes. Darn her hide. He decided to go back to the room and take a 20 minute nap until Grace got out of her test. Maybe she would go with him when he went to see how he did on the exam.

Of course she would. Grace always did what he suggested; Mary hardly ever did. Mary always had a plan and when he went along with it, he was always glad he did. He thought, if she were to have a theme song it would be "Hey, Look Me Over," a song made popular by Lucille Ball in the play "Wildcat." He wondered what Grace's would be. She was always trying to please everyone, but in a quiet, almost invisible, non-attention getting and timid way. Her speech teacher at the end of her first speech had given her an "A" for content and a "D" for delivery. He told her she was too mousey.

Grace was equally beautiful but in an unflashy quiet way. He really couldn't think of a good theme song for her unless it was "Tiptoe Thru the Tulips." Their table was never the center of attention. He never dated, or wanted to date anyone else after meeting Grace, even Sandy. And when he was with Grace, he never thought about Mary. But when he was alone and trying to study, it was Mary who interrupted his concentration, a habit developed in the summer. He constantly thought about the special times they had shared together.

As he walked back to the dorm he continued thinking about Mary. It was like the first page in A Tale of Two Cities by Charles Dickens that started out, "It was the best of times. It was the worst of times." He had spent countless hours dreaming about her, and avoided her like the plague whenever he could. If he knew she would be some place, he made sure he wasn't. He did not want to be just another member of her male harem, stable, team, fan club, or whatever. He was 25, a trimester from graduating. He was ready to start looking for a partner for life, a true love. Lately, he found himself picking up other people's babies and enjoying cuddling with them or giving them their bottle. Maybe there was something to this biological clock thing.

When he got to the room, Benny was there packing for the trip home. He was riding to Denver with Lane. Pete lay down and watched Benny. "How do you think you did on the test?" he asked.

Ben smiled and said, "I gave the old doc lots to think about. Did he say anything about me after I left? I was the first one finished," he said proudly.

Pete remembered the professor saying that Benjamin had a great imagination and that he had set the school record for completing a final exam.

"Yes. In fact he was quite complimentary, Benny. He said you even beat Susan." (There was no need for a last name. A couple of times during his lectures Dr. H. had paused and said, "Isn't that right, Susan.")

Benny looked surprised, then smiled and continued his packing. Slowly it dawned on Pete that Benny was packing up all his stuff and the pyramid was gone. Pete himself was only taking one duffle bag (also called a sea bag).

"Why are you taking so much? Afraid Santa or the elves will break in and steal our stuff?"

"I'm not coming back"

"What?"

"I have chosen a new career path."

"Well Lah Tee Dah. Don't you sound fancy."

"I am going to be a fireman." Pete let out a groan and rolled over on the bed. Benny was suddenly enjoying himself. He continued with a twinkle in his eye. "It was between that or becoming an astronaut." He was joking about the latter. He explained that he had relatives in the Denver Fire Department who were after him to apply, and he had concluded that academics was not his strong suit.

Pete sighed. "I wonder what kind of clown they will saddle me with next time." Benny gave him a one finger salute.

Actually, Pete had someone in mind before fifteen minutes had gone by. He hoped he could talk Tom into replacing Benny. Tom was a good student whose roommate was a popular athlete and their room often became a gathering spot making it hard for him to study. Tom was definitely the cream of the crop. (Choices)

Half an hour later Pete sadly helped Benny carry his stuff to the parking lot to wait for Lane. They had become good friends. When it came time to say good-bye, they shook hands, and exchanged phone numbers. Pete said, "Thanks for waking me up this morning. If I read about Denver burning to the ground, I'll know you got the job."

Benny grinned. "And if you hear about a rocket ship missing the moon and hitting Mars or Pismo Beach, California, you'll know I took that occupational path."

At that moment Lane showed up and loaded Benny's stuff in his car. Pete stood in the parking lot and watched until the car was out of sight and even a few minutes after that. Then he turned and walked back to the dorm. As he walked he pondered over how people came into his life, became very important, and then went out of his life forever.

Pete looked at his watch. Grace should just about be getting out of her test. He would walk over and wait in the hall until she came out. Then they could walk over to Dr. H.'s office and see how he had done. As he got to the room where she was taking the test, he could hear a voice say, "Time's up. Pencils down. Proctors, collect the papers." She was the third person to come out of the room. She smiled when she spotted him and trotted over to give him a hug. He told her, "Let's go down and see how I did." As they approached the room, he started to get nervous.

Suddenly he was afraid to look. The grades were posted on the door. He told Grace to check for him. He stood back with his fingers crossed looking towards Heaven. "You got 172 on the test," Grace said. There was a possible 200 points.

Pete got out his calculator. "That is about 86%. Not an "A." Need 90% to be an "A."

"Maybe not," she said. "That is the 2nd highest grade in the class. And the 3rd highest is a 158. Sa Su"

"What was the highest grade?"

"Su Cu got 200."

He knew who Su Cu was. Sue was always the best student in any class. He hated her. She should be on "Jeopardy" instead of going to Fort Lewis and ruining the curve for everyone. Then he remembered that this professor always threw out the highest and the lowest test score in figuring the curve.

Grace continued to study the list. Pete was just getting ready to jump for joy when her face clouded and she said, "Oh No!"

His joy vanished as quickly as it had come. Had she read the wrong initials? He felt like the cold steel of a sword had pierced his gut. "What is it?"

"Be Fu has 16 points. That's got to be your roommate. He's in that class and there are no other Be Fu's. The next highest of the lowest grades is a 73 Ch Hu."

Pete quickly scanned the page and confirmed that he had indeed got an "A" on the test. This would be the first time in his life when he got straight "A's". Then remembering the professor's comment; he repeated it. "I don't believe Benjamin had an adequate grasp of the subject matter presented on the quiz." Pete paused. "I believe that dispels one rumor."

"What rumor?" Grace asked.

"I heard they would give 20 points if you showed up on time and spelled your name right."

"Do you suppose he misspelled his name?"

"I believe the city of Denver is in big trouble." (In his mind, he pictured Denver as a pile of ashes.) "Good-bye Denver."

During a quick scan Pete "just happened" to notice that Ma Ch got a 143. That would be either a B- or a C+.

They walked over to the coffee shop and to Pete the atmosphere was completely different. Now he had another "A" to his credit and he wasn't sitting at a table by himself, but with an attractive girl that he really liked and she was showing no signs of wanting to leave. Elvis had been replaced by Brenda Lee singing about knocking or rocking around a Christmas tree and then came Bobby Helm's "Jingle Bell Rock." Too soon it was time to part. He walked Grace to the parking lot. She had borrowed Linda's car. Linda was working a shift at the A & W and had finished testing the day before. Grace had dropped her off before driving up the hill. Now it was time for Linda's shift to be ending and she needed to go pick her up.

Grace invited Pete to come visit her on New Year's and he promised to try, without really believing it would happen. He planned on skiing nearly every day with his brother, and she lived in the opposite direction in a different state some 30 miles from a town called Gallup. He couldn't ever remember being there, but knew it was on the famous Route 66 because it said so in a song. He wished her a Merry Christmas and kissed her goodbye. Then he headed for his room to pick up his duffle bag and go on to Bryan's room to wait.

Pete had started spending a lot of time with Grace this trimester. She was the opposite of Mary in nearly every way. She was tall, quiet, religious, shy, sincere, studious, loyal, and not interested in being a social butterfly. She too was beautiful but in a quiet unflashy way. You had to be close to Grace to see and appreciate her beauty where Mary grabbed your attention from a block away . . . or farther . . . even if you didn't have exceptional vision . . . or binoculars.

At Fort Lewis there is a beautiful little chapel. It has large windows looking out on the town below. The chapel contains an organ and is never locked. It was one of Pete and Grace's favorite places to go. Grace would sing and play the organ and Pete would join in when he knew the words.

Grace was there on several scholarships including not having to pay tuition if she maintained a certain grade point average. . She was only 17 and he met her in a class that was supposed to be limited to seniors only: average age 23. There were nine students. The class consisted of eight men all seniors and one girl who was a freshman; but no one in the class knew the girl was a freshman because she did not wear a freshman beany or act like a first year student.

Pete met her on the first day of the senior seminar on Russian history. He was running late for class. In fact he was running to get to class when he dropped his books. He was carrying everything he needed for two classes, so he wouldn't have to go back to the dorm. In an instant he was back on his feet having scooped up his load and was running with everything but his pen which still lay in the grass where it had rolled unnoticed. He was two minutes late when he burst into the small seminar room with a table in the center and nine chairs around it. There were seven men and one girl sitting around the table. Dr. Duane A. Smith, looking younger and healthier than most in the room, stood at the end of the table next to a white board which he was writing on. He reached down and crossed off the last name on a list that was on the table.

"Lady and gentlemen, I do believe I have the honor of introducing Mr. Wheatley."

A red faced Pete quickly sat down in the first and only empty seat which happened to be next to the girl. He hurriedly got out his spiral notebook, then started frantically looking for his pen. It was missing. He probably lost it when he dropped his books and was scooping them up. He knew he had it when he left the dorm. He loved that pen. It would write in three different colors making it easy to emphasize things the professors thought was important.

"Is there a problem Mr. Wheatley?" asked Dr. Smith.

"Yes. I've lost my pen. I have nothing to write with."

"I have an extra pencil you may borrow," the girl said.

As he reached for it he looked into her face. A beautiful face with the shiniest, sparkliest eyes he had ever seen. He thought he had seen that face before: in a dream, back when he was in high school. But that would have been impossible he found out later. She would have only been ten. The minute his hand touched the pencil he felt a slight jolt which he attributed to static electricity. At that time, he did not realize what an impression she had made on his subconscious.

When the bell rang he was the first one out the door. He wanted to see if his pen was near where he dropped his books and he did not want to be late for his next class. The special pen which wrote in three different colors was there, and he got to the next class on time. As he sat down and opened his notebook he realized he still had the pencil. He had not meant to keep it even though she had said he could. She said she had plenty more. He took notes with his pen, but he kept staring at the pencil and thinking about the girl who had loaned it to him.

That night was the first time in months he didn't dream solely about Mary who now shared his dreams with pencil girl. During the day his mind drifted to thoughts of pencil girl with the shiny eyes as much as it did to Mary.

Pete really wanted to see her again, but he didn't even know her name and the class didn't meet again for several days. He told Lyle who had been his summer roommate about the mystery girl with the shiny sparkly eyes.

"Call her up. Ask her to the football game tomorrow," Lyle suggested.

"I can't."

"Why?"

"I don't know her name."

"No problem. Go over to the girl's dorm and tell them you want to see the girl with the shiniest sparkliest eyes."

"I believe I'll pass on that wonderful suggestion," he said. "I'll just have to wait until the class meets again next week."

Pete spent most of the afternoon in the library. While he was there Lyle came in, walked by his table and dropped a folded single sheet of paper on the table and kept walking like a character in a spy movie. Pete unfolded the paper. There were two words written on it in bold print taking up most of the paper: "GRACE COUSINS." In smaller letters was written, "Commit to memory and destroy. Swallow if captured." Pete got up and followed Lyle out of the library at a discrete distance. "What is this?" he said when he caught up with him in the hall, while holding up the paper.

"I am inclined to believe it is the name of a girl with sparkly eyes," said 008. "Although, I haven't personally witnessed this particular phenomenon or the Northern Lights, but I'll take your word on both accounts."

"How did you get it?"

"Oh I just happened to be walking by Dr. Smith's office and noticed it was empty. So I went in and . . ."

"STOP! I don't want to know. Then I'd be an accomplice and probably get kicked out of school." Pete started wadding up the note, getting it to a more swallowable size in case he was apprehended before he could get to a garbage can. Fortunately he did not have to swallow it.

It took Pete a while to build up the nerve to go over to the girl's dorm and talk to her, and only then when Lyle said he would go with him. But when they got to the girl's dorm, Lyle said he would wait outside. Pete was told at the front desk that there was no Grace Cousins there. He was sure Lyle had pulled a fast one on him. He headed for the exit with murder on his mind. To his surprise, Lyle was waiting for him. "Lyle, there is no Grace Cousins in that dorm. You know what they say about payback, Lyle. They say it's a bi..."

Lyle interrupted him. "I've got an idea. I bet she's a town girl. Why don't you go over to the main switchboard and ask if they have a number for a girl with sparkly eyes."

"I don't think so. And that ceases to be funny. Actually it never was."

"Sorry. Come on. I've got a few minutes. I'll go with you."

"Okay, but this time you go in."

As they reached the office where the switchboard was located, Lyle entering first said, "My ex-roommate would like to phone Grace Cousins and ask her for a date. **BUT , . . .** I tried to talk him out of it. I think I hear my mother calling me. And I'm late for my date with Gwen. Gotta Go." And he zoomed out of there.

Pete could not figure out what happened. He stood frozen in place. He couldn't see who Lyle had been talking to because the switch board blocked his view. The girl on the switchboard stood up.

It was Mary. Mary had several part time jobs. She worked the switchboard for a couple of hours on weekends and evenings and she still worked in the cafeteria. Her expression seemed to say you can run, little man but you can't hide. I own you. He felt like a little puppy trying to get out of a pen and almost making it. Mary looked it up and handed him the contact number for Grace. (She was boarding with the Maderas who had moved to Durango from Gallup the year before.)

Mary had a smile on her face and acted both cheerful and condescending. "I think Grace would be the perfect girl for you." Pete's inference was she thought Grace would be a safe place to store him. Pete had the feeling Mary was interested in him, but just not at that moment. There were a few more things on her bucket list still to be checked off before settling down.

Pete went to the student center to use one of the pay phones. One of the Maderas answered on the second ring. It was Linda's brother.

"May I speak with Grace please?"

"GRACE, PHONE," yelled the voice.

It seemed like an eternity before she came on. He almost lost his nerve and hung up several times while he waited. He might not have phoned at all had Mary not been so nonchalant, cheerful and helpful, almost daring him. It was like she was saying give it a shot, you'll realize that no one can compare to me. Pete certainly did not want to show up to the game without a date now. And Mary knew he was going to ask Grace. If he showed up with someone else, she would know he had partially failed and was there with a second choice. And she would of course be even more confident. His thoughts were interrupted as Grace came on the line.

"Hello, this is Grace."

"Hi." SILENCE. Suddenly the cat had his tongue and he couldn't think of a thing to say and sign language would be no use over the phone.

"Who is this?" she said after a moment of silence.

"Pete."

"Pete who?" He was tempted to say McGillicutty or the famous phone line, is your refrigerator running, but he didn't.

"Wheatley." He remembered Dr. Smith introducing him as Mr. Wheatley. After another uncomfortable moment of silence on the other end, he added, "Mr. Wheatley."

"I'm sorry, Mr. Wheatley. Whatever you're selling. I am not interested. How did you get this number?"

"I'm a student." (Silence) "I'm in one of your classes." (Silence) "I'm not selling anything." (Silence)

She interrupted the silence. "I don't remember giving out my number in any of the classes. Which class?"

"Russian History."

"Okay. I am taking Russian history. Which one are you? I haven't learned any of the names yet." (To a 17 year old girl they all looked like they were too old for her . . . except . . . there was that one magic moment with the late guy . . . but it couldn't be him. She had seen him walking around and chatting with Miss Popularity several times and even saw them at the A & W her first day on the job. They had been Linda's customer. Since coming to Durango she had several dates with boys Linda had set her up with. She liked one who was very nice and could see the relationship progressing. She was trying to think of a polite way to discourage this Wheatley character.) "Mr. Wheatley, I appreciate the call, but I'm seeing someone who . . ."

He interrupted her. "You loaned me a pencil. I'd like to return it." (*That was a lame thing to say,* he told himself.)

"OH! MY GOSH. HI THERE. Do you need another one?" (*That was a stupid thing to say,* she thought.)

"I really wanted to ask you to the football game tomorrow, but I don't have any transportation to pick you up. But maybe we could get together sometime next week. I'll see if I can borrow a car."

"Linda and I are in the chorus and the chorus is going to sing in the middle of the ball match at the half pint."

"I believe they are calling it halftime these days," Pete said diplomatically.

"We are riding to the contest in Linda's car. I love football meetings." (She had attended one game in her life. She had talked her father into taking her. She had not really understood what was happening on the field at all.)

"Would you sit with me during the game? When you're not singing."

"I'd like that."

"I'm in D Dorm Room 206. If you phone when you are leaving the house I will meet you in the parking lot."

She did. He did. And they had a wonderful time during the first half although it became more than obvious to Pete she knew as much about football as he did about knitting. Absolutely nothing, except it had something to do with two girls named Pearl.

During the halftime performance, Pete noticed Mary was also in the chorus and not standing too far from Grace and Linda. When the chorus members came back into the stands he followed Mary with his eyes and saw her sitting next to someone that he didn't recognize. He wasn't sure if the man was a student at the school or not. He nicknamed him Mystery Man. Surprisingly it didn't bother him at all. He didn't feel even a twinge of jealousy. In fact, he felt a little sorry for the mystery man who was probably about to get his heart broken or his life turned topsy-turvy. He later learned Mystery Man's name was James Herriot.

Grace returned to sit next to him. Suddenly the world was a wonderful world and he enjoyed the second half as much as the first half even though it started snowing and would take an abacus to figure out how many points Fort Lewis lost by. He escorted Grace down to the parking lot where Linda was waiting impatiently. On the way back to his room he passed Mary waiting outside one of the dorms. Her date had gone in for something. She appeared to be slightly intoxicated. Probably the best way to watch a game on a cold wintery Colorado day.

Pete never dated anyone else after that. Mary would flit in and out of his life in five to ten minute sessions. But the meetings were more like old friends sparring, trying to get the best of each other in a friendly way. But afterwards, he was left with an ache in his heart. Thoughts of her no longer dominated his thinking, although there was still a bond with the slight possibility of something greater hanging over their heads.

Pete's growing affection for Grace after the initial jump start was a gradual thing. He liked being with her. He liked her. When he was with her, Mary was not a problem. But there were the times when Grace wasn't there that thoughts of Mary slipped in unbidden.

With Grace it was a head over heels, 180 degree change of direction. She told the boys she had been going out with that it was time for them to trot along; she was no longer available or interested. She arranged to move on to campus at the beginning of the next trimester, so she and Pete could be closer.

This put a strain on her relationship with her friend Linda who had not only talked her into going to Fort Lewis but had arranged for her to stay with the family and even got her the job as a carhop at A & W. Linda had worked there for over a year, and it was her influence that got Grace the job over several other more qualified applicants.

Grace really didn't like the job. Too many customers wanted to flirt. They would say things she found embarrassing. When one of the customers made a suggestive and particularly inappropriate remark to her, she "somehow" lost her balance, tripped over something, and he found his root beer with ice-cream "floating" on his lap. The same day, in fact, within minutes, she tendered her resignation. The owner did not try to talk her out of it. It was only her second day on the job and one week before classes began at the college, where she loaned a pencil to . . . someone. Before Linda talked her into going to Fort Lewis she had been planning on attending Ozark Christian College in Joplin, Missouri.

CHAPTER 4

Denver Bound

Pete could have probably driven to Denver in his little Nash Metropolitan, but that would have meant reinstating his insurance which he suspended to save money at the first of the trimester when he arrived on campus. Driving by himself in a tiny little car over the high mountain passes in the dead of winter did not appeal to him. Wolf Creek Pass that lay between Durango and Denver was 10,856 feet above sea level.

He and two others had responded to Bryans note on the bulletin board in the student center asking for anyone going to Denver to join him and share the costs. Actually there were a couple of similar offers, but Pete chose Bryan's because his car was the largest and he was a non-drinker with a good reputation. Bryan was to furnish and drive the car; the others would each pay fifteen dollars. (According to the computer the purchasing power of fifteen dollars in 1964 is equal to one hundred and twenty dollars today: 2021. But what does it know?)

Bill Bolton, known as Bilbo to his friends was the last to show up. He said he had been "shopping." Then it was load Bilbo's Bags in the trunk and head for Denver. It would have been safer to wait until morning, but they were young, felt invincible, and were anxious to get home for Christmas. Because the sun had already gone down, they didn't notice that the skies were darkening.

The boys were in a jovial mood: laughing and joking as they drove off the mesa and out of Durango. After all it was Christmas, the tests were over, and they were going home to spend the holidays with family and friends. They even chanted a favorite beginning of a summer poem from their childhood as they drove off the hill. "No more classes. No more books. No more teacher's dirty looks." Bryan looked at his watch. It was 6:10 P.M.

Bill pulled out a bottle from a pocket of his ski jacket somewhere between Bayfield and Pagosa Springs. He took a drink and said "Merry Christmas." Then he invited everyone to salute the upcoming holiday. Bryan declined. Tim took a healthy swig. Then it was Pete's turn. Whisky had always been difficult for him to swallow, especially without making a face. He really didn't want to, but he did not want to be the wet blanket. He had been accused of being such by some of the younger guys because of his strict attention to the books and not participating in some of the pranks and other activities. (They had no way of knowing about some of his activities at the University of Alaska, which rivaled some of those of a character named Ferris Bueller in a movie made 10 years later.) He held the bottle to his lips and pretended to drink. Tim banged him on the back and said, "Good Man, Old Pete."

The blow on the back caught Pete by surprise. It also caused the bottle to hit his teeth and his mouth to open wide causing him to inhale a large slug of unexpected whisky which gushed down his throat like a flash flood in the desert. When the choking and coughing had ended Bill looked at his half empty bottle and declared that Peter Pig had to skip the next four rounds.

That was okay with Peter Pig. That giant slug consisted of the most liquor he had consumed in the last three years starting after he set the family record for drinking too much champagne at Cousin Diane's wedding. Champagne was diabolical. It tasted like soda pop, making it easy to drink too much. According to the rest of the family, he had made a complete ass out of himself, which he found quite insulting. That wasn't the way he remembered the wedding. He remembered having a wonderful time and being the life of the party. Everybody was his friend and everybody loved him. Diane's sister Lorraine declared when it was her turn to get married, he wasn't invited, and she would get a restraining order against him if necessary. Diane said she wished she had thought of that. The cruelty of his cousins, plus the fact he woke up the morning after the wedding with the worst headache of his life, made it easy for him to become a nondrinker.

Later, Bill produced a second bottle. Pete was thinking that Bill Bolton's last name should have been "Bottle." Bill Bottle could still have had Bilbo for a nickname. "Bilbo Bottle" had a nice ring to it, he thought. By this time Pete's first giant swallow had been absorbed by his body, which was not accustomed to alcohol, and a warm mellow feeling was coursing through his body, and his personality was changing.

There are mean drunks and obnoxiously super friendly drunks. Pete fell into the second group. Pete the life of the party and weddings was back. He was now clever, uninhibited, and in love with the world. He still disliked the taste of the whisky, but loved the uninhibited feeling the liquor gave him. He didn't want it to end, so he gladly accepted his turns when he was allowed back in the rotation.

As the car hurtled through the night they talked about everything: classes, sports, the weather and . . . GIRLS. Pete found Tim and Bill's knowledge on this subject mind boggling. They knew statistics like heights, measurements, strengths, weaknesses to be exploited, true hair color, times of the month, degrees of promiscuity, and plans for the holiday. What one didn't know the others did.

Bryan and Pete didn't add much to the conversation. Bryan because the weather was making it necessary for him to focus all his concentration on keeping the car on the road and moving towards their goal. Pete didn't add much to the conversation because he was only an authority on three. Well, not exactly an authority, but he had dated three of them and knew how tall they were.

That is not to say he didn't find the subject of the other girls on campus fascinating, enlightening, and in some cases shockingly surprising. In fact he was enjoying it and bringing up names for discussion that he had wondered about.

Then the face of Sandy waving him good bye in the coffee shop came to mind, and he said her name. Tim said he heard that her boyfriend had asked her to marry him and she had said she would think about it over the holiday. *I bet that was what she was going to tell me,* Pete thought. He wished he hadn't asked her about the test.

Then one of them followed up with he heard George say at breakfast that he was riding to Albuquerque in the same car as Mary Christmas, and George predicted she would be eating out of his hand before they reached Aztec. He even declared that she might want to change her name to HAPPY NEW YEAR after that. The others laughed, but Pete suddenly felt sick. George had a reputation for being the campus lover. The girls had nicknamed him Lover Boy and Gorgeous George.

It was like a one-two punch to the gut. Pete felt like he was going to throw up. Tim looked at Pete and said, "You don't look so good. Hey Bryan, pull over! I think this guy is going to be sick!"

They were on the top of Wolf Creek Pass. Bryan pulled over and Pete fell out and staggered behind the car. For the next five minutes he tried to throw up, but nothing would come out. Then on Minute Six a volcano erupted. Pete thought he saw everything he had ingested in the last six months come flying out his mouth. However, the cold night air revived him, and he climbed back in the car feeling much better, almost euphoric. There were some unkind and insensitive remarks made about what he had done to the air quality in the car. Bill suggested that Pete be put out in South Fork or Alamosa. Tim seconded the motion. Bryan was considering it until Pete said through chattering teeth that he wouldn't get out unless his money was returned.

"Would you take a check?" Bryan asked.

"N-n-n-NO."

"Do either of you other two want to pony up Pete's fare?" Bryan asked. There were no takers.

During the period they had been stopped on top of Wolf Creek, no other vehicles passed. It seemed like the rest of the world had had more sense than to be out and about on snowy, icy, Colorado mountain roads in the middle of the night. During that ten minutes Pete had been out of the car he became covered with falling snow. He was able to brush most of it off before getting back into the car. Soon his feeling of euphoria left him and he started shivering and couldn't stop. *This isn't going to be a Merry Christmas,* he thought, *if I die of pneumonia. W*orst of all he couldn't get George's brag out of his mind: "She'll be eating out of my hand before we reach Aztec."

"*I hope she bites that hand before you get to Aztec!*" Pete shouted.

"What are you talking about? We're not going to Aztec." Tim declared moving as far away from Pete as possible. Tim was thin, nervous, and only about 5' 7". "Hey Bryan, I think this guy is delirious. His teeth are chattering; he is really shivering and he is saying things that don't make sense."

Bryan got out and went to the trunk where he kept what he called an emergency box and pulled out a heavy blanket which he wrapped around Pete.

"We're out of here. This snow storm is starting to get serious," Bryan declared as he climbed back in the car. "And we don't want to get stuck up here." At the bottom of the pass was a sign next to a blinking light warning people not to attempt the pass unless they had chains or a 4-wheel drive vehicle.

"Do we have snow chains?" Tim asked.

"Not exactly," Bryan said.

Nobody in the car wanted to know what that meant. But they were already over the pass, so that was just a moot point . . . they thought.

The trip over Wolf Creek had convinced Bryan that he did not want to turn at Del Norte and take the shorter route across the state to Denver: the hypotenuse of the triangle. He opted to stay on 160 and go through Alamosa to Walsenburg where he could catch the interstate north into Denver. Chances of help would be much greater if things started to go wrong.

How that car full of students managed to make it through the stormy night is one of God's miracles. Maybe Bryan was an angel, or more probably he was someone competent God had arranged to be available. He certainly seemed to be the only one with any common sense in the car.

Bryan looked at his watch as they approached Denver. It was 1:30 in the morning. The 380 mile trip had taken two hours longer than usual. Everybody but Bryan had slept on and off, but they were all awake now and had been since Colorado Springs. Pete was the first to be dropped off. It was near 2:00 am when they pulled into the outdoor parking lot of the apartment where Pete's parents lived.

Bill suggested one last round. There was hardly any left in the bottle, so each was instructed to take a "baby" sip. But that was all it took for the non-drinker. He was suddenly back in a party mood.

"HONK THE HORN, Bryan," he shouted. "Let everyone know that Party Pete is back in town." Fortunately, Bryan did not comply. But Pete shouted, "MERRY CHRISTMAS," at the top of his lungs while he was waiting for Bryan to get his bag out of the trunk and then Pete started to sing.

"We're out of here," Bryan told the others as he hurried back into the car. "The last thing we need is to get arrested for disturbing the peace." He pressed the accelerator and the car started moving towards the exit.

"He sure looks pitiful dragging his sea bag through the snow to the entrance," said Bill.

"Maybe we should wait and see that he gets inside," said Bryan. "I'd hate to read that a Fort Lewis student froze to death after being abandoned by his friends." He took his foot off the gas, put the car in park, pulled on the emergency brake and turned off the engine.

Tim was turned around in his seat watching Pete out the rear window. "What's he doing now?" Bryan asked.

"It looks like he is serenading the whole apartment. OH DEAR."

"What is OH DEAR," Bryan asked anxiously.

"He appears to have entered into a contentious discussion with someone on a 2nd floor balcony. OH OH."

"What is OH OH?" Bryan asked fearfully.

"He appears to be giving "The Finger" to someone on a second floor balcony . . . with both hands."

"That seems like strange behavior for someone who calls himself Party Pete," said Bilbo.

"That guy up there on the 2nd floor looks awfully big," said Tim. "OH NO!"

"What is OH NO?" shouted Bryan.

"The man on the second floor is starting to throw things," Tim announced.

"We ARE out of here," said Bryan just as something that could have been a boot landed on the hood and bounced off.

"His aim isn't very good," Tim commented. "He missed Pete by a mile."

"He put a sizable dent in Bryan's hood," Bilbo observed.

"SACREBLEU!" shouted Bryan using a French oath as he opened the door. He started to get out intending to whip both Pete and the asshole on the second floor. Bryan loved his car and was proud of how it looked. He waxed and polished it once a week. At that moment they heard the distant sound of a siren heading in their direction.

"I bet someone has called the cops," Tim said.

The sound of the distant siren was no longer so distant. Bryan jumped back in the car.

"Gentleman, start your engine," encouraged Bilbo.

The instructions were unnecessary. The car leaped forward crushing the first boot just as its mate landed on the car's roof. They peeled out of that parking lot.

"His aim isn't improving," Tim pontificated. "He is letting the boot go too soon and not following through with his arm."

"Shut up," demanded Bryan, "if you don't want to walk the rest of the way." The parking area must have been sanded because the car shot out of the parking area, hit the road, skidded, and headed east lickety-split. Bryan's goal of trying to outrun the siren and flashing lights came to an end eight blocks later. Bryan pulled over to the side when their pursuer was just three blocks away, prepared to take his medicine. Then his eyes got big as saucers, and a smile formed and expanded from ear to ear as an ambulance flew by on a mission of mercy.

When they got to Tim's house, Bryan noticed there was a boot on his roof as he was getting Tim's suitcase out of the trunk. The laces from the boot had got tangled with his ski rack. Then he gave Tim the boot in more ways than one. "Tim my heart and Black Diamond (his name for his car) can't take this. I think you two better find another ride back to school in January."

"What about Party Pete?" Tim asked looking at the boot in his hand. It was a nice looking Redwing hiking boot.

"If he gets within ten feet of Diamond, he may need some extensive dental work."

"I'd pay to see that," Bilbo said.

"Bryan, would it be asking too much for you to go back so I could look for the other boot?"

Bryan snatched the boot out of Tim's hand and threw it in the middle of the road. "Does that answer your question?" Tim nodded. "Get in the car, Bill. You're next."

As they started to drive off Bilbo the bartender, who was the most responsible for the problems, observed, "I don't think that guy Party Pete should drink."

Bryan slammed on the brakes. "OUT"! Then he jumped from the car and ran around to the trunk and pulled out the Bilbo bags in haste and set them on the sidewalk. "You can spend the rest of the night at Tim's." Then he got back in his car and drove off.

"I never knew he could be such a grump. Did you see how rough he was with my bags?"

"At least he didn't throw them in the street like he did with my boot."

CHAPTER 5

Grand Arrival: Party Pete

Back at the apartment, Pete was proving the wisdom of Bilbo's statement as he wove his way through the lobby, entered the elevator, and pushed the button for the fifth floor. It only took him two attempts. It was darn lucky that he did not hit the 2nd floor button where waited a big, barefooted man who had pushed the down button and was planning on breaking a couple of middle fingers.

On reaching the 5th floor, Party Pete wove his way down the hall singing a ribald ditty Bilbo had taught them about Santa Claus and The Tooth Fairy to the melody of "Here Comes Santa Claus." Being in a happy playful mood he knocked on every door as he passed or pushed the doorbell.

He got to his parents door at the end of the hall and knocked. There was no response. He knocked a little louder. And at the same time he sang, "Merry Open the ding dong door, TRAH LAH LAH LAH LAH, LAH LAH LAH LA" to the tune of Deck the Halls. He was an unqualified success. No less than six doors opened and there was talk of "lynching," followed by "tar and feathering," with "eviction" thrown in for good measure. The door to 512 opened, his mother's hand shot out and jerked him in, and the door closed at the speed of light. He was sure he was already in the apartment when he heard the sound of the door slamming.

It took a minute for him to get his bearings. “My duffle bag is still in the hall, and I think I may have just got whiplash,” he said. The mother opened the door and pulled the bag into the apartment. She noticed several of the neighbors looking in her direction. It looked like they were having a town or neighborhood committee meeting.

Pete’s father stood in the middle of the living room with a scowl on his face. Normally, the look would have terrified Pete. Tonight it struck him, Party Pete, as funny. Perhaps it was the fact his father was wearing only an undershirt and skivvies exposing skinny little legs. “Pops,” he started out. (This was a no no, a BIG NO NO. The boys were told at an early age that when addressing him, they were only allowed to call him “father,” “dad,” “Sir,” or “Mr. Wheatley.”) Pete was anxious to tell his father that for the first time in his life, maybe several lives if there was anything to this reincarnation theory, there was the possibility that he had straight “A’s.” He had even written and practiced a little speech while waiting for Bilbo in Bryan’s room.

It started out, “I have come home from the wars to celebrate the Christmas Yuletide with my precious sibling and those two from whom whose loins I have sprung. It is my great pleasure to announce . . .” (Here he was going to imitate a fanfare: “DUH DUH DUH LUT TUH DUHH” and tell them about the straight “A” trimester. He had been going to school for 20 years and never had that kind of report card.)

He did not get to finish. His father cut him off right after the loin springing. “There was no loin springing. You were adopted,” he shouted, “from the Bakersfield Public Zoo during Adopt-a-Monkey-week. We will discuss your behavior in the morning. EARLY in the morning!!!“ With that he spun on his heels and stomped back into his bedroom. His mother shook her head sadly and followed her husband.

Pete couldn't blame them. Prior to his time in the Marines he had never earned grades higher than "C's" and he was always in some kind of hot water. It was usually for mischief and pranks like short sheeting his parent's bed, putting a whoopy pillow under the cushion of a teacher's chair, exploding cigarettes, phoning people and asking if there refrigerator was running or if they had Prince Albert in a can, etc., etc. In a hundred different ways he had been an excellent argument for birth control.

The other brother, Alan, was just the opposite: outgoing, hardworking, great athlete and intelligent. Alan was coming home from another college where you had to be in the top 10% of your high school class to even get in, not to mention things like high SAT'S. Alan, three years younger than Pete, was completing his pre-med studies this year and was already accepted by the University of Washington's med school. The brothers liked each other, but were not like each other.

Pete stumbled into the bathroom, brushed his teeth, and headed for the other bedroom. He fell asleep on top of the bed fully dressed leaving his gear in the middle of the living room where someone might trip over it. Another "No No."

That morning the father was as good as his word. He came into Pete's bedroom at 5:30 a.m. First there was the job of getting his gear out of the living room, which the father had stumbled over but had not fallen. Next came a series of lectures starting with "Never, Never use his father's toothbrush." (He probably shouldn't have smiled during this part of the speech.) Next came a lecture on temperance, which Pete thought ironic as his father had never gone to bed without downing several martinis. He did have to admit that to his father's credit, he never started before 5:00 p.m. (I believe the sun is over the yard arm, he would say.), he never missed a day of work, and he did his drinking at home.

They had just started in to Lecture 3. Pete was going to have to go to each person whose door he had banged on and rang-ed on and sanged on and apologize, and ask for forgiveness. This was not only going to be embarrassing but hard as Pete had amnesia about nearly everything that happened after the unscheduled stop on top of Wolf Creek Pass. In the middle of Lecture 3, the phone started ringing. The mother got up to answer it glad to be away from the arguing. Pete, who had a splitting headache, was starting to talk back. The result could only be a scene of disagreeable consequences.

"Hi Mom," came the voice over the phone. She smiled. "I have some terrible news." The smile vanished. "My car broke down just outside of Twin Falls, and I won't be able to make it home for Christmas. Joe, who was riding with me, lives here and he and I will be rebuilding the engine. His father has agreed to let us work on it in their garage and there are bunk beds in Joe's old bedroom."

"Can't you take a bus or a plane? We will send you the money."

"No. I have got to get it fixed before I do anything else. But if you want to send money, I'll get their mailing address. I'll keep you posted on the progress. Tell Pete I hope there are lots of pretty girls on the bunny hill and I hope he isn't still stuck at the snow plow level. Gotta go. I'll call you later. Love you."

The woman was sniffling when she returned to the breakfast table. Pete and his father stopped their arguing and stared at her questioningly. "That was Alan. His car broke down and he won't be home for Christmas."

"Damn, that's just great," growled the father jumping up from the table, throwing down his napkin and up his arms while stamping out of the room. The woman got up and followed him.

Pete was left alone at the table; he felt badly. He knew everything except the car breaking down was his fault. They were good people, and 90% of the problems lay on his doorstep. When they came out of the bedroom, he would apologize, ask their forgiveness, and do everything in his power to make this a good Christmas for them.

Pete could hear their conversation and felt like he was eavesdropping on them. He went into the living room and turned on the "Today Show," more to cover up the conversation from the bedroom than anything else and respect their privacy. Unfortunately, his father had the type of voice that penetrated and he wasn't holding back. One of the penetrations Pete heard was, "The one we like can't make it, and old (It was a phrase he had never heard before, but it sounded derogatory.) for brains staggers in and tries to get us kicked out of the apartment and . . .(he lost the next few words and then caught) and uses other people's toothbrush."

"*The one we like . . .* " *That* statement struck home. He actually found the comment about the toothbrush rather comical, but the part about "the one we like" went straight to his heart and completely changed Pete's attitude from wanting to make amends to wanting to get out of Dodge, in this case Denver. He had really been looking forward to spending the vacation skiing with his brother and spending time with his parents. Christmas really had no more significance for him than any other holiday except it was longer, there were also presents and happy childhood memories. His parents had never been church goers, so the importance of Jesus' birth had never been part of their family celebration.

Because his parents had never been church goers, he had never been one either. During most of his life he had been a non-participating believer, then an agnostic, and finally as a college student, he had matured to the belief that there was no God.

His mom drove his dad to work because she needed the car for some shopping. She wanted to get it done right away because another big storm (even bigger than the last one) was predicted to be coming in and she didn't want to be out on the streets when that happened.

Pete phoned Benny and asked if he would drive him to the bus station. He told him that his brother's car, a green 1946 Chevy, had broken down, so he was going back for his car. That way he would have options over the break. He went to the apartments between the elevator and his parent's apartment and apologized to those that were home. Most of them were very nice. Then he went back and wrote three letters of apology and slipped them under the doors of those who had not been at home. He had just finished and returned to the apartment when Benny buzzed from the lobby.

When Benny dropped him off at the bus terminal, he had an hour to spare before the bus to Durango was scheduled to leave. He thought about the note he had left on the dining room table.

Dear Folks,

A few of the guys came by and want me to go on a short ski trip with them for a few days.

Pete

To back his story, he went down to their storage cage in the basement and got out his skis, poles, and boots.

CHAPTER 6

On The Road Again

Pete was the first one on the bus and glared at the others as they entered. Even though it was practically a full bus, no one asked if the seat next to him was taken. It probably helped that he had his briefcase and jacket lying on the seat next to him. How ironic he thought. What all these other clowns are hurrying to, I am running away from: FAMILY. He opened his briefcase and took out a spiral notebook. He felt the urge to get his thoughts on paper. He would keep a journal of this Christmas. He wrote for a while and then drew a rough map starting with Durango at one end and Denver at the other.

The driver of the bus reminded him of St. Nicholas. Even though he didn't have a beard, he was short, round, lively and charismatic with a cheery greeting for each passenger as they mounted the bus, including Pete and reminded him about the line from the poem that mentioned a "little old driver so lively and quick."

It was starting to snow lightly as the bus pulled out of the depot and headed south: just a few flakes drifted down. The bus was scheduled to follow the same route he had just traveled the day before: Colorado Springs, Pueblo, Walsenburg, Alamosa, Wolf Creek,

Pagosa Springs, and Durango. He wasn't sure where it would go after that. Maybe Farmington, or Gallup; he didn't care.

By the time the bus got to Colorado Springs the flakes were large and thick, but still falling gently. His mood was improving thanks to that of the driver and the rest of the folks on the bus, especially a little girl a few seats away. She was as delightful, cute and animated as Shirley Temple had been in any of her movies. He guessed her to be in one of the first three grades at school, most likely kindergarten or the first grade. She was continually talking about going to grandma's or presents, or singing about something up on the house top, Rudolph, or Decking the halls. Every few minutes she would look back at him, smile and wave. The first few times he ignored her. Then he made a single wave (one direction) hoping that would stop her. No such luck. Soon he was responding with a double wave (back and forth), then a wave and a grin. Before she got off the bus in Pueblo he was waving, smiling, and even returning her "Merry Christmas" with ones of his own.

There were now quite a few empty seats on the bus after a lot got off at The Springs and Pueblo, the two main Colorado cities on the route: most getting off and few getting on. He amused himself, as so many loners do with contemplation, day dreams, and wishful thinking. He was feeling sorry for himself and wondering what his Christmas would be like. He'd probably ski all day, by himself, find a restaurant and eat by himself. Then he would find a hostel to spend the night. His little Nash Metropolitan was much too small for his 6' 1" frame to sleep in comfortably.

Pete found himself wishing that he was a character in one of those old time stories about Christmas. He fantasized about church, large family gatherings, yule logs, Christmas pudding, cutting down a tree in the forest, decorating it, popcorn, stockings hung by the chimney, caroling, etc., etc.

The ones he and his family celebrated were rather plastic in comparison. It was nice to get together with his brother and folks without worrying about school, but there was no true feeling of Christmas. He compared that to the family with the little girl and her two older brothers. They had left the bus in Pueblo where they had been met by happy family who lived east of there between the towns of Ordway and Fowler. With their departure a great amount of the Christmas spirit left the bus with them and the emphasis went from Christmas to storm.

Pete was thinking that if it was snowing this hard in Durango, he might have trouble getting his little car off the hill. The clearance under his little car was only 6 ½ inches. He could end up high centered or just not able to move. It seemed like everything he did this Christmas just got him deeper and deeper in trouble.

It reminded him of the time he got into some quicksand in Alaska when he was working for United Geophysical. Everything he did to get out, just sunk him deeper and deeper. Fortunately a fellow worker came back to see what had happened to him. Together they managed to get him out with the aid of a rope and one other worker.

He had been thinking about getting his car and driving back to Denver to be with his mom and dad, trying to make them happy and make up for Alan not being there and Party Pete showing up at two in the morning. But this snow was playing havoc with that plan. He had already been missing his folks, but now that it looked like he wouldn't be able to make it back, this feeling intensified. He was really wishing he had stayed at home.

Between Pueblo and Walsenburg the storm seemed to up its game. The large flakes were starting to pile up on the ground and the wind was becoming a significant factor. People were starting to talk about the storm as though it were a person, and quite a formidable one at that. The bus was now only about a third full. The snow had continued to fall slowly and was building up on the edges of the road, but Colorado has the best road crews in the world and the road was fine on the Interstate.

Forty-eight miles later in Walsenburg, two got off and none got on. It was there the bus quit heading south and was now heading west straight into the heart of the storm and no longer on I-25. The strain was starting to show on the driver's face as they headed west towards Alamosa. Pete thought Nick was no longer looking lively and quick. It was becoming obvious to all that Colorado's crack highway department was having a hard time staying ahead of the falling snow. The bus made it to the top of and over La Veta, one of Colorado's easier passes, but not without a struggle.

On the western side of the pass with no mountain to protect them, it seemed like the storm had doubled in power. It was too much for the road crews to maintain. The bus was only going about 30 miles an hour as they headed down the west side of the pass following a snow plow and a caravan of cars. Before catching up with the parade, the bus had slid slightly a couple of times and all aboard, or at least a majority of them realized they could very easily slide off the road. There was no traffic coming the other way and Pete realized they must have closed the pass.

Pete had the same emotional feeling of dread he sometimes got in an airplane before takeoffs or landings, when there was stormy weather. There was only one lane clear and no one tried to go around the slow moving plow. They were just thankful it was there and making it possible for them to keep moving. This Christmas was turning into a disaster and one Pete would remember the rest of his life.

When the bus reached the floor of the valley, the storm seemed to be taking a break and for the last few miles into Alamosa it seemed like everything was going to work out all right. Pete recalled hearing a professor say this valley was the highest agricultural land in the United States. Looking out the window he even cracked a joke to himself saying they probably planted snowballs. Then he told himself, "Pete, don't quit your day job."

The streets of Alamosa were packed with snow. It looked like the city road crews had given up. Cars parked on the side of the road looked like giant humps of snow. Pete was thinking if it had snowed this hard in Durango, he would wait until daylight before going up on the Enchanted Mesa for his car. He would spend the night in the depot. Come to think of it, he would be lucky if he could even get his car off the mesa. He was glad he had phoned Allstate and had his insurance reinstated before leaving his folks apartment.

Pete had been wishing for the last half hour he had stayed at home. In his thinking, "home" was still where his parents were, even without Alan. The earlier spirit of the happy travelers and the time to think, had made him see things from his parent's point of view. In all fairness, he had to admit he had not returned in a manner one would hope from the fruit of their "loom" or was it "loins."

It came as no surprise when the driver trudged out of the small building which served as a terminal in Alamosa and announced there would be a delay. Wolf Creek Pass was closed, but the plows were hard at it and off duty personnel had been called in to assist and get it re-opened. The driver said the bus would not leave for at least four hours, and he recommended everyone go get something to eat and check back then.

Pete returned four hours later after spending the time in the town library. He had not felt like eating, and he loved libraries. The news was not good. The highway crew had lost a snowplow in a small avalanche and there was no possibility of the pass being open before the next day. Even that was doubtful.

"What can I do?" he asked the man behind the counter.

"We'll give you a ticket back to Denver and refund your money, or you can ride a giant "U."

"What is that, a unicorn or a lady sheep?" he asked. Those were the only two appropriate "u" sounding words he could come up with on the spur of the moment. (Well, maybe scholars would challenge the use of the word "appropriate.") He was tempted to say that the bus company (Greyhound) was going to the dogs. Pete had never been very good at resisting temptation.

"Ho Ho. Very funny," said the agent without much enthusiasm. (Pete doubted his sincerity.) "You can take the bus south to Albuquerque, transfer to a westbound as far as Gallup, and then transfer to a northbound which will take you through Farmington to Durango. It requires two transfers, and an extra 400 miles, but in the long run, may be the quickest way to get there. To use a football term, you would be making an end run around the tall mountains."

"Forget it," Pete said. "When does the bus leave for Denver?"

"Tomorrow . . . It is trapped on the other side of Wolf Creek."

Pete sighed in resignation. "Oh Well! When does the bus leave for Albuquerque?"

"Thirty minutes. We're rerouting the bus you were on."

"I'll take the Big U." When he climbed aboard the bus, he said "Hike." The driver had no idea what he was talking about.

Thirty minutes later he was on a bus headed for Albuquerque with the paper work in his wallet that guaranteed he was paid all the way to Durango and it covered the transfers. *Now if the weather will only cooperate,* he thought, and it mostly did. He was proud of himself. Adversity had thrown many hurdles in his way, but he was still moving. He felt like running up and down the aisle singing about the wheels on the bus going round and round. Ten miles south of Santa Fe, the 2nd wave of the storm started making an appearance, but gently, much like it had started in Denver when his bus was leaving there.

Pete changed buses in Albuquerque and was then heading west on an almost empty bus. It had been held up for some couples coming up from the south and going to Flagstaff, AZ. The bus was approximately 30% full.

Being in Albuquerque reminded him that Mary had flown home to Michigan from that city less than 24 hours earlier and had been driven there in the same car with Lover Boy George. He hated Lover Boy and he hated the fact he was jealous, but he couldn't help himself. Thoughts of Mary were in charge of his subconscious. He thought about the first time he had heard Mary's name. It was six months prior to him meeting her.

It was in January of his first trimester living on campus that he first became aware of the neat name, "Mary Christmas." He had gone down to his friend Tom's room to see if he wanted to go to lunch. The door was open and Tom waved him in. There were several others in the room visiting Cheto. Tom said he would be ready in ten minutes as soon as he finished a chapter he was working on. Pete sat down on Tom's bed to wait. Tom was sharing the room with a popular athlete named Cheto who was a gifted running back with a great personality. Therefore, that room was often the gathering spot for the jocks, making it hard for Tom to concentrate. He often went to Pete and Benny's room or Ken's and Marv's to study.

William Bradford Bentley the third came down the hall and entered the room without knocking or being invited. William Bradford Bentley the third was from Boston and thought of himself as superior to the local yokels, cowboys, Indians, and Mexicans he was surrounded by, but he made an effort to fit in, even though he probably felt like he was slumming. He had been quarterback of his high school football team and had chosen Fort Lewis because of its less than stellar record in football. He figured he could walk on and be a starting quarterback at a little college that most folks had never heard of. However, there was a lot about being raised in Boston that had not prepared him for life out west.

Some of his attempts to fit in were legend. Pete remembered hearing about the time William Bradford Bentley the third walked into a room where a couple of the students who happened to be of Mexican descent (Don & Juan) were playing cards. They were also drinking cokes and eating jalapeno peppers. William Bradford Bentley the third asked what the peppers were and Don told him they were Colorado Pickles and "to eat them correctly, you had to immerse them in the cheese dip, then put the whole thing in your mouth and chew real fast." Then Juan demonstrated. Without being invited, William Bradford Bentley the third grabbed one of the largest, dipped it in the cheese sauce which had been enhanced with Tabasco Sauce, popped it in his mouth and chewed real fast. For 30 seconds nothing happened other than the chewing real fast. Then William Bradford Bentley the third stopped chewing. During the next 30 seconds his marvelous Boston bean (brain) kicked in telling him something was amiss, something terrible, on a par with the sinking of the Titanic, the great Chicago Fire, the eruptions of Mt. Vesuvius or Krakatoa. His eyes popped out, sweat poured down his face, and his mouth was ablaze. What he hadn't swallowed, he spit, shooting it clear across the room. He ran from the room to the drinking fountain in the hall screaming "WAH-TAH WAH-TAH NEED WAH-TAH LOTS WAH-TAH!"

Don turned to Juan and commented that East Coast Gringo seemed to have trouble pronouncing his "R.s" correctly. Juan agreed. Don then said it would make it hard for him to speak Spanish. Juan agreed. Don was picking up the chili that William Bradford Bentley the third had spit out and had landed on Don's bed. "He has terrible table manners," Don stated. Juan agreed. "I don't think we should invite him to share snacks with us anymore," Don opined. Juan agreed. Don said, "He just left without even saying good-bye." "That was certainly rude," Juan said. "It's your play, I discarded the queen."

But that wasn't the only famous William Bradford Bentley the third story. His roommate's name was Roger. Roger was a Mormon from Utah and couldn't stand William Bradford Bentley the third and his superior attitude. Roger had put in for a change of roommates after the first week and expressed **his** willingness to move if William Bradford Bentley the third wouldn't. He even offered a reward for anyone willing to trade with him. For some reason the administration was dragging its feet. I suspect it was because they couldn't find anyone who would agree to room with William Bradford Bentley the third.

Roger was having a little trouble with constipation. It was suggested by one of his wives (not true, just a little Wheatley humor), that he try a little prune juice. Roger bought a quart bottle and some little paper cups. He then poured some prune juice in a cup and sipped on it while he studied.

William Bradford Bentley the third returned to the room and noticed the bottle of prune juice on Roger Roommate's desk. William asked what it was for. Roger told him he had read an article where a quart of it would raise a person's IQ 10 points if drunk all at once. (The reason for the lie was Roger did not want to admit he was having trouble with constipation to Blabber Mouth Bentley the third fearing the news would soon be spread all over the campus.)

'Let me taste it," said William Bradford Bentley the third and picked up the bottle and took a sip before Roger could stop him. William Bradford Bentley the third liked the taste.

Roger Roommate was mad. "Take the bottle you stupid eastern #$%. Now I'll have to go buy another. Drink the whole thing. If you raise your IQ 10% you might make it to the lowest rung of the human level, but I doubt it. You will probably top out at monkey. I don't want it now that you have had your mouth on it. Chug a lug it all if you are man enough."

For some reason, William Bradford Bentley the third's feelings were hurt by something Roger had said. I suspect it was the "monkey" comment. He would show Roger he was man enough. He would chug the rest of the bottle right in front of him. But not today. He had a history test the next morning. Ten percent more brain power wouldn't hurt the cause. He would wait and drink the rest of the bottle in front of Roger right before leaving for the test.

The next morning everything went as he planned until William Bradford Bentley the third was three quarters of the way across campus. He suddenly switched to Plan B, as in "(B)athroom." Unfortunately he was not able to employ Plan B successfully, arriving too late at the destination. He missed, not only the test, but all his afternoon classes, football practice, supper, and everything else for 24 hours.

Roommate Roger was quoted as saying he would have to revise his hypothesis on the level prune juice would raise someone's intelligence. He concluded it was much closer to 90%.

Back to my story about the first time I became aware of a Mary Christmas. William Bradford Bentley the third came into the room excited and asked, "Have you seen the two new girls that just entered? One is from Colorado, and she is an A+. Maybe two pluses. **BUT . . .** the other is from Chicago and she is off the chart good looking. She is a fifteen on a scale of one to ten. And get this he declared, throwing in dramatic pauses, her name . . . is . . . Mary . . . Christmas."

(*Great name*, Pete thought. At the University of Alaska, he knew a guy named Larry Christmas, but this beat that.)

". . . and I'd crawl three miles on my belly over rusty razor blades just to smell where she last tinkled," Boston Bill continued. (He might not have said "tinkled.")

"On that note, I am out of here," Tom said jumping up from his desk.

"I'm already half way out the door," Pete put in, "but I'm not as hungry as I was before Boston Billy joined us".

"Maybe we should call him Boston Belly," said Tom

The bus hit a larger than usual pothole and Pete was jolted back into the present and the storm again. They were ten minutes west of Albuquerque. The snow was falling so thickly and heavily that the wheels on the bus were only going round and round at 30 miles per hour. The snow was now falling as heavily as in Colorado.

Wherever he looked outside the bus, all he could see was white: snow on the ground and snow falling through the air. The bus's headlights could not pierce the snow much further than 50 feet. It gave the illusion that the bus was in a gigantic white room, isolated from the rest of the world.

Pete was reminded of a Hank Williams song he had heard the late Johnny Horton sing called "The Lost Highway." He sang it to himself in his mind.

Yes, he thought, like the fellow in the song, he was on the lost highway. He leaned his seat all the way back and tried to sleep. He couldn't. He had never been able to sleep in a chair or a sitting position, unless he didn't want to . . . like when he was studying for the last test two days earlier.

Looking around he noticed the last seat in the bus stretched clear across and it was unoccupied. Pete got up and went back to it and was able to lie down. He was soon asleep, but it was not a good sleep. It was fitful and full of bad dreams. He kicked and tossed and even rolled off the seat once. That woke him up. He was upside down with his feet on the seat and the rest of him on the floor. He got up and walked back to his seat near the front.

The wind with, no high mountains to block it, was running wild and having its way with the highway and could best be described as a blizzard. Then around Prewitt, the storm seemed to slack off. Later the driver told them they were passing Thoreau which he pronounced as "Thru" and if they didn't get in trouble going over the Continental Divide they would be in Gallup in the next hour. As they were going over the divide the driver called out, "LOOK AT THAT." Two semis that had been heading west, the same direction they were going, were both off the highway, one in the ditch on the right and the other in the median. Fortunately, they were both upright.

"This place eats trucks in the winter when the weather is bad," the driver said. The snow was no longer falling as hard and seemed to be tapering off, but the driver kept the speed under 45. Pete could tell by the driver's face that the trip had been hard on him. Thirty minutes later they pulled into Gallup.

CHAPTER 7

Gallup Café, Can't Pay

Pete was the only one to leave the bus in Gallup. The time was around 4:00 a.m. The depot's lobby was small, about the size of a large living room with a counter and a pinball machine and some cold hard benches. It did not take long for his sea bag, boots, skis, and poles to be unloaded. No one got on and the bus was quickly on its way. Pete and a young Navajo named Steven were the only ones in the little building which was used by both Greyhound and Continental Trailways. Steven, the night man, was playing the pinball machine and Pete sat on a hard bench shivering and wondering why such a small building was so hard to heat.

There was a four hour wait until his bus was due, so Pete asked if there was an all-night restaurant within walking distance. Steven said there was one just across the street. Pete asked if he could leave his briefcase and Steven told him to put it behind the counter.

When Pete went out, he received a pleasant surprise. It had quit snowing and there were no clouds. He could see the stars above and the city's Christmas decorations below. It was almost like a fairy land. Everything glittered and sparkled. The difference between what it looked like when he arrived and what it looked like now was like that movie where the girl and her dog were blown from Kansas to Oz. The accumulation on the ground he guessed at about two feet. A pickup truck went slowly by and he heard the familiar sound of tire chains that he remembered from his two years in Alaska. One chain had not been cinched up tight enough and banged against a fender.

In front of the café was a group of three large men. They were swaying unsteadily and speaking unnaturally loud in a language he couldn't understand but thought was most likely Navajo. It could have been Hopi, Zuni, Gibberish, Tongues, or Babel for all he knew. His knowledge of the Bible definitely had some gaps he decided. He nicknamed the group "The Carolers" in his mind.

He hoped they weren't saying, "Let's scalp this tourist and take his wallet." They must be Eskimos he decided. What right thinking Indian would be out in weather like this? He thought about the three wise men that followed the star. These would have had to follow a snowflake. And they really didn't look or act all that wise. Wise would have gone into the café or stayed at home beside the fire. (He didn't realize that they had entered the café earlier and been rudely escorted out by a couple of miners who were trying to flirt with the waitress.) Why did his thoughts keep returning to things religious? Most likely, because it was the reason for the season.

He hurried past The Carolers and into the café making sure he did not make eye contact with any of the group. The café seemed old and dingy, but warmer than the bus depot. Two unfriendly looking men sat at the end of the counter next to the register drinking coffee. They looked up as he entered, sneered, and went back to their attempts to engage the waitress in conversation.

Pete took a seat in one of the booths. The waitress glanced up from the magazine she was reading then went back to it. Apparently, he decided after waiting for several minutes, if one wanted to order they had to go to the counter. He started to get up, but then the waitress made the long walk over. She had a scowl on her face.

"What's wrong, the counter ain't good enough for you?"

"And a cheery good morning to you, Madam." (Silence) . . . "I'm fine, thank you. Thanks for asking. Nice little place you have here."

Pete looked her up and down quickly. Her uniform looked like it hadn't been washed in over a week. Her teeth were slightly stained, probably from cigarettes. It was obvious to Pete that oral hygiene or any other kind of "giene" was not a high priority with her. She was somewhat overweight, in her late 30's or early 40's, with a killer body: starring two large breasts which she seemed quite proud of. They were pushing against the buttons on her uniform every time she took a breath. The badge over one said Mable. He thought about asking her what the other one's name was, but didn't. It was an old joke and he figured she'd heard it a hundred times.

She took a deep breath. It was harder for them, but the buttons held. Pete wondered if they had been sewed on with fishing line. She had undoubtedly put on weight since she bought the uniform or she was wearing someone else's outfit. "If you are done staring, would you like to order?"

Pete could see his wit and charm was wasted on her, so he ordered just enough to let him remain in this warm building. "I believe I will have a doughnut and a coffee with cream."

"ANYTHING ELSE?" she asked after she returned with the coffee and doughnut. The doughnut looked like it had seen better days, probably in the Truman administration. (That's a joke, son. He thought to himself.) It was probably "day old" . . . a week ago. However, the coffee smelled good, although a dark stain made the cleanliness of the cup suspect.

"*ANYTHING ELSE,*" he thought about saying, "a tetanus shot," but held back. The room was warm and the bus depot was not,

He pulled a book out of his pocket that he had found in the bus station when he was putting his briefcase behind the counter. It was by Louis L'Amour. It was good. The coffee had warmed his body and he was no longer shivering. He couldn't stomach the doughnut and slipped it into his pocket to throw away when he got outside, or use as a weapon if attacked by The Carolers. He read for half an hour until he came to some missing pages. Pages 75-94 were missing. Dang! Lilith was trying to join the wagon train and Cleave was trying to track her down because of her beauty and an inheritance she was to get. With a sigh, he put the book down and got up to pay. At the register Pete reached into his back pocket for his wallet.

It was not there! His wallet was gone! How was this possible?

He felt through all his other pockets. Nothing. He started to sweat. He was on the verge of panic. He felt like shouting, "WATAH, NEED WATAH." He repeated the search. Where could it be? The waitress and the two men were watching him. She looked as though she were watching a familiar movie. It was a movie called "The Deadbeat." He ran back to the booth and felt around the seat, behind the cushion, and on the floor. Where was it? Had he left it at the bus depot? Maybe he had put it in his briefcase, but he didn't think so. By turning all his pockets inside out he came up with fifteen cents and the despicable doughnut. That was embarrassing.

"Don't like our doughnuts?" Mable asked.

"I was saving it for later," he replied as he handed her the fifteen cents. "Could you trust me for the rest until I can get over to the depot and pick up my wallet?"

"NO!" She reached for the phone like she was going to call her boss or the police.

One of the customers who had been trying to flirt with the waitress stood up and said, "You want me and Harry to take him out back, Mable?"

"No she doesn't! And you'd better step back," Pete said. "I have this doughnut. I don't want to hurt anybody but if forced to, I will."

They were not intimidated or impressed with his sense of humor.

Then an idea occurred to him. "Wait," Pete said. "I have got this great LOUIS L'AMOUR book. It was a present from my mother on her death bed. She said, 'Son, you have got to read this book. It's great.' Look, it's worth more than what I owe. The price is on the cover." He purposely "forgot" to mention the 19 missing pages fearing they might decrease the book's value.

Harry said, "I love that author. I'll buy the book for what Captain Doughnut owes."

Mable hesitated, then said, "Leave the book, I like this writer too. Sorry Harry." She was starting to read as he hurried out of the café. He hoped she didn't get to Page 75 before his bus got to town.

He hurried back to the depot. The "Eskimo Carolers" were gone. Had they found his wallet and gone off for a potlatch? Not only was his money in the wallet, but also his bus ticket. He was stranded. Stranded and broke. As he stumbled across the street, he thought about his grandmother.

What was it his Grandmother Anderson used to say? Oh yes, "Cheer up, things could be worse." He didn't see how. It was two days before Christmas. He was stranded in a strange town full of mean looking drunks and waitresses; he didn't have any money and his family had most likely disowned him. Maybe Grandma's advice was okay for her day, but she was currently out of sync with today's society. How could things possibly get worse?

This question was about to be answered. He learned how when he got to the depot. His duffle bag wasn't where he had left it. *Oh dear God,* he thought. *The only thing I have in this world is the clothes I am wearing and a stale doughnut that was probably left over from the "Last Supper." There it was again, another Bible reference.*

Steven, the Navajo who was in charge of the depot, appeared to be in a foul mood. He was throwing things around and cussing. At least Pete thought it was cussing. Steven was doing it in a language Pete didn't understand. It was like watching the old "I Love Lucy" show when Ricky would go off on some tirade in Spanish. Steven appeared to be looking for something.

"My wallet is missing," Pete said.

"Well doesn't that just put the icing on the cake," Steven responded. "My book is missing. I know I left it on the counter when your bus got here. A thief must have snuck in and taken it while I was in back getting some freight to load on the bus. All I found were pages 75-94 where the thief dropped them next to the front door. ."

Pete wanted to ask him if Lilith got on with the wagon train and if that gambler had caught up with her, but thought better of it.

"You didn't see my book, did you?"

Pete shook his head and tried to look innocent. "Maybe the bus driver took it."

Steven cursed. "I never did like that guy. His eyes are too close together and he is always sneaking around and not helping me with the freight. This isn't the first time things have showed up missing around here. Let's go across the street for a cup of coffee. I'll pay. We'll figure out what we can do about your situation. Give me a minute to lock up and turn the sign around. There are no buses scheduled for two hours."

"OH NO," Pete cried out. "Let's figure it out here. I twisted my ankle," he lied.

Pete was beginning to think that his chances of living until the sun came up were getting slimmer and slimmer. The waitress was probably still reading THE book and that would be the second thing Steven noticed if they went to the cafe. If she had come to the missing pages, she would certainly not hesitate to tell the world how she came in possession of the book. Harry and the other guy would back her up. AND . . . Pete would lose his only friend in this town.

He promised God that he would never ever tell another white lie. He remembered another of grandma's favorite sayings: "Oh what a tangled web we weave, when first we practice to deceive." Perhaps maybe grandma wasn't as far out of sync with this modern society as he first thought.

He let out a low *fake* moan and grimaced as he sat down bravely stifling the reaction to the pretend pain in his pretend sprained ankle. From the seat on the bench, Pete noticed his skis leaning against the wall. "At least they didn't steal them," he said.

"Who? What? Steal what?" Steven asked.

"The ones who stole my duffle bag. They didn't steal my skis and poles."

"Your bag and boots are in back," said Steve. "It was just easier to leave the skis where they were."

What a relief Pete thought. I'll have some clean clothes to be buried in.

Steven interrupted his thoughts. "You haven't seen my book, have you? It's called How the West Was Won."

It was like being dropped through a hole into a frozen lake. He had never actually had that experience. But once in Anchorage he had attempted to join three of his friends who wanted to become members of something called the Polar Bear Club. To join, they thought all you had to do was swim in a lake or the ocean in the middle of the winter. They had been drinking and weren't really sure of the rules. There were three of them. The lakes were frozen, but they found a place where Cook Inlet starts up Kinik Arm where the saltiness and the tides kept the water from freezing solid. He only made it as far as a toe on one leg and the shin on the other, and that only because he lost his balance and had to kick the shin foot out to catch himself. He had made the mistake of **testing** the water with his big toe and the rest of his body had decided the inlet had flunked that **test**. He told his friends, who all dove in but didn't make the swim, that he Pete was a member of the Owl Club. Its members had to be wise enough not to jump in freezing water. He said they (his buddies) qualified for the Dodo Club (named after the foolish extinct bird) whose members were dumb enough to jump into large bodies of water in freezing weather. They suggested he was a member of the Chicken Club. But like Grandma says, "He who laughs last, laughs best." He was the only one of the group that did not get sick. They created a club called the Chicken Club, and made him president. When they got back to the camp job, his new name was HEN-rieta.

Steven asked him to remember the last time he had used the wallet and trace his actions from there. The last time had been in a snack bar in Albuquerque. He had bought a Coke, some chips and a Snickers right before getting on the bus to Gallup. He had taken his ticket out of the wallet to show the driver. Then he put his billfold back in his pocket and mounted the bus. He remembered distinctly taking the ticket out of his wallet and showing it to the driver. He remembered not being able to sleep and going to the seat in the back of the bus. He remembered a fitful sleep and dreaming about being chased by the Abominable Snowman whose name was Frosty and waking up upside down with his feet on the seat and the rest of his body on the floor of the bus. *I bet that is when I lost it,* he thought. He told Steven.

Steven phoned the depot in Holbrook and left a message for the driver to phone back when he arrived. There was nothing to do but wait. They visited for a while and then Steve went back to the pinball machine and Pete started reading Page 75. It was a good book; he'd have to finish it someday.

Forty-five minutes later the phone rang. He ran to stand next to Steve. It was someone wanting to know the price of the fare to Salt

Lake. The phone tingled a couple of times in the next half hour, but when Steve picked up the receiver, they were greeted by a weak dial tone and static.

"I hope the phone doesn't go out again," Steve commented.

AGAIN! Pete thought. He was picturing his grandmother's face telling him that things could be worse. He thought of Job in The Bible and wondered if he had such a helpful and encouraging grandmother telling him to cheer up because things could be worse.

CHAPTER 8

Wallet and Phone

The phone rang again; it was the driver. Pete heard Steve explain the situation to the driver. Steve handed the phone to Pete. "He has gone out to check the bus. I reminded him about you going to the back of the bus to stretch out and sleep." It was five minutes, a long five minutes before the driver came on the phone. His wallet had been found, on the floor in the back of the bus along with a magazine on the history of the Alamo, which said one of the heroes to lose his life was Elton John. The magazine did not say if he was killed by the Mexican army or a group of music lovers.

Pete crossed his fingers and asked, "Is there any money in the wallet?"

"Yes, do you want me to count it?" Pete said "yes." It was all there.

They made arrangements to have it on the next bus heading east and he could pick it up at the Gallup depot. Pete would not be going anywhere until that wallet arrived. He tried, but not too hard, to get the driver to take out $20 for a reward, but the driver declined saying, "My reindeers are itching to get on to Winslow and Flagstaff.

Merry Christmas to all, and to all a 'Good . . . Morning." And he hung up.

Pete looked at Steven, "I don't think his eyes are too close together."

Pete looked at his watch. It was a little after five. The bus bringing his wallet was not scheduled to arrive until the afternoon. And the schedules, because of the storm and the tremendous amount of snow on the ground, were more wishful thinking than something one could count on.

Pete had given quite a bit of thought on the bus to visiting Grace over New Year's and possibly driving her back to campus. It surprised him, but now that both girls were absent from him, his thoughts turned to the dark haired girl nearly as much as the blond. Thoughts of Mary were exciting: but they always left him with a feeling of deep longing, hurt, and exhaustion. Thoughts of Grace were pleasant and left him feeling refreshed and contented. Maybe he'd give her a call. Because he had been up so long it hadn't occurred to him others might still be sleeping.

Pete borrowed some change from Steve and dialed the number Grace had given him. It rang twelve times before it was answered by an unhappy, gruff, male voice. "**YES!**"

"May I speak with Grace, please?"

"**NO!**" That was followed by the slamming down of the phone.

Pete turned to Steve. "Whoever answers their phone is a man of very few words."

"He has very good volume though. I could hear him clear over here," Steve said.

"That doesn't surprise me. I think it may be several hours before hearing returns to my left ear. Is there any chance I can borrow $10 from you until my wallet gets here?"

"No."

They bargained for half an hour and finally came up with a deal where Steven loaned Pete $25 using the skis as collateral. Pete agreed to pay $5 interests on the loan. Pete turned a couple of the dollars into change and then went back to the payphone. It was now approaching seven o'clock.

The phone rang six times before it was answered, this time by a woman. "May I speak to Grace?"

"It's a little early for that," said the voice.

"Please! This is Professor Dingledorf. It relates to her scholarship."

"Hold on," the voice said. There was a l-o-n-g period of silence, so long he had to feed a few more quarters into the phone.

Finally Grace came on. She sounded sleepy like she had just been awakened. "Hello. This is Grace. Who are you?"

"I am Jingles the Christmas Dwarf, here to grant your greatest Christmas wish."

"Good-bye Jingles the Christmas Dwarf or Dingledorf or whoever you are. I'm hanging up."

"WAIT! Don't hang up." Pete remembered the first time he had talked to her on the phone and said, still trying to be cute and charming, "This is Mr. Wheatley. You loaned me a pencil." (Silence) "Did you miss me?" (Silence) "How are you?"

"F-i-n-e," she said slowly, dragging out the word. The voice did sound familiar.

It wasn't the same reaction he had got last time he used that sentence. She sounded strange, a little distant and was acting funny, like she was trying to tell if he'd been drinking. **Oh Dear**! He wondered if he had called her while he was in his cups or she had called Denver and got his mother.

"Is something wrong? You sound different," he asked.

"I'm not sure. I never expected you to phone this soon . . . or this early . . . especially this early. What time is it in Denver? It is a little after seven here. Are you calling to tell me you can't come down on New Year's?"

"No."

Her voice brightened. "Are you calling to tell me you can come for New Years?"

"How about Old Years?"

"What are you talking about?"

"I'm not in Denver."

"Where are you?"

"I'm in Gallup at the bus depot, and I'll be here all day." (SILENCE) He did not hear the sound of joy he had been expecting and hoping for. The only thing coming over the phone was SILENCE. He broke into an explanation about his brother's car breaking down and deciding to go to Durango to get his car and Wolf Creek being closed and the rest of what happened, leaving out only the parts about him drinking too much, having trouble with his parents, and running away from home. He ended with, "I'll be here all day and wondered if you wanted to get together for a while." (SILENCE).

His imagination filled the void with all sorts of possibilities. She is worried that I have come to spend the entire vacation. She has reconnected with her old boyfriend. Maybe he is with her right now. Maybe he was the person who answered the phone the first time. Then a voice came on but it was not Grace. It was the operator demanding some more quarters. *Okay*, he thought but this has to be the last time as he dropped his final change into the slot.

He couldn't figure Grace out. Why the silence? Was she giving him enough rope to hang himself? She hadn't hung up. This was the first time since their first date that she had not just jumped positively on any of his suggestions enthusiastically. It made him realize that he had been taking her too much for granted. He would never do that again if he were lucky enough to . . . The operator came on again and when he didn't have any more change he was met with the sound of a dial tone. That operator sounded like and reminded him of Mable across the street. Perhaps they had attended the same charm school.

He told Steven that he had a quick errand to perform and he would be right back. Everything looked the same outside but no longer seemed like a fairy land. This was a horrible little town he thought. He walked into the café. The lady behind the counter was different. She was shorter than Mable, wearing a clean outfit, thin, and bustling about. "Good morning. May I help you, Sir? Just sit anywhere. I'll be right with you."

He told her that he was looking for Mable. At that moment Mable came out of the kitchen. She was wearing a long coat and had snow boots on. Her shift was over.

Mable stopped when she saw him and glared. There was a frown upon her face and she looked ready to do battle.

Pete held up his hands. "Before you say anything, I have come to pay my bill like I promised. My wallet has been found." He paid for his coffee and round rock with a hole in the middle pretending to be a doughnut. He gave her a tip that was equal to the whole bill.

She was stunned. "Why didn't you keep going?"

"I was never trying to cheat you. I really lost my wallet. You can ask Steve at the bus depot if you don't believe me."

"I believe you." She smiled and reached into her purse. "I bought you a present." She handed him the book. "I'm sorry, but there are some pages missing." She laughed, "Merry Christmas."

On his way back to the depot he was trying to decide where to put the book so Steve would find it without connecting its temporary disappearance to him. When he entered the building Steve said "You had a phone call. You are supposed to phone Grace. She said you know the number."

Steve gave him change for a five dollar bill: 3 ones and 2 dollars' worth of quarters. When Steve was getting the change Pete slipped the book under some brochures at the far end of the counter.

Pete dialed the number. The phone was answered on the first ring. It was answered before the first ring ended. A breathless voice started talking before he could even say hello. "I'm sorry to have been gone so long, but I had to talk Mama into letting me borrow the car. The snow is quite deep out here, and she doesn't like the idea of me driving, but I persuaded her."

"What! You mean I had been talking to myself for all that time?"

"And quite eloquently I imagine," she retorted.

Was she trying to be funny? He had never noticed her having a sense of humor before. She had always treated him more . . . uh . . . "reverently." After all, he was a senior and seven years older than she. He had been expecting an apology for leaving him hanging on the phone, not humor . . . at his expense.

She interrupted his thoughts. . . "Got to go. I'll see you in an hour, good Lord willing. Bye." There was a click and then a dial tone before he could say anything. Pete was in shock. Was this the quiet, shy, mousey girlfriend he had known for the last 16 weeks? Was she turning into a Mary? There was a new song that was being played on the country radio a lot this month by some guy named Buck. The singer was comparing his relationship with his girlfriend to someone grabbing a tiger by the tail. This Buck didn't sound too bright. He wondered if maybe he, Pete, was in the same category. He walked outside for some fresh air. Nothing about the place had changed, but he thought to himself, what a fine little town this is.

CHAPTER 9

Grace, Ranch, Tree & Tire

Ninety minutes later, a car pulled into the parking lot and "tooted" for him. *I guess her mother never gave her the lecture about pulling up in front of a date's house and honking,* he thought. As he ran for the car, he grinned to himself recalling his mother's efforts to instill a little etiquette in her two sons.

Grace smiled as he entered the car. "I'm so glad to see you. I would have been here sooner, but the road is awful, and mother changed her mind aboutlettingmecomeunchaperoned,and . . ."

"Hey, hey. Slow down girl. These poor old ears can't listen that fast."

"W – H – A – T W – O – U - L - D .... Y – O – U L – I – K – E T – O – D - O F – I – R – S – T - ?"

"Hmmm. Do your vocal chords have a speed and volume we haven't heard yet?" (Again he mused over her seeming lack of reverence for him, and he could hear in his mind that guy Buck singing a warning about the tiger.) Apparently this new behavior wasn't just limited to the phone. She was on her own home turf and tapped into a different degree of confidence. He'd have to straighten her out when they got back to school.

"Why don't you show me the town? I don't really care what we do, I just want to spend time with you until my buses and wallet get here."

"Yes, I bet spend is the key word with me doing the spending." She laughed. It was a pleasant sound. He was liking this change in her personality.

"I've got a good idea. Does this town have a library?"

"Oh no you don't, Buster. It has an excellent library, maybe the best in the state because of Octavia, but you are not going to see it today. Half the time I have been with you has been spent in a library, but now we are on vacation, Christmas vacation. No libraries and no talk about school work. I have a surprise for you, but first I have a couple of presents to buy and errands to run. It was part of the deal I had to make to get the car."

No . . . Buster! What has she been snorting? He wisely didn't express those thoughts. He decided to play along, *in for a dime, in for a dollar.*

"OH GOOD! I love shopping and I REALLY like surprises. I'll be happy to go along with you and give you any suggestions on what expensive gifts to give a young man, say of my approximate age and interests," he said with a twinkle in his eyes.

She smiled. "Unfortunately, I do not need any consumer buying tips. I have already bought your present, but I could use a big strong man to carry a couple of packages."

The "couple" of packages and few errands turned into "many" and the poor lad's arms were aching by the time they returned to the car. "If a hernia is my surprise, I don't think I love surprises anymore." Now he knew why married men never went shopping with their wives. He had always disliked everything about shopping and could not, for the life of him, understand why he was having such a good time.

"Oh Hush, there weren't that many packages, but because you've been such a good boy, I'll take you to a library and then out for something to eat. My treat." He completely missed the fact she had said "a" library and not "the" library.

The car started south away from the center of town and up a long 3 mile hill that had been partially cleared by a truck with a blade on the front and some kind of material in its bed which it was sprinkling on the road. From the top of the hill he could see it was a long ways down to the bottom on the other side. Grace didn't hesitate, just shifted down a gear and kept on moving. He could see far ahead that it looked like it might be snowing.

"They built this library a little far from the center of town, didn't they?"

She laughed. What a pleasant sound he thought. It almost sounded like singing. "The library is out at the ranch, and so is the lunch. You have plenty of time. I want you to meet Mama, . . . AND . . . she wants to meet you."

Oh Oh, he thought. An older friend, Larry, had warned him that when they want you to meet their parents, it is time to get out of Dodge. Unfortunately for Larry he had not followed his own advice and was raising and at the mercy of five lords a leaping: the wildest little boys Pete had ever seen. If the song was correct, poor Larry still had five more lords to go. Every once in a while Pete would see smoke coming out of large mounds of snow. "Look," he said in an attempt to be funny, "The snow is on fire."

She smiled. "Before the storm, you would have been able to see hogans out there. Indian houses," she clarified.

"I know what hogans are." He hated when he said something to be funny and people thought he was serious.

The farther they progressed, the more desolate the landscape became. He was starting to feel like an unwilling volunteer on an Arctic expedition. "Don't you think we ought to go back to Gallup while we still can?" She didn't say anything. "I've lost my appetite." She didn't say anything. "Actually, I had this wonderful meal at the café across from the bus depot, and I'm still full."

"I hope you didn't order one of their doughnuts," she warned.

The scenery was starting to remind him of pictures of Antarctica and the North Pole he had seen in the National Geographic. She continued to ignore most of his comments and kept driving. It was taking her full concentration. "There is a law against kidnapping." No comment. "Are we going to see penguins?" No comment. "Are there any polar bears out there?" No comment. "Does the word "hypothermia" mean anything to you?"

"Oh pooh," she said.

"*Pooh.* My sentiments exactly, only I spell it starting with a 's' and ending with a 't.' What happens if we get stuck?"

"My man will get us out, or maybe someone will come along and help."

Maybe? That wasn't exactly the reassuring answer he had been hoping for. They had not seen any other vehicles in the last few minutes other than the big truck with the blade on the front heading north back to Gallup. "Have you ever put chains on?" Grace asked.

Pete groaned. "Yes. Once. Five years ago . . . in a parking lot . . . that had been freshly graded . . . It took me 45 minutes, and I damn near froze to death. And the pain when the feeling came back into my fingers was a twelve out of ten. Also, I was properly attired for the ordeal, which I am currently not. I have no gloves or other warm clothing. I am dressed for riding on a bus, not wrestling around in the snow trying to get chains on a tire. The bladed parking lot had hardly any snow and outside this car it looks to be well over two feet."

"You certainly have a great sense of humor."

"Yes. That's right. I do, but I have not been employing it. I have been completely serious in my comments, and I vote that you turn this car around at the first safe opportunity. I am putting my foot down." He stamped against the floorboard for emphasis.

The stamp had no affect other than a smile from the driver. "Did my parents put you up to this?" he asked. She did not answer, just smiled. By this time they were twenty miles south of Gallup. "I wish you would turn this car around at the first opportunity." She turned the car off the highway between two pine trees. "Is this the first opportunity? It doesn't look like much of an opportunity. Are we taking a short cut? People often have bad results when they take short cuts." His voice seemed higher than his normal speaking voice.

He lowered his voice to sound more authoritative. "Grace, this does not please me. What you are doing is technically known as kidnapping throughout the courts of our land, in all civilized countries and . . . where is the road?"

"Somewhere down there under this beautiful snow," she answered.

"Beautiful snow! I don't think so. This is ugly white snow and perchance, is this ugly white snow covering a road with a grade ditch on either side?"

"Yes."

"How deep is the grade ditch?"

"Don't ask."

"I won't. I am more than willing to forget that question. How about this one? How do you know where the edge is?"

"I don't know exactly, but whoever made these tracks seems to know what they were doing. If we can stay in these tracks, we should be fine. I stayed in them going to town and it worked okay."

"IF?" For some reason his mind turned to stories he had heard about lemmings. It was rumored that they would follow the tracks

of their leaders' right off cliffs to their deaths. "Are there any cliffs on this road?" he asked.

There had been no big truck with a blade on the front and dropping road salt out the back to aid the traction on this road. No, "*road*" wasn't an accurate description. "Path" would be more accurate. They were on a *path*. Even path might be too glorious a name for what they were on. There was only tracks made in the snow by one or more multiple vehicles. Quite possibly driven by certified imbeciles. The first car had made the tracks and all of the other travelers stayed in the same tracks unless they met another vehicle. Then they would each veer to the right relinquishing their left hand rut and as soon as they were passed, they would get in the original ruts.

Pete was starting to sound like a broken record with a single theme. "Are we turning around? Are we looking for a place where we can turn around? Are we going to die? How far until we get to a place where we can turn around?"

"No and No and No and Eight miles," she said answering all his questions in one burst. "Eight miles to the ranch." He glanced at the speedometer and then at his watch.

At their current speed the eight miles would take the better part of an hour. At the four mile mark they met a pickup truck. Each vehicle relinquished one rut and they safely passed and got back in the two ruts going down the road. However, the snow had stopped and the clouds were starting to clear. He could see blue sky. The car picked up speed.

Possibly to keep from having to answer so many questions, Grace turned on the radio. "Frosty the Snowman" was playing and she sang along. *My that girl has a pretty voice,* he thought. The car was now whizzing along at 30 miles an hour, safe because the tracks in the snow acted like railroad tracks. There was a large break in the clouds and the sun shined through. "Jingle Bells" came on the radio.

"Roll down your window," Grace said as she rolled down hers. He followed suit.

I'm living a dream Pete thought. This must be the way it feels to be "dashing through the snow in a one-horse open sleigh." He joined her and sang along. Silent Night was the next song on the radio. Grace slowed the car and they raised the windows. Pete quit singing and just listened to Grace. The music had the same effect on him that a lullaby has on a baby. He felt safe and calm.

The road, or path, went up and down over the hilltops and thru the valleys. He was reminded of a song they used to sing in grade school about "over the river and thru the woods to grandmother's house we go." He asked Grace if there were any rivers for them to go over. She said "no" and he said "that's too bad."

She looked at him like he was losing his mind. "Maybe they are on the floor," she said.

"What?"

"The marbles you have apparently lost."

Then they went over one hill, a little taller than the rest. Before them lay a pleasant little valley. In the valley were two houses, a little store, a barn, a corral and some out-buildings. The place looked so pretty and snug that he fell in love with it instantly. It was love at first sight.

"The red house on the south side belongs to my uncle and aunt. They also own the store." She turned to the north and parked in front of the green house. "This is where Mama and Daddy live." The house appeared very large to Pete. There was a 4' stone wall around it made of red rocks. The car hadn't even come to a complete stop before a plump little woman with a large smile came out to greet them.

"Mama, this is Pete."

"So I gather. Looks a mite paler than in the pictures you showed me. Come on in, Son, and have a cup of coffee and something to eat."

"Thank you, Mam." The lunch was only sandwiches, chips, and soda pop, but Pete couldn't remember ever enjoying a meal more, even though he was thoroughly interrogated by the Mama. At one time he asked her, "Mrs. Cousins, are you a detective with the Gallup Police Department or an agent for the FBI?" She was not thrown off course. "No, I work for a dentist. He's closed the office until after Christmas. What is your opinion on how the president is handling the war in Vietnam and do you floss regularly?"

After lunch, Grace made her mother close her eyes while they carried in the packages from the car. They took them to Grace's bedroom and hid them in the closet.

"I'm quite disappointed it was not necessary for me to close my eyes too," he joked.

Grace laughed and retorted that in his case it would be much better if he closed the mouth and left the eyes open. Then she recited a poem about an owl.

THE OWL

A wise old owl
Sat on an oak
The more he saw
The less he spoke
The less he spoke
The more he heard
Why can't we be
Like that wise old bird

Pete was amazed at her spirit. He was seeing a different Grace than the one he was used to. This one was not mousey, but full of spirit, witty, lively, and laughed a lot.

Apparently the mother thought they had been in the bedroom long enough because she called for them to join her. When they joined her in the kitchen she told them it was time for him to sing for his supper, uh lunch.

"I tried that at breakfast. I was not a success. I think the trouble was that Mable was not a music lover."

"I think the trouble was that she was," chuckled Grace.

Pete ignored her pitiful and insulting attempts at humor and addressed the mother. "How many songs do I owe you for a baloney sandwich, a few chips and a Shasta cola? After lugging packages all over Gallup for you, I think we are square."

The mother did not seem impressed with his argument. "Malin, that's Gracie's father, is supposed to get the tree for us when he gets home from work, but he phoned and he has to work late. I don't want him to have to do it in the dark after a hard day's work. Would you mind picking out a tree for the house?" She pointed to the south which was both the direction of the forest and store.

Pete was amazed. "You mean that little store even sells Christmas trees?" The two woman laughed at him. It was the kind of laugh one might hear if he accidentally had his shoes on the wrong feet, but it wasn't a mean laugh. "Wait a minute," he said. "You mean go out into the woods, find a perfect tree, cut it down and bring it back to decorate. WOW!" That was an integral part of the perfect Christmas he had fantasized on the bus. Maybe there was something to this Law of Attraction he had read about where you attract the things you think about.

"Yes," said the older woman, interrupting his thoughts. "It's not too far. The best trees are out past the barn and on the side of the hill. Don't you cut your trees?" she asked.

"No, we usually go down to the Christmas tree lot and buy one." He thought to himself, my dream is coming true. I am going to have an old fashion Christmas. It will be just like the ones in the books where they walk through the snow to the forest and cut down the prettiest tree to decorate. He had forgotten for the moment that he wasn't staying. "I'll be happy to get the tree for you, Mrs. Cousins, and a Yule log, and some holly, and some mistletoe and . . . "

"WHOA, sailor! You will not be getting any mistletoe, and I don't really think we need a Yule Log either. What time did you say your bus is getting to Gallup?" That brought Pete back to earth and the real world. Pete remembered Grace telling him one of her mother's sayings was, "Here's your hat. What's your hurry?"

"The bus with my wallet won't arrive until late afternoon, and I don't have to meet it. The bus going north is much later, so I'm good for a couple of hours."

They found him some coveralls, gloves, over boots, a scarf, a knitted cap, and a single bladed axe. Except for the axe, he felt like a little boy whose mommy has over bundled him up before allowing him to go outside and play in the snow.

The snow started falling again as they set out across the pasture to the forest of pinon pines and cedars. The snow was knee deep, but they were young, happy, and frolicking like a couple of young colts. They inspected each candidate with the care of a judge at a Miss America Beauty Pageant or National Dog Show. At last they made their decision. The winner stood 73 inches tall and looked perfectly full from each direction. The happy boy from the city cut down the tree and the two proudly headed back with the trophy. They arrived back at the house with a beautiful tree, happy hearts, and cold feet. The mother was pleased with the choice, but had to get a friendly jibe in. "I think a beaver could have cut down the tree faster," she said with a smile. While the couple warmed themselves with a cup of hot chocolate and sitting in front of the heater. The mother went down to the storage room and got the stand for the tree.

"Now young man, before you leave, would you trim the bottom of the tree, carry it into the house, put it in the stand, and set it in the corner of the living room next to the piano. Pete saluted and said "aye aye." Then he turned to Grace and said, "I thought you said it was your father who was a sergeant in the Marine Corps."

Pete was in such a good mood that it seemed a joking matter, but he remembered rebelling against his own mother when she had asked him to do chores around the house. He vowed to be a better son.

The mother mentioning his impending departure came as a shock. He had been having such a good time helping them prepare for the Christmas of his dreams! He did not want to leave. It was like being forced to put down a book whose story you are enjoying and deal with the real world. He glanced at his watch. His departure time seemed to be rushing down on him at the speed of a high balling passenger train.

They saved the branches he had trimmed to make a wreath for the kitchen window. He carried the tree into the living room and set it up in the stand. He screwed in the supporting screws while Grace tried to hold it vertically and the mother kept issuing instructions: "it's leaning to the right, move it more to the left, no-no-no, that's too far, etc., etc." When they were finished, and it was placed in the corner next to the piano, it looked beautiful. Pete could just picture the happy scene that night when the family decorated it. In his happy scene the mother would be issuing orders, the father would be carrying them out and Grace would be at the piano playing and singing Christmas carols. Suddenly the smile on his face disappeared, to be replaced by an expression of sadness as he realized something would be missing: him.

The mother noticed the change. "Would you like another cup of hot chocolate before you leave?" the mother asked kindly.

"Yes, thank you," was what he said. What he thought was "leave-leave-leave." "Leave" has certainly become Grace's mother's theme song. He excused himself to go put the axe away in the garage. Coming back he passed the car which was waiting to return him back to Gallup. "Well old paint," he said as he patted it on the fender while passing, "I wish you had thrown a shoe or had a flat tire or . " He stopped dead in his tracks. An idea had occurred to him. What was it his sainted grandmother used to say when she wasn't talking about things getting worse? Oh yes, "The Lord helps those who help themselves."

He looked up at the store. There were a few pickups and one car, but he didn't see any people. However, in the backseat of the car were a boy and a girl and they saw him. Just in case anyone was watching he pretended to drop something. He bent over and pretended to look for it in the snow. Then he straightened up and went on to the house. He had a new bounce to his step and was attempting to whistle Jingle Bells. It sounded more like "toot toot toot" than Jingle Bells. The dog from across the road trotted down thinking he was being called.

Such had been Pete's haste that he hadn't spotted the kids or notice an Indian who had been on his knees adjusting snow chains on his truck. Perry had seen the white man do many strange things but this was a puzzle. If this man dropped something in the snow and was feeling around with one hand, why was the other hand on the tire? He would keep an eye on this stranger for his friends. Perry turned to the kids in the car, "Did you see that?" They nodded. He decided to stay and see what would happen next.

Back at the house, Pete stalled as long as he could, but the old woman kept them on schedule, and way too soon they bid her good bye and went outside and got into the car. Grace started the engine and let it run for a moment to warm up. Looking up towards the store they noticed a group of Indians staring at them.

"Do you always attract this much attention?" Pete asked.

"No, never. Maybe you are the attraction. Wave goodbye to your friends."

She let out the clutch and the car started forward. THUMP-THUMP-THUMP She stepped on the brakes. "Something is wrong!" she said. "I wonder what it could be."

"It sounds like a flat tire to me," he ventured.

They got out of the car. "Pete, you are right. Look," she said pointing at the tire.

The right rear tire had "mysteriously" gone flat. Pete decided the time had come to demonstrate some dramatic acting ability. "Oh No!" he shouted in a manner he had seen in a melodrama. He raised the back of his hand to his forehead and allowed an expression of despair to cross his face. "Now, (He paused for effect.) I shall be late and miss my bus. DARN! DARN!! DARN!!!"

"Not if you hurry and change the tire," said a voice behind him. The mother had been watching from the kitchen window and came out to see what the holdup was. Grace handed Pete the keys and he walked to the trunk and took out the jack, lug wrench and spare tire.

"It is best to loosen the lug nuts before jacking the car off the ground," he pontificated, "otherwise the whole wheel will turn if the nut is on too tight. And these nuts look like they are on **very** tight." He emphasized the word "***very***."

He slipped the wrench over the first nut and strained. It did not budge. "See, it is a good thing we did not jack the car up first. This job could take a lot longer than I thought it would."

The mother snorted.

Then he took a deep breath, braced himself, took a good grip on the wrench and pulled for all he was worth. He was really putting on a show of manliness. His muscles were bulging, sweat popped out on his forehead, the car rocked slightly forward.

The mother was not fooled. "You might be more successful if you attempted to turn the lug nuts in the other directions," she said. She signaled for Perry, Benny and Frank to come over. They had been watching from up by the store in amazement. She said something to them in Navajo and they went to work immediately changing the tire. Except for the nut Pete had tightened, they all came off pretty easy. That nut took two of them. They were like a well-trained pit crew. One jacked the car up, while another took off the tire and inspected it while the third slammed on the spare. (This was in the days before spares were smaller and called "doughnuts.")

The one called Perry examined the tire and said it looked like the valve stem had jiggled loose, and he would tighten it and refill the tire with a pump he carried in his truck, so it could serve as the spare. Pete didn't think this jiggle theory was possible and that he might have an ally. All he had done was take off the cap and press down on the valve stem. Perry returned and gave the tire to Benny to put in the trunk. He looked at Pete and shook his finger at him as though scolding a very naughty child. Then he smiled and stuck out his arm to shake hands. During the handshake Perry palmed him a little round valve cap Frank had found it near where the car had been parked. As they shook, he whispered, "She is a very pretty girl and gave him a wink."

"What was that all about?" the mother demanded when he returned to the ladies.

"Oh, he was just making fun of me for turning the nut in the wrong direction."

"I should think so," the mother replied. "You'd better get started."

"Yes, Mam." They got in the car and were soon on their way. As he turned around for one last look at the pleasant little valley, he noticed the mother talking to Perry. He hoped Perry wasn't ratting on him.

Five minutes later, Grace said, "That's odd."

"What? Something wrong with the car?" he asked hopefully.

"No, but it looks like Perry's truck back there. He lives in the other direction."

CHAPTER 10

Town, Wallet & Sarge

The trip to town was quite pleasant. The clouds had cleared and there was blue sky. The sun was doing a good job on melting the snow and making the roads, paths, and tracks slushy.

When they got to the bus depot Grace said she would wait in the car because it shouldn't take long. Pete was nervous because he had been thinking of all the things that could have gone wrong: bus crash, agent forgetting to send it, someone stealing the money out of it, etc., etc.

There had been no bus crash; the agent hadn't forgotten to send it; and no one had stolen money out of it. The package was there with Pete's name on it. He was elated.

The agent, who looked and acted remarkably like Deputy Barney Fifth on the Andy Griffith show, asked to see some form of identification. Pete deflated like a flat tire whose valve stem had "jiggled" loose.

How was he going to prove who he was? The proof was in the package that he was not allowed to access. He suggested phoning Steven. Steven did not answer.

After twenty minutes, Grace got tired of waiting in the car and came in to see what the delay was. "She will tell you who I am": Pete said. "Grace, who am I?"

She looked at him like he had lost, not just a few, but all of his remaining marbles. "Nutsy the Clown?"

"No, really. Tell the man who I am so I can get the package."

"Sir, oh noble sir, his name is Peter G. Wheatley. He just happens to resemble Nutsy the Clown. I believe the word describing this phenomenon is doppelgangers."

The agent looked at Pete and declared, "I don't know you, and I don't know this smartass woman. She could say you are President Johnson and it wouldn't make it true."

"He is not President Johnson," Grace volunteered.

"Grace, that is not helpful," Pete said.

The agent agreed that Pete wasn't President Johnson and Grace wasn't being helpful, but he still wouldn't turn over the package. He said it was his "fanny" on the line if Pete weren't the real Pete. It was at that moment, Pete noticed his skis and poles still leaning against the wall where Steven had placed them, and that reminded him about his sea bag in the back room. He described it and told the agent that it was in the back and had his name and address on it.

"Not good enough," declared the agent. Pete continued, "It is held closed with a combination lock, and I know the combination. (The agent was weakening.) I will tell you the combination and if it opens the lock on the bag with my name on it, you can open the package, take out my wallet, and you will be able to tell by my driver's license that I am who I say I am." The lock worked and the agent opened the package took out the wallet and checked the driver's license.

"Thank you Mr. Wheatley," he said as he handed over the wallet.

Pete quickly re-opened it to see if everything was there. To his surprise it was, including the $20 he had told the driver to take.

What's with these people around here, he thought. With only a few exceptions, they are all un-normally decent?

He got the driver's name and left an envelope for him with $20 in it. He put the money he owed Steven in a different envelope and left it in the agent's care, knowing it was probably as safe as if it were in the Bank of England. He smiled as he made up an imaginary scenario in his head where Steven was trying unsuccessfully to get the envelope from the agent. Pete's bus was running late, and he now had 3 hours minimum to kill and a beautiful girl to kill them with. (He hadn't thought once about Mary since joining up with Grace.)

Grace asked if he'd like to meet her father who was in charge of the silversmiths at Tobe Turpen's Trading Co. Pete nodded. He was not anxious to say goodbye to her. He had met the father and the uncle when they came to pick Grace up at Thanksgiving. He came away with the impression they were two, hard of hearing old coots who were more anxious to get back on the road than talk to him. Grace's dad thought Pete's last name was WHEATIES, like the cereal. That meeting lasted maybe two minutes.

When Pete and Grace walked into Turpen's, which was humongous, a tall thin man in his late 40's or early 50's, detached himself from a group and headed in their direction. He was Pete's height, had grayish-black hair, wore glasses, and carried himself with the bearing of a military man with a little cowboy thrown in. He had a big smile on his face when he saw his daughter. "HELLO GOURD HEAD," he greeted her loudly from across the room with his pet name for her from the time she was born.

"Daddy, do you remember Pete? You met him when you came to pick me up at Thanksgiving."

The old man stuck out his hand and said in a voice loud enough to be herd in every corner of the store, "HELLO POST TOASTIES."

Grace turned red with embarrassment. "Pete is waiting to catch the bus to Durango. And I would appreciate you not calling me Gourd Head."

Pete saw his chance to get even. "Don't feel bad, Sir. She doesn't like to be called Nutsy the Clumsy Clown either."

"Is that what they are calling her at that college?"

"Not at the college, Sir, at the A & W."

The old man's face looked puzzled, and Grace's flushed a brighter shade of red.

The man was quite pleasant. He showed them around the large establishment and introduced them to every worker in the building and half the customers. It was obvious he was super proud of his girl. He had quit school in the 8th grade, and she was going to college on scholarships. The tour ended up in his office and they were having a nice chat when the phone rang. Malin answered it. The voice was quite loud and Pete thought he recognized it. The old man's side of the conversation contained a lot of and seemed to be limited to "Yes dears."

"That was your mother. She wants you to start home right now. She says she wants you to get back before it gets dark and the road becomes too icy. She says several cars have already slid into the ditch out there and she expects the roads to get worse and become a sheet of ice." Pete wondered how the mother knew where to phone. Grace offered to take Pete back to the depot, but her father said he would do it when the store closed, and she had better do as her mother said.

I'm getting the feeling, Pete told himself, these folks are either not too anxious to lose their daughter, or I am not exactly what they are looking for in a prospective son-in-law. The two men stood side by side on the store's front porch as Grace pulled out of the parking lot on to the highway. A blue pickup did so also. It looked familiar.

"Do you recognize the Indian driving that truck?" he asked the old man.

"Yes. That's Perry. He lives out near us. What a lucky coincidence that he is going back right now. He'll make sure Gracie gets home safe. Funny, I didn't see him in the store."

"Yes. Lucky coincidence," Pete echoed.

When the store closed, they climbed into Malin's truck and headed through the still snow-covered streets to the depot. There was still plenty of time before the bus was to arrive. Pete had given up on his old fashioned Christmas. He told the old man to let him out in front of the depot and not to worry about sticking around until he caught the bus. Malin said, "Normally I wouldn't leave until you were safely on the bus, but I promised to go out and get a Christmas tree when I get home and Donna never forgets one of my promises." He kind of shivered as he thought about trekking through the deep snow in the dark with only a flashlight and an axe.

"You know," he said slyly, "I may just sneak over to the Christmas tree lot and buy one. When I get home I'll hide it in the back yard and when Donna starts asking when am I going after the tree, I will say right now, then find a warm place to wait a few minutes, then bring it in. You want to come with me?"

"To the ranch?"

"No, to the Christmas tree lot."

"I've got a better idea," Pete said. "Why don't you just use the one I cut for you this afternoon? It would save a lot of extra work and sneaking around."

A look of joy crossed the wrinkled old countenance. "Boy, you were sent straight from Heaven."

(That was something Pete had never been accused of before.) "Would you put that in writing for me, and sign it."

"This calls for a drink. You have time before your bus, and now, so do I. You do take an occasional drink, don't you?" The way he said it gave Pete the impression he would look upon a "no" answer with the same disfavor he might towards one who was an admitted communist or girl hater. Pete thought back to his last conversation with his father.

"Mr. Cousins, does the name 'Old Booze for Brains' mean anything to you? (He had not been able to remember the word his father used.) That, of course, is a false accusation, but I have been known to step from, though not fall off, the proverbial wagon. In short Sir, I do not totally and religiously adhere to the teetotaler's doctrine of complete abstinence from the fermented spirits."

The old man just stared at him. "You're full of more shit than the Christmas goose. Did you swallow a dictionary? Bet your folks are sure glad they sent you to college. Well, do you, or don't you?"

"Out of deference to your age, Sir, and the fact you have a long drive, and I a limited time allocated to me by the impending arrival and departure of my northbound public conveyance, I shall not, in the words of the plebian intellect, drink you under the table." Pete didn't know the true meaning of half the words he was spouting, especially "plebian." The old man didn't either, but he understood the last four. (Did I mention math . . .)

"Drink me under the table! Why you smart mouthed college dandy . . ." He tried to think of a famous quote to match the lad. After a brief pause he came up with a line from a poem written by Mary Howitt from her The Spider and the Fly. "Won't you come into my parlor, said the spider to the fly," he quoted as he pulled up in front of his favorite watering hole. The old man seemed quite proud of his ability to bring forth a famous literary quotation on the spur of the moment.

As soon as they were seated in the lounge, a sexy looking barmaid sashayed over to their table. She was drop dead sexy and Pete was wondering how she managed to get her blouse buttoned or fit into her slacks. She bent over slightly giving the men a breath taking view of her cleavage. Pete was the first to catch his breath and be able to speak.

"Coors for me and a sarsaparilla for my little friend." He wasn't sure what sarsaparilla was, but he had seen one of the good guys in an old cowboy movie order it, then beat up everyone in the bar for making fun of his choice in liquid refreshments.

"What!" cried the old man, choking on the word? The barmaid looked as surprised as the father. No one had ever ordered one of those before. She had no idea what it was. This was hardly Malin's first visit to the lounge and he always ordered a Manhattan.

Pete continued as if nothing were out of order. "And if you are out of sarsaparilla, maybe a Roy Rogers or a Shirley Temple." He winked at her and said in a low voice, "It's the little fellow's birthday. You had better make it a double: two cherries." He remembered his parents saying the same thing to a waitress at a fancy restaurant on a family reunion when he was seven and Alan was five.

"The usual," shouted the old man when he finally found his voice. He was just about to get mad when he noticed Pete's face had a grin on it. Malin realized he had been had, and a grin crossed his face which turned into a smile followed by a chuckle then outright laughter. "You just about got my nanny goat," he declared.

"Just about? I got you good."

By the time the barmaid returned with the Manhattan and Coors, both were laughing and enjoying each other's company. One drink led to another. As soon as his glass was empty, the old man ordered another round. The memory of his last encounter with liquor and the trouble it had caused was still fresh in Pete's mind. There were four cans of Coors in front of Pete and only one of them, was not completely full.

Malin pointed at the barmaid who was across the room showing her wares to a group of cowboys by bending slightly, breathing deeply and walking like Marilyn Monroe. "What do you think of Sasha, son?"

This has to be a trick question Pete thought. He is looking for a reason to tell me to stay away from his daughter. Pete slowly looked the woman up and down feasting on every inch of her killer body. "Well," said Malin.

"WOW! Nice taste in shoes," Pete said pointing at her high heels.

"Nice shoes!" Malin cried. "You need a shot of testosterone. Boy, I didn't even notice she had feet." It didn't look to Pete like the cowboys noticed if she had feet or not either.

The old man had been in the service during World War II, and looked back on those days as the high point of his life. As is the habit with old age, he tended to remember mostly the pleasant aspects. "Boy, were you ever in the service?"

"Marines."

That did it. The word "marines" had pushed the old man's buttons. He started telling war stories, beginning with his first day of boot camp and progressing all the way toward the day he had foolishly left the service. Pete could not have gotten a word in edgewise if he had wanted to, which he didn't. He had only been a six month reserve, and still had to attend monthly meetings and go to summer camp for two weeks every year with the Denver unit. That did not stack up very well against storming ashore in places like Bougainville. He knew many of the regular marines tended to look down on reserves, as being worse than swabbies (sailors) and doggies (soldiers) and only a tad better than civilians, which is what they really were (citizen soldiers).

When the old man finished, he started to question Pete about his time in the service. Pete did what came most naturally: he fabricated and exaggerated. In boot camp he had been given enough Marine Corps History to make his tales ring with authenticity. All his life, Pete tended to make it a policy not to let truth come between him and a good story.

It wasn't long before Malin realized that this quiet young man sitting across from him was a hero in the mold of Sergeant York, Audie Murphy, or Chesty Puller.

"Son, you're a ding dong hero! Someday I'd like to see that Congressional Medal of yours." The old man saluted. Pete smiled modestly, returned the salute and asked Malin about Bougainville. The old man was having the time of his life and was soon heart and soul back in the Pacific fighting the Great War. Pete had started calling him Sarge. This pleased the old man and got them both off the hook. Pete was uncomfortable calling Malin by his first name and Malin was uncomfortable being addressed as "Sir" or "Mr. Cousins." So from then on, the old man was simply "Sarge" in Pete's mind.

Pete's mind was on Grace and the old fashioned Christmas he had almost had. He felt like a dog that had been dragged from the fireside and put out into the night: the cold lonely night.

Malin interrupted his thoughts. "Boy, how come you are so far from home on Christmas?"

Pete had been so successful with his fiction so far, he saw no reason to return to the truth. "My folks have gone to Hawaii for the winter, and my brother is staying with friends in Palm Springs, so I thought I would go back to my cold, drafty, lonely dormitory room and study."

Perhaps a more sober man would have seen through this marvelous concoction, but not an old Marine who had been drinking and discovered his comrade is also a Marine and a modest hero to boot. "That's awful. That's no way to spend Christmas. You are coming home and spend Christmas with us."

Pete made a feeble protest, mostly for show, but nothing would have dislodged him from his chair until after the northbound bus left for Farmington and Durango.

"Son, you had better phone the ranch and let them know we're leaving Gallup."

Pete did not want to be the person to phone, but he could tell the old man was not looking forward to talking to his wife in his present condition or from his present location. Pete was hoping Grace would answer as he dialed. But it was not to be. It was the mother.

"Hello, this is Pete."

"Hmph. Do those new fancy buses have phones on them now?"

"I missed my bus. Uh . . . you see . . . Mr. Cousins bought me a bon voyage drink, and we got to talking, and time flew by, and before we knew it, I had missed the bus. I would gladly wait in the cold, drafty, lonely, unfriendly bus depot, but I am worried about Mr. C. He was . . . very thirsty, and I am not sure he is in any condition to drive home safely."

From the other end of the phone came a deep sigh. Pete continued. "As I was saying, I missed my bus . . . and . . . he . . . invited . . . what I mean to say . . ."

"Oh hush. Your room has been ready for hours."

"What?"

"I had a feeling you might be staying. When I saw someone Grace said earned straight 'A's' this trimester turning the lug nuts in the wrong direction, I knew something was up and that you were scheming for ways to stay. I would have invited you then, but I wanted to see how you would swing it. If I had known you were going to liquor up Papa . . . but Papa's never needed much of a reason. Boy, I love my daughter, and it gives me great pleasure to see her so happy. I believe she's laughed more this afternoon than in the last year. But let me give you a warning."

OH, OH, Pete thought. Here it comes. He was expecting something like, "If you hurt her, we will hunt you down and . . ." The possibilities were endless. But it wasn't a threat. It was a warning. A true warning.

"Watch out for Auntie. Now, you two get out here. There is a dinner and a Christmas Tree waiting for you." She hung up and Pete returned to join Malin.

The lounge had filled and there was a band tuning up as Pete returned to the table. Malin said he needed to go to the head, as he referred to the restroom. As soon as he left, Pete went over to the table with the cowboys and negotiated a trade: his full cans of Coors for their empties. When Malin got back, Pete was sitting in front of six cans of Coors and one half-empty glass of a Manhattan. "Looks like I out drank you," Malin said.

Without saying a word, Pete took each can, one at a time, and turned it upside down on the table, to prove it was empty.

"What did you do, fall asleep in there?" Pete asked.

"Must have. Looks like you beat me. I can't finish that last one. You can sure put it away, Son." Pete smiled modestly, or what he thought would pass for modestly.

"I think we better go." He wanted to get away before one of the cowboys came over and let the cat out of the bag.

As they passed the cowboy's table the men stood up, cheered, and wished them a VERY, VERY, MERRY, MERRY CHRISTMAS.

"Sure is a friendly bunch in here tonight," the old man said.

"Yes, I'm impressed with how nice everyone is." Pete agreed.

"One even thanked me," Malin said. "Why would he thank me?"

"I think he was talking about your service in the Marines. I noticed once he was talking to Sasha and she pointed in your direction."

"What about the one who told me 'pleasure doing business with you, Sir.' Why would he say that?"

"When I was in the restroom he and one of his friends were discussing presents for their wives as they were washing their hands. I told him you were a big cheese at Tobe Turpen's and would see they got a good deal."

"Thanks Son." He nodded in appreciation. "Christmas is a wonderful time of the year."

Pete walked behind the old man as they headed for the truck. Sarge walked a perfectly straight line and his speech was normal, BUT Pete had seen him consume a fair amount of alcohol. Pete was trying to think of a diplomatic way to ask Sarge if he could stand on one foot, close his eyes, and touch his finger to his nose. He couldn't think of one. He decided to really cinch up the seat belt, do some bodacious praying, and prepare to die. Maybe if he was lucky they would carve "He Died for Love" on his tombstone.

When they got to the truck, Malin said, "Would you mind driving? I'm feeling a little tired after trying to keep up with you and the Christmas rush in the store."

"I would be happy to. I would be overjoyed. Praise the Lord. I have always wanted to drive a big truck like this." This was not completely true.

During his three years in Alaska, Pete had driven nearly every kind of vehicle imaginable over every kind of road condition and in every kind of weather. He was really only nervous when someone else was driving, and he had no control over the conveyance. He did slow down when approaching other vehicles because he didn't trust **them**, but traffic was light as most folks had the good sense to stay home.

Pete drove and Sarge talked about the war. Pete kept the speed down because the roads had turned icy. He pretty much tuned Sarge out and thought about Grace and what a wonderful Christmas it would be. Therefore, he can probably be forgiven for smiling at the same time Sarge told about being wounded in the posterior by a piece of shrapnel. Unfortunately the headlights from an oncoming truck lit up the inside of the cab at that particular moment.

"BOY, I notice you grinning at my injury. I don't appreciate that. A wound in that area can be quite painful and is not a laughing matter." Malin thought to himself, I'm glad I didn't tell the kid about getting a social disease in New Zealand. He might have laughed us right off the road.

"Sorry Sir. I was smiling because I am happy. Hope you are not in too big of a hurry. That Chevy in front is all over the road, and I don't want to risk passing it."

"If I was more in a hurry, I'd get out and walk. Are you sure you ain't Barny Oldfield, or Bobby Unser's . . . grandma." Pete moved the truck up behind the Chevy and started looking for the opportunity to pass.

That seemed to satisfy the old man. He started telling Pete something about the M1 rifle being superior to the M16. It seemed like both men were traveling down different roads in their minds.

Just then the Chevy lost control and after several attempts to regain it, slid off the road into the ditch. Pete found a safe place and pulled off the highway. They walked back to see if anyone was hurt. The driver and passengers were all okay. Malin declared they were drunk as skunks. Pete thought that was an unusual expression. He could not remember ever reading about skunks consuming alcohol. Malin declared they shouldn't be driving. He took their keys out of the ignition and threw them out in the snow. "By the time they find those keys, if they find those keys, they will be sober enough to be driving."

"It will probably be spring," Pete said.

"When we get to the ranch, I will let the police know where there is a car full of people in the ditch."

They got back in the truck and started down the road. Malin started to tell him about some battle, but Pete's mind drifted to Grace, the ranch, the old fashion Christmas and the fun they would have. His grin seemed to extend from ear to ear and beyond. Hopefully, Sarge would not remember any other injuries.

After an unusually late dinner, Christmas records were put on the stereo, and they decorated the tree while Perry Como was singing about being home for Christmas; Bing Crosby about a white Christmas; and Andy Williams about silver bells. There was a cozy fire on the hearth, and some friendly bickering about the placement of ornaments, but it was done in the spirit of Christian fellowship, and most of the time they were singing along with the music on the stereo. Grace had a beautiful singing voice which was pretty much covered up by the rest of them, who couldn't carry a tune in a bright new shiny bucket. When they finished, there was not a prettier tree in the land.

By then it was time to turn in. Grace's mother asked if Pete wanted some hot chocolate. He really didn't, but said he did because he did not want the fun to end. Sarge looked at the boy in surprise, "Do you drink that stuff?" he said. "I've got something better in the liquor cabinet. It will help you get to sleep."

Pete passed on the suggestion and the woman seemed very pleased. The old man shuffled off to the bedroom mumbling something about the next generation being a bunch of pussies or pansies. Pete couldn't tell which. He hoped it was pansies.

CHAPTER 11

Problems

The next morning, they ate an early breakfast, admired the tree again, and Sarge went off to work. The ladies started making strawberry jam and cookies. Pete went out to shovel the walks, chop some firewood, and Grace showed him how to make a wreath. About ten o'clock, he drifted up to the Trading Post and watched the aunt and uncle trade with the Indians.

The Indians arrived using all means of transportation. Some on foot, others by horse, some in wagons, but the majority were in pickup trucks.

When he left the store, there was still an hour before lunch. He remembered seeing some mistletoe when they had gone for the Christmas tree the day before. A walk up there would give him an excellent chance to think about some problems that had been bothering him.

The air was cold, but the sky was clear and the snow crunched noisily under his feet. He liked the sound. The snow was deep enough that he used the trail they had broken the day before. On a day this wonderful it was hard to believe he had any problems, but he did, and any one of them could get him kicked out of this paradise. To keep them straight he numbered them and wrote them in his little pocket-sized notebook. He got out the little notebook that fit in his shirt pocket and started to read.

1. The Indian Perry knew he had let the air out of the tire.
2. He had to get in touch with his parents and let them know he would not be home for Christmas and that he was all right.
3. What if Sarge found out he had lied and his parents weren't in Hawaii. Pete realized everyone did not have his appreciation for a good story that deviated slightly from the unadulterated truth. Grace knew they were in Denver, but she didn't know he had told her father they were in Hawaii. He couldn't tell her he had lied to her father. She thought he was wonderful and always took the right and noble course.
4. What if Sarge found out he was only a reserve, had never been in combat, and had lied about all the medals and brave deeds?
5. Who was Auntie, and why was everyone warning him about her?
6. He had to get some presents for these people.

He found the mistletoe but none of the answers to his problems. On his way back to the house, he gave a lot of consideration to one of his grandmother's favorite sayings: "Honesty is the best policy." He didn't know about the "best," but it might be the "safest." He even considered becoming a truth teller, but decided that he better taper off gradually like Uncle George did with cigarettes. Uncle George had a plan of gradual reduction that would have him free of the nasty habit in ten years. Anything quicker than that, he reasoned, would be too great a shock to his system. Pete came to the conclusion that any round of sudden truth telling might prove to be too great a shock to his system also, but vowed that once he lied his way out of this situation, he would only tell teeny weeny, harmless, little white lies. Maybe Uncle George's problem was that ten years had been too abrupt. It was all moot anyway. Uncle George had passed away from lung cancer before his theory could be proved.

CHAPTER 12

Town Trip, Phone Call & Memories

While they were eating lunch, Pete asked if they knew anyone going to town he could ride in with. He explained that he needed to buy some presents and he could ride back out with the sarge. The mother frowned, and then went for her car keys.

"There will be no more riding home with Malin for you. I think I can kill two birds with one stone, and keep two birds from getting stoned, by giving you the car and having you bring Auntie out when you come back."

Grace looked unhappy. "Mama, wouldn't it be better to let me sort of break Aunt E. to him gently? And what about N. S.? He isn't coming with her, is he?"

The mother nodded.

"Oh no," Grace wailed.

This was the second time Auntie had been mentioned to him with the implication he was going to be sorry. He wondered if she were like Bertha Mason the crazy insane woman they kept locked in the attic in the play they had presented at school: "Jane Eyre." If so, he would just as soon forego the pleasure. And who was this N. S.?

His thoughts were interrupted as the mother continued. "You know what happens when either your friend here or Auntie ride out with your father. There seems to be an uncontrollable urge to stop at the village tavern. Besides . . . what could Auntie do to a famous war hero who can drink 10 beers and walk in here as sober as a judge?"

Pete swallowed hard, but didn't say a thing. Grace did not look convinced. The mother had a twinkle in her eyes as she handed him the keys. "Sarge says you are a good driver. Drive carefully . . . Audie."

"Audie?" Pete felt like the camel who has just felt one of the last extra straws being loaded on to his back.

When he got to town, the first thing he did was phone Denver. He informed his mother that through a very unusual sequence of circumstances, he was stranded in New Mexico at the home of one of his classmates and would not be able to get home in time for Christmas. Then he told her he realized he had not been a very good son and would try to do better in the future.

She told him Alan had phoned again. The car was just about fixed. They had been working pretty steady on it and had recruited help from a car club Joe had belonged to in high school. Alan predicted he would be home by the 26$^{th.}$ Also she said, a Mary has phoned several times. **BOING.**

He hadn't even thought about her since getting to Gallup, now there she was messing with his mind again.

Parents & Mary

His parents had met Mary at the end of the summer session and after a rough start, had loved her. She had ridden with him as far as Denver where she took a bus on to Illinois to be with family during the short break between the summer session and the fall session. It had been a wonderful trip. They stopped and visited her roommate and best friend who had dropped out of college. They stopped at several interesting tourist sights, hiked to a water falls, swam in a lake and basically took advantage of being young, in love, (at least he thought he was) and in Colorado in the summer.

After dinner that night in Denver, they walked over to a nearby park. When they got back to the apartment his folks had already gone to bed. They went into a multipurpose room that served as an office and a guest bedroom. They put on some records and looked at slides and photo albums. It was after midnight when there came a banging on the door. Pete went to open it and there stood his father in a bathrobe. His face was red and Pete swore he could see steam coming out of his ears. The old man stated there would be no entertaining young ladies behind closed bedroom doors in his apartment. Pete was directed to the porch where he was told his sleeping bag was waiting for him. Were it not for the interruption, Pete believed they would have stayed up all night talking, looking at pictures, and listening to music.

At breakfast the next morning there was tension, but Mary did away with most of it in the first five minutes by saying she was so glad there were still people around who were sticking up for propriety, and letting them know how much she enjoyed looking through the family slides and albums. She apologized for the closed door, by saying it had just been done because she knew they were sleeping and didn't want the music to bother them.

Later the next morning they walked to the bus depot downtown which was well over a couple of miles but seemed so much shorter that morning. Her hair was in braids, and she had not bothered dressing up for the trip home. No one could be blamed for mistaking her for some hippy girl who was backpacking, bus taking, and hitchhiking around the country. Pete suspected that was what his parents thought. They probably thought Pete picked her up as she was hitchhiking and made up the story about her being a student at

Fort Lewis. They suspected that Pete sometimes wasn't completely truthful with them.

Pete carried the backpack for her as far as the bus depot. They laughed and joked and skipped and greeted nearly everyone they passed and wished them a "Good Morning." At the depot they waited together until it was time for her to get on the bus. Then he gave her a hug and a quick kiss as she paused before mounting the bus. She promised to let him know when she arrived home. She also promised to let him know if she needed a ride back to school, but gave him the impression that she would need one and was looking forward to that need. He noticed that she took a seat next to someone who was wearing a uniform and talked him into moving over so she could have a window seat where she and Pete could see each other better until the bus pulled out. He marveled how she could get anybody to do things and how she could move them around like chess pieces.

She forgot to phone when she arrived. Pete just chalked it up to her being her. Pete spent a good part of the first week planning on interesting places they could visit on their drive back to Durango. The next week he was starting to feel that he was being taken for granted or she had found another way back to school. He might have phoned her but realized he did not have a phone number or an address for her. During the week before classes were to start, he phoned Karen whose parents lived in Aurora and asked if she would like a ride to campus. She accepted. Karen was smart, had a great figure, and . . . a reputation, according to Bilbo and Tim. Pete just wanted to not look like he had been left at the altar, so to speak.

The very next day Mary phoned saying she would be arriving in Denver in two days. She was all bubbly and told him that she had told her family she had met this boy who might be the one, and they were all excited for her.

What he wanted more than anything else was to say, I'll meet you at the bus depot. But he had asked Karen; she had accepted and even cancelled out of a ride back with several girlfriends. As far as Pete was concerned, he was locked into his agreement with Karen because . . . because it was the right thing to do. When he told Mary that he wouldn't be able to give her a ride from Denver to Durango there was a minute of disbelieved silence. He told her that when he didn't hear from her he had assumed she made other arrangements. He did not tell her about asking Karen. Then Mary said in a hurt tone, "I'll see you at school. Excuse me, I have some other arrangements to make," and she hung up.

The first time he saw Mary at the college after that she said, "I hear you invited Karen to ride with you from Denver. Is she as friendly as they say?" Then she turned and walked away before he could respond.

But Mary wasn't the type to stay mad. Her mad lasted a week. She even realized she might be partially responsible for Pete not waiting to hear from her. Whenever they would pass each other she would smile and say "Hi," or, if there was time, ask about his parents, or bring up some memory from the summer or just ask how he was doing and share with him what she was up to. But there was no more tossing little pebbles at his window and inviting him to come out and play or share an adventure. It had bothered her that it was always up to her to initiate something or suggest the date, although they had never called them dates. AND there was this girl named Grace who always seemed to be present.

Now with everyone back on campus, Mary's agenda was busier than ever and her calendar overflowing with requests. One, Pete called the Mystery Man, seemed to have moved to the front of the line.

A & W

Once, before classes started, Mary was driving off the hill in a convertible someone had loaned her and she saw Pete walking along the side of the road in the same direction. Once again he had cancelled his car insurance to save money and wouldn't be driving it. She stopped and offered him a ride saying, "Hop in Cowboy, I owe you one." It turned out they were both going into town to purchase similar items. They spent the afternoon shopping for things they would need for the trimester and ended up at A & W.

It had been a delightful afternoon, almost like last summer, but not quite. They shared a cheeseburger, fries and a large root-beer float. Linda, their carhop was perfect. They spent much of their time watching and laughing at another carhop who seemed very unsure of herself and not happy at all. Pete couldn't take his eyes off her. There was just something about her. They decided she must be a high school junior or senior.

Linda came up to their window to see if they needed anything else. Mary said, "I don't think Miss Bumble is going to make it." Linda smiled, "Her name is Grace, she is my best friend and this is her first day on the job."

Pete remembered when he was in high school getting a job with Chicken Licken, a fast food place on the corner of Rosemount and Foothill Blvd, a mile from their house. He worked there after school and on weekends. Maxie Rosenberg, the owner, was always yelling at him to work faster and there was the greasy smell of frying oil. He hated that job and when the opportunity to go to work for a pharmacy as a clerk and delivery person came up, he jumped on it, and switched jobs at the speed of light. For over a year he felt like throwing up whenever he was around anything being fried in oil.

A truck pulled up next to the convertible on Pete's side and Grace came up and took their order. As she turned to go put in the customer's order Pete smiled at her and said, "Hang in there, Grace. It gets easier."

Mary waved at her and added, "You're doing great, Grace. Next time we are going to ask for you."

Linda was watching and smiled gratefully. "I'm still here. I can hear you," she said laughingly.

"You were great, we just thought Grace needed something positive. First days are tough," Mary said handing her the money.

Linda picked up the tray but handed back the money. "No charge. This one is on me. You are a great and kind couple. This is the first time I have seen Grace smile all day." They drove out of there very happy. This had been a great day.

That was the first time Pete or Mary ever saw Grace. They remembered it because it was the last time they ever did anything together in Durango. Grace remembered it because it was the best part of a horrible day for her. (Never underestimate the power of a kind word.)

The Shirt

Back during the summer, Pete had several shirts that needed ironing. His very favorite, was a red-checkered, short-sleeved one, he wore 40 % of the time. But he didn't iron it; he just wore it and let the wrinkles gradually disappear. This was not acceptable to Mary. She offered to iron it for him. He accepted. This worked for about three or four times. She did a good job, but was not always prompt about getting the job done. In fact, the red shirt was in her dorm room at the end of the summer session when they left for Denver. She promised to return it first thing when they got back to school.

Several times after returning to campus Pete would see her and ask about the shirt. She always had some excuse like the communal ironing board was being used, the iron wouldn't work, or she hadn't been able to get to it. He told her not to worry about ironing it, just get it back to him. It didn't happen.

Then shortly after the homecoming football game which he attended with Grace, and Mary attended with Mystery Man (James

Herriot) she presented him with a flawlessly wrapped package. He could pretty well tell by the feel what was inside.

"It's my shirt, isn't it?" She nodded. "Thank you," he said.

"Your welcome. I'm sorry it took so long." Pete hugged the package, then put it in his briefcase.

"Aren't you going to open it?" she asked.

"No, I'm late for class."

She looked disappointed for about five seconds than turned and walked off.

"Thanks again," he shouted at her retreating body.

She did not turn around, just waved her hand in acknowledgement that she had heard him. When he opened it later in the dorm, there was his favorite shirt, perfectly ironed. Not a wrinkle in sight. There was only one problem. It had been cut up into two inch squares. On their next date, Pete told Grace about what Mary had done to his favorite shirt. Grace had never seen the shirt because it had been in Mary's possession since before Grace came to Durango. Grace said she would like to see it. When he showed it to her, she was shocked. Then she said, "May I have it? Maybe I can make something out of it."

"You mean like a handkerchief, or a book mark. There's not enough to make a dust rag. I guess the buttons are still good." He handed her the corpse. "Good by Old Paint," he said to the pile of scraps that had once been his favorite shirt.

Two weeks later, Grace told Pete, "I have a present for you from me . . . and Mary."

"What is it? 100 dust rags, 20 handkerchiefs, or 80 bookmarks?"

"None of the above."

It was a shirt, his favorite shirt. It was held together with some kind of magical tape. The pieces had been perfectly aligned and when Pete put it on you couldn't tell it had been damaged.

They waited two days until they knew Mary was on the serving line. Then for the evening meal Pete and Grace joined the cafeteria line. This was not usual for Grace because she still lived in town with the Maderas. The couple did not say anything, but acted as if nothing unusual was happening. However, one member on the serving line dropped her serving spoon on the floor and her eyes got big as saucers while her jaw opened so wide that her chin nearly hit the ground. (Perhaps a slight exaggeration.)

The relationship was never the same after that, it was cordial and had morphed from being tense, to two old "friends" fencing verbally with each other like in a Hallmark movie, with the possibility of something more in the last five minutes of the show. But like I said, there were no more little pebbles being tossed against the window to get his attention and invite him out on an adventure. And Pete was continually with Grace, a shy, quiet, pretty, young freshman who fell head over heels in love with him. And there was his friend Sandy, just waiting to sweep in and pick up the pieces when both girls dumped him.

Another impediment in the Pete and Mary saga was a dark horse had entered the race. He was a tall young man from the area who was temporarily taking a break from school and wanted to be a veterinarian. I don't remember his name, so I will call him Mystery Man or James Herriot after my favorite vet and author in literature.

In those days there was an outdoor walkway on the second floor level connecting the dorms. One day Pete was walking on it to class and he spotted Mary on the ground level throwing little pebbles at a 2nd story window. He called out asking if he could help. She told him she was trying to get ahold of James and whose room he was in. Pete entered the dorm, walked down the hall, knocked on the door and told the man who answered that there was a young lady trying to get his attention. James hurried to the window, pulled the curtains, and smiled happily. He had been trying to get her on the phone while at the same time she was under his window trying to get his attention. Earlier in the year he had visited a buddy of his on campus, met her, and they were soon seen together almost exclusively.

Pete continued his walk to class feeling good. He wanted what was best for her. His friend Sowers a retired policeman who was now working security at the college had told him his summer girlfriend was seeing a really good person from a fine local family. That pleased Pete.

His parents knew nothing about their current situation. They could not believe such a charming girl as Mary was interested in Pete, nobody could. She **had** looked pretty scruffy when they met her, but her personality was at 100%. Both his parents had fallen completely under her spell as had anyone who knew her for over five minutes. As beautiful as she was, it was her sparkling personality that was her greatest asset.

On any phone call with his parents, the first thing said was always, “How is Mary?” or “What is Mary up to?” or anything about Mary. Even Alan who had never met her, but in learning about her from the parents, would work Mary into any conversations over the phone or in letters. Pete guessed this was at the urging of his mother.

After the **BOING**, Pete just wanted to get off the phone from his mother. He realized he did still care for Mary. “Tell Dad, Merry Christmas, and Mom . . . I love you.” (He could not remember the last time he told her that.) He meant it with all his heart, but somehow it didn’t sound sincere to him when he said it.”

On the other end of the line, the woman had to sit down. What was he trying to do, give her a Christmas heart attack? The family had always assumed love, but hardly ever expressed it. And Pete had been the most unsentimental of them all. What were they doing to him down there in New Mexico? Had he joined a cult? Was he becoming a flower child? She wanted to tell Pete she loved him too, but she was out of practice; it had been too long. Instead she said, "I want the phone number where you are."

Pete wasn't sure he wanted to give it to her. In fact, he was sure he didn't. but he had just promised to be a better son and meant it. "Okay Mom, but they have got a kind of funny joke down here. They told me I would only be allowed to receive calls from my Aunt Mary. So if you phone and they ask who you are, you will have to say Aunt Mary. If they say Where are Pete's parents , you are supposed to say Hawaii. It is complicated. Think of it as being like a password. I'll explain it when I get home." He hoped he could think up a good and believable fabrication.

"You certainly have interesting friends. Get home as soon as you can. And son, thank you for . . . uh . . . what you said." She had trouble using the "L" word too. There was a slight pause, then a chuckle, followed by, "Aloha." That's a good one Jean, she thought to herself: Aloha ha.

Mary

Later in the day, Mary phoned the apartment in Denver from Illinois to wish Pete and his folks a Merry Christmas.

Normally if anyone treated her like he did, they would be history. But there was just something about that boy: true, he was five years older than her, but he seemed so inexperienced and naïve, she considered herself the mature one in their relationship. She felt he might be the one she wanted for the father of her children and to spend the rest of her life with . . . **BUT** . . . after . . . after she settled down. The catch was, that she was not quite ready to settle down . . . just yet. There were still a few more things on her pre-marriage bucket list and there was James. But it was darn annoying and inconvenient that she had to keep rescuing that poor sap Pete from sweet young things that were ready.

The mother answered the phone and was delighted to hear from Mary. She had no idea Pete and Mary were currently no longer an item, and Mary didn't tell her. Under Mary's gentle grilling, she let it slip that Pete was spending Christmas with a classmate in Gallup because a terrible snowstorm was preventing him from getting back. However, he was expected back in a couple of days. She told Mary she would be glad to take a message.

"No thank you, Mrs. Wheatley. I need to deliver the message personally. Could you give me the phone number where he can be reached?"

There was something so pleasant about the girl that the mother had fallen completely under her spell. "Okay, but you are going to have to say you are his Aunt Mary. They have some kind of joke going on down there and you have to use the code."

Joke uh, Mary thought after she had hung up. *Taint funny, Magee*. She knew exactly who the "classmate" was. Poor foolish Pete. He kept trying to find other girls. He just didn't seem to realize he had been spoken for. In the vernacular of the stores, she had put him on lay away or she had earned the right of first refusal. He reminded her of a little puppy who kept slipping out of his pen and running around the back yard thinking it was free. It looked like it would take a little special attention to get this puppy back where he belonged. She had let this relationship progress just a little too long. She couldn't believe that in the beginning she had encouraged it thinking that the timid little freshman would be a safe place to store him temporarily. Maybe she could divert his attention to Sandy.

Mary's call to Gallup proved unsatisfactory. A rather gruff voice informed her that Mr. Wheatley was away for the afternoon and the time of his return was indefinite.

Meanwhile Pete who was looking for a solution for six problems, had no idea that a seventh was about to make all the others seem inconsequential.

Shopping For Presents

Meanwhile, Pete was currently roaming the streets of Gallup trying to pick out appropriate gifts for each member of Grace's family. He always had difficulty selecting presents, and this year was proving no exception. For Grace, he wanted something romantic enough to please her without upsetting her parents. He was starting to think of her more and more as a possible partner for the rest of his life and less and less as just an amiable study partner and someone to take his mind off Mary. He finally gave up on the perfect present and settled for some books. One was an exercise book. Like most exercise enthusiasts he enjoyed sharing the joys of physical fitness with others. The other books were one of Christian poetry and the other a picture book of Christmas around the world. For the mother he bought a large bouquet of roses and for Sarge, a bouquet of Four Roses. He didn't know what to do about the aunt. Too bad he didn't still have THE Louis L'Amour book.

CHAPTER 13

Auntie, N. S. & Snively

(It is rather appropriate that Auntie shows up in Chapter 13.)

Like the cities of San Francisco and Seattle, Gallup is a city with many hills. There the similarity ends, Pete thought to himself as he pulled up in front of a trim little white house with green shutters. He was about to meet the infamous Auntie that he was warned to look out for. Grace had tried to clue him in the night before. He tried to recall what she had told him.

Hank and his wife Daisy had three daughters. The oldest was a hard worker and very responsible. She was smart and had a subtle sense of humor seeing amusing things others missed. That was Grace's mother, Donna, who he had already met and always seemed to be three steps ahead of him. The youngest was tall, clever and lived on the east coast in New York. Chances were he would never meet her. She was married to a truck driver.

The middle daughter's name was Elouise; she was the infamous "Auntie" he had been repeatedly warned about. At one time Elouise had it all going for her. She was beautiful. She had a nice figure. She was popular. She was witty. She was engaged to a handsome young lawyer who many thought might go far in politics. He had beat out all the competition and won her heart completely. She became a teacher and her only problem was she was too kind and the children would often take advantage of her.

Then for some reason she needed an operation and a blood clot formed in her right leg causing it to grow three times the size of the other. It was quite painful and affected her personality. She walked like someone with a wooden leg. Handsome Jack the lawyer broke off the engagement. He left town shortly after he learned she had bought a bull whip and was practicing with it. She decided that all men were no damn good. She allowed as though there might be three possible exceptions: Jesus, Billy Graham, and Duane who was the truck driver her youngest sister had married. She tolerated Sarge only because he was married to her oldest sister Donna. Her own father was a player, and he and Daisy separated. But Daisy would not give him a divorce. He produced a second set of children with an Indian woman. Each one of the kids from this union was outstanding and successful. Daisy moved in with Evelyn who had sworn to never marry and they most likely spent their evenings bad mouthing most of the male gender. Daisy passed away on Mother's Day in 1963 and Auntie lived alone with her pet parrot.

One day Auntie was walking down the hall to her class, after the bell had rung. She had gone to the office to borrow a yardstick. She overheard two students walking behind her discussing the way she walked. Somehow students in the upper grades did not feel they had to worry about or obey First Grade or Kindergarten teachers. That came to a flaming halt that day. One was telling the other she walked like that pirate in Treasure Island with the peg leg. He even called her Long John Silver and imitated her walk. Something snapped inside her brain. She whirled around brandishing the yardstick she had been carrying like it was a cutlass.

"WELL SHIVER ME TIMBERS, YOU SCURVY LITTLE BILGE RATS," she roared. "YOU GET TO CLASS OR I'LL

BEND ME CUTLASS ACROSS YOUR STERN SIDES." With that she brought the yardstick she was carrying down hard on a nearby table containing Lost-and-Found items. Fortunately it did not shatter.

BANG! The noise was nearly as loud as her curse, and it was heard in nearly every room. The two students ran for the sanctity of their class.

She never had any problems after that. Over the years students made more progress during the year they were in her class than any other in their educational experience. AND they insisted that their children, and grandchildren be put in her room when they entered school. She taught there for 30 years. Whenever the principal had to be away, Auntie was left in charge. The principal was always welcomed back with open arms, especially by the men teachers. She was never bashful about sharing her opinions and thoughts.

Pete's thoughts were interrupted by the sound of a ship's bell attached to the house. On the porch stood a large woman with a scowl on her face. She had a sea bag strap over one shoulder and a parrot sitting on the other. Then quicker than he could get out of the car she started hopping down the steps with one leg doing 80% of the work.

She tossed him the bag and stood by the passenger's door. The bag hit him in the chest with all the force of the heavy medicine ball at the gym when Big Al threw it. He was knocked back into the car. "You're late," she growled. "You're late," repeated the parrot. She pointed to the bag. "If anything is broken, you will have to replace it." "Replace it," echoed the parrot. "Now stow it in the aft hole," she said pointing to the trunk. "Aft Hole," said the parrot making it sound like something else. He put the bag in the trunk. It was heavy. Then he walked to the driver's side and started to get in. Pete was not very comfortable around birds . . . or pirates. When he was five years old he had been attacked by a rooster. This was his first pirate.

Auntie was still standing outside by the passenger door. "Now what?" he asked.

"A gentleman always opens the door for a lady," she explained like talking to one of her first graders. One moment a roaring old sea salt of days gone by, and the next Miss Manners. He hurried to open the door hoping the pirate would remain at sea or wherever it had gone and the bird would stay on its side of the car and not try to attack him. If it did, they were sure to end up in a ditch. He felt about birds like some people did about spiders or snakes.

"Mam, would your bird like to ride in the back seat or the trunk," he asked.

The woman scowled and the parrot did something with its feathers that seemed to puff it up to double its size. It opened and closed its beak several times making a snapping sound like castanets.

"Snively, I've seen Nose Snapper perform amputations for less respectful remarks than that."

"Just kidding, and the name is Wheatley," he said with a nervous laugh. "heh, heh, heh"

"So am I," she chuckled: "HO HO HO. His real name is Tweetie Pie after that adorable little canary in the comics. He really is a sweetie pie."

As they headed south Pete noticed she looked much younger than Grace's mother and when she was Miss Manners, she was quite a charming conversationalist. Her hair, which had to be dyed, was flaming red. Her body, except for the bad leg, seemed to be in great shape. He remembered reading a book called THE 3 FACES OF EVE about a lady with multiple personalities. He wondered if that was the case here or if she was doing the good cop bad cop thing with him. He wished he had listened more closely to the inadequate warnings about this woman. He was once again starting to wish he had stayed in Denver. As they drove along the parrot contented itself by imitating different sounds. He could sound like a telephone, a car horn, a siren, a turn signal and many others. Twice Pete thought his turn signals were on and once he pulled over for an emergency vehicle that wasn't there.

They were half way to the ranch and visiting pleasantly. She was telling him what a fine girl Gracie was when he noticed her voice changing. It was getting deeper, less courteous, more gravely, and less friendly. It was sounding more like a man's voice than a woman's: a man looking for trouble. Pete took a quick glance at the woman and found his pleasant traveling companion had morphed into someone else. The eyes that met his glance were full of anger. A feeling of claustrophobia came over him. He became aware of how small the space in the car really was. And it became smaller as she released her seatbelt and slid over next to him. She grabbed his arm with a grip that would have done justice to an NFL linebacker like Eric Meany, and whispered something into his ear. Pete could smell garlic on her breath.

"Would you like a Certs?" he asked. He had bought a roll hoping to test its effectiveness with Grace.

"Thankee," she said snatching the roll out of his hand. She took out two and gave them to the parrot. Then she put the roll in her purse. "I'll save the rest in case I ever need them."

"I wasn't offering you the whole roll." (She glared at him.) "But that's all right. Look on it as a gift . . . or a peace offering."

To say this woman made him nervous would have been an understatement worthy of the Guinness Book of World Records.

Auntie smiled. It was an evil smile. "Would you like to see my knife?" she said. "I call it Man Stabber."

"**NO!**, I would definitely **NOT** like to see your knife."

She chuckled and whispered, "Boy, have you ever been to sea?"

"Yes."

"Oh," she said surprised to find a virtue in him. "Who did you sail under?"

"Uncle Jim." (His Uncle Jim was a geologist who had a small sailboat, the Jolly Dolphin, which he sailed from the marina to Catalina, a whopping 22 miles, once a month with his wife and two daughters.)

"Never heard of him," she said. "You still can't marry my niece."

"Okay."

He must have answered too quickly because it aroused the old girl's suspicions. "Pretty quick to answer there, Snively. You're not trying to blow me off, are yee?"

"Wheatley, the name is Wheatley."

He'd heard that Auntie tended to give people nicknames, reflecting what she thought of the person. "*Snively?*" He wasn't sure he liked his new nickname. And what in the world was a "snive" or a "snively." He was pronouncing it with a long "I" in his brain. Auntie pronounced it with a long "I" half the time and a short "I" half the time. Then he remembered a phrase from his early childhood when he had stubbed his toe. After the first half hour his mother had growled, "Peter, quit your sniveling." At that moment his thoughts were interrupted by a not-too-gentle tapping of knuckles on the side of his head.

"Boy," said the aunt. "Are you listening to me?"

"Yes Sir . . . I mean Mam. You said I couldn't marry your favorite niece."

"That was ages ago. Are you sure you are a college student. You seem to have the attention span of a gnat."

Pete wisely didn't say anything.

After a long moment of silence the aunt said, "Try to remember this little rhyme. Any hanky-panky and Auntie spanky." There was another long pause then the aunt asked, "When are you leaving to go back to wherever you came from?"

At that moment, the parrot moved to her left shoulder, the closest shoulder to Pete, and leaned in the direction of his nose.

"NOW," Pete declared while simultaneously tromping on the brake. "I'm leaving NOW! Tell Grace I got an emergency call from Denver." They had just passed a store and gas station. He would drive back to it and try to hitch a ride back to town. Auntie could either drive the car to the ranch or make arrangements for someone to come and pick her up.

Because of the icy road, instead of the car coming to a stop so he could make a U-turn, it took off like a whirling dervish. The next few moments were filled with screaming and squawking by the passengers as Pete tried to regain control of the vehicle. He almost made it. The car after several complete revolutions ended up in the ditch at an angle.

"Well, this is a fine How do you do," said the aunt. "Where did you get your license, in a Cracker Jack box?"

"How do you do Cracker Jack Box," said the parrot.

The parrot had ended in the back seat on his back where he had toppled. The aunt looking pale and a little shaken had slid to the other side of the car either because of centrifugal force or the angle the car was now resting. The seatbelt and a death grip on to the steering wheel kept Pete in place.

Remembering her question about when he would be leaving, the aunt said, "Tomorrow will be soon enough to leave."

"Soon enough," repeated the parrot from the back seat. Because his wings had been clipped, he was not able to fly back to the aunt's shoulder.

"Do I **have** to stay until tomorrow," Pete asked.

"Yes," said the aunt.

"No," said the parrot. It must have decided it wanted no part of this crazy young man. Pete was thinking, *This parrot is starting to lose it.*

Pete had been planning and hoping to stay a few days, but his mother sounded as though she really missed him he rationalized, and it sounded like his brother might make it for part of a week. They would be quite disappointed if he showed up without a nose or they read his name in the obituary. But down here in New Mexico it was like a crazy world peopled by old Marines, Indians, a too clever mother, a loony aunt with multiple personalities, an attack parrot, and Gracie. He calculated that was one reason for staying and four against: 20% for, 80% against. (Did I mention that math was not my best subject? Amazingly, I did that calculation in my head.) The ranch was also 30 miles from the nearest town. He could end up shot, stabbed, or de-nosed and the body or nose probably wouldn't be discovered until spring, if at all.

After about five minutes, two pickup trucks full of Navajos stopped. It seemed everyone in the trucks had the last name Yazzie except for one Tsosie, two Begays, and a Dubois. They were amazing. In twenty minutes the car was back on the road and checked out. They refused any pay, but one said he wouldn't mind having the delicious looking green chicken that was sitting on Auntie's shoulder. This did not please Auntie, or the parrot, which had gone strangely quiet and had no comment.

They were soon on their way again. Auntie suggested that they not tell anyone, like her sister, about this little adventure realizing it might not have happened if she and N. S. had stayed on their side of the car. Pete agreed. He didn't want the others to know he was responsible for putting the car in the ditch.

Auntie, satisfied that she had made her point, reached out and turned on the radio. The station was playing Christmas songs with very few commercials and Auntie was singing along with gusto. When she was not sure of the words she would fill in with her own creations, unless there really is a verse in Deck the Halls that goes "Fifteen elves on a snowman's chest. Yo ho ho and a bottle of rum."

Pete was starting to get suspicious about the bottle of Nyquil that she kept pulling out of her purse and sipping. She had told him it was for a terrible cough. Then she coughed to add authenticity to the statement. But it dawned on Pete that she never coughed again on the whole trip, even though the sipping kept happening.

When they reached the ranch, Auntie bailed out after issuing orders for him to bring in her sea bag and where to stow it. And of course there was the re-warning about what would happen to him if anything was broken. Pete couldn't believe anything that was even half fragile had survived the ride out or her tossing the bag around. Pete sighed. In his mind, he was supposed to be the hero of a Hallmark Christmas and here he was being treated like a cabin boy, stevedore and porter.

As he struggled into the house with Auntie's bag over his right shoulder, he heard the sisters talking. The Aunt was saying that this one didn't seem to have much gumption, "and he is a terrible driver. Put us in a ditch."

So much for your promise, Pete thought.

Auntie continued. "Grace should throw him back, like the catch and release policy they have for fish on the Animas River. Why I bet the sissy doesn't even have a tattoo."

"I wanted one, but my mother wouldn't let me have it," Pete said stepping into the kitchen. The second it was out of his mouth, he wanted it back. He realized it was a mistake. It would certainly do nothing to change the aunt's estimation of his manliness or gumption-ness. He remembered Grace saying that Auntie had some tattoos. He tried to recover. "I was in pre-school at the time . . . and . . . we slid on some black ice when Nose Snapper made a move at my olfactory entrances."

"And he can't keep a promise," mumbled the aunt.

"Your Aunt Mary called while you were in town," the mother said. **BOING!** "She sounded awfully young to be your aunt."

Pete knew exactly what had happened. There was only two girls he had given the Denver number to. One was here in New Mexico and the other was in Illinois. His mother was putty in the hands of the one back east.

"Mrs. Cousins, it is kind of a funny situation. Both my parents have a sister named Mary. My dad's sister is the same age as he is, I mean two years younger, what I am trying to say is they are in the same age range. My mother's parents had a little girl late in life, and her name was . . . is . . . Mary. We call her "Young Mary" and we call Dad's sister "Old Mary," when we are talking about her, but not to her face. Then we just call her Aunt Mary. You must have been talking to Young Aunt Mary."

"See, I told you he was flaky," the aunt said.

At that moment, Grace came into the kitchen. She smiled when she saw him. She had been in the living room wrapping packages with the record player covering up the sound of his return. Pete thought it sounded like Andy Williams singing about it being the most wonderful time of the year, and with the appearance of Grace, suddenly it was. Grace showed him to the aunt's room and he followed and set down the heavy bag with a thump.

"Oops. Your aunt said she would skewer me if any presents in her bag were chipped," he commented. "Judging by the weight," he said rubbing his right shoulder, "one, or even two of you may be getting cannon balls for Christmas. Un-chipped cannon balls he added quickly and hopefully."

"Oh pooh. Don't take Auntie too seriously. Most of what she says is just an act. She's really a little pussy cat. She's all talk . . . or 'meow.' Some of the older girls in the family got married before finishing school, and she's afraid I might too. She's just trying to scare you."

"She's doing a remarkably good job."

At that moment the door swung open, and there stood the aunt. Pete excused himself saying he had to go to his room and wrap some presents he had purchased today. Grace offered to help.

"Not in his room you don't," declared Auntie.

There is everything we need in the living room where I was wrapping when you two got here," Grace volunteered.

When they got to the living room Grace said suspiciously, "I thought you told me you had the clerks wrap today's presents."

"Then why did you offer to help?" He countered.

She didn't answer. Pete said, "I just wanted to get away from Captain Long John Gestapo."

The aunt had stayed in her bedroom to unpack. Pete and Grace sat on the couch in front of the fireplace. They could see outside through the window. It had started to snow again. Big, lazy flakes floated gently down in slow motion. For the rest of his life, whenever he tried to recall the scene, he used the term "snow-motion."

Perry Como was singing about being home for Christmas when a truck turned in. It was Sarge. Sarge insisted that they all have a round before going over to Bert and Belle's across the street. Grace and her mother had coffee. Sarge and Auntie had a couple of shots of Jim Beam. Pete held a can of beer which he mainly just pretended to drink. When he thought no one was looking, he poured the contents down the drain and half-filled it with water from the tap. But someone was looking; it was the mother; she smiled with approval.

They were all in a great mood as they left the house to trek across the street. They were all wearing boots but the women were carrying sacks with shoes in them. The snow was falling harder. They had just reached the road when Pete said he wanted to go back and get his jacket. "I'll go too," said Grace, "and make sure he doesn't steal the silverware or peek at any presents."

"I think I'll go too and get my heavier coat," said the aunt turning to follow the couple.

"NO you won't," said the mother, blocking her. "We can give them a few moments to be alone."

"Grumble grumble," came from the aunt, but she did as she was told. Her older sister was one of the few persons in the world that exerted any kind of control over her.

The first thing they heard as they re-entered the house was the music. The aunt had stacked some records on the player in her room so the parrot wouldn't hear them leave and get upset. Grace waited in the kitchen while Pete retrieved his jacket from the bedroom. Then he said, "Wait there, I need to use the bathroom." Pete headed in the direction of the bathroom, but stopped in the living room. He had felt something in his jacket pocket that gave him an idea.

In the parrot's room one record finished and another started. It was Nose Snapper's favorite, some orchestra playing music of the sea backed by sounds associated with the sea. In the kitchen, Grace was starting to wonder what was taking Pete so long and why he told her to stay in the kitchen.

Suddenly Pete's voice called out, "Grace, come here." His voice didn't sound normal. What could be wrong? She hurried into the living room. "STOP," he called out when she reached the center of the room. "STOP!" Called the parrot from the other room. Grace stopped. His voice had still not seemed normal. "Look up," he said. She looked up. Somebody had hung some mistletoe above the spot she was standing under.

She started to speak. "Somebody has put . . . "

That was as far as she got. She stopped cold as she realized who had and why she had been told to stop in that particular spot. The parrot was in another room imitating sounds associated with the sea along with the record. There was the sound of waves, the warning cry of a foghorn, and the calls of seagulls. The song playing was Ebb Tide. Every element and detail was indelibly etched in her mind.

Pete stepped up to her. She was not looking at him but still looking at the ceiling above her and the mistletoe. She could feel his body coming closer to hers but still not touching, as he waited for her to look down. She became aware of her heart pounding harder and harder; beating faster and faster. The blood coursing rapidly through her body was stimulating all her sensitive areas.

Time seemed to stand still. It was like watching a giant wave building up just prior to crashing on the shore. She looked down; their faces were inches apart. She felt his arms go around her as their bodies melded together. Then as their lips met, the wave exploded upon the beach. There was no holding back. She responded as though it were the most natural thing in the world. She had no idea where she learned to move like she was moving.

For Pete it had been a different story. He had done it more as a joke on the aunt. He figured to give or get a quick peck on the cheek or lips and then hurry over to the party across the street. There he would drop hints where the aunt could hear like "I wonder who hung the mistletoe in the living room at the other house," and "There sure are some good kissers in this family."

What he got was entirely different. Like everything else that had been happening in his life these last few days, the situation seemed to be out of his control. It was like he and circumstances were being manipulated by a force far greater. It was like being caught in a riptide or a strong current. He felt like he was a character in a story, doing whatever the author typed on the paper. It reminded him of floating in the ocean relaxed and letting the current take him wherever it wanted.

When he stopped just short of her, his mind was racing a mile a minute. This thing had gotten out of hand. What had he gotten himself into? He had to get out of here. But the force wasn't having any of that. When Grace's gaze quit looking at the mistletoe and found his face, he had never seen anything so beautiful. It was like a magical fog had surrounded them isolating them from the rest of the world.

As she reached out and touched him, his body automatically took the last step towards her. Their bodies touched, and his arms went around her. Then as their lips met, and the powerful wave took them in its grip, all he could do was hold on for dear life and enjoy the ride. He believed he could smell salt sea air and hear the distant cry of seagulls, the call of a fog horn and waves breaking on a faraway beach. There had also been rockets bursting overhead and the sound of bells: a ship's bell, a channel buoy, a telephone . . . *telephone?*

The fog evaporated and there they stood holding each other up in the middle of a house surrounded by snow 600 miles from the nearest ocean and gasping for air. The phone **was** ringing. Grace asked him to answer it because her legs were a little unsteady. He said his were too and after all it was her family's phone, so the call wouldn't be for him.

He was so wrong. "It's for you," she said. And held out the phone.

Who could it be? The only person he had given this number to was his mother. Grace's mother had mentioned a long distance call from back east someplace. His hand was shaking as he reached for the phone. He could only think of one person who was back east, might phone, and could talk his mother into giving her the phone number. He didn't want to talk to ***her,*** *especially in front of Grace. His heart was still pounding from that kiss.*

"Hello, this is Pete."

He recognized her voice instantly. It was an unhappy voice. It was an angry voice.

"Snively, by my watch, you've been down there unchaperoned twenty minutes. Remember the poem about Hanky, Panky, and Spanky?" Before he could answer, she continued. "Comprendo?"

He breathed a sigh of relief. Nay. Joy. "Si si, Senora. How wonderful to hear from you, and what a great poem it is. You must be the poet laurate of New Mexico."

"Do you want me to kick your ass up into your shoulders?"

"I'd rather have one of your famous hugs or delicious shortbread, fruit cake, or plum pudding."

The aunt was furious. She did not know what to say next. Every insult she hurled at him, he turned into a compliment to her. Finally she gave up, "Just get your sorry butt over here," and she hung up slamming down the receiver.

Pete walked back to Grace. "Her Ladyship requests our presence in the drawing room," He held out his hand to help her up from the couch where she had sat while he was talking to the aunt.

"Shall we," replied the girl.

"We shall. The Duchess did seem insistent," he replied.

In the magic moment they had experienced under the mistletoe, Pete and Grace had become one, with the smoothness of waves blending far out at sea. With the fire burning low, the music playing softly, and the lights of the most beautiful Christmas tree in the world, which he had brought in from the forest, blinking merrily, two young hearts had shared a brief moment they were never to forget.

As they were crossing the road Pete said, "By the way that was a very nice kiss."

"*Nice*" she thought. That was like calling Mount Everest a hill. She was shocked. She had been expecting him to say something like that was the kiss of the century, the kiss of my life. But she was up to the challenge. She wasn't going to let him get away with that. She faked a yawn and said "I'm saving my "A" game for someone a little more exciting. Don't feel badly, you might get better . . . someday. You're still young."

Well played he thought. This was not the same quiet, timid freshman that he was used to, and a professor had called "mousey."

CHAPTER 14

Christmas Eve: Party and Battle

It had become tradition that Christmas Eve was spent at Bert and Belle's across the street. On Christmas morning each brother had a special private celebration in his own home with his own family. And then in the afternoon they would all gather for a Christmas dinner together as long as their mother was alive.

Pete and Grace hurried over to the other house where the uncle was ruling with benevolent joy over his married daughters and their families. He reminded Pete of old Fezziwig the jolly employer of young Ebenezer Scrooge in Charles Dickens' The Christmas Carol. His profile was not too dissimilar from that of a snowman's but it did not keep him from being able to outwork any man in the community. Fezziwig was sitting in one of the rocking chairs with his brother Sarge sitting in another next to him. Pete marveled how two brothers could look so different. One looked like a marshmallow and the other like a piece of over-dried jerky.

Most of the women were in the kitchen visiting and working. There were two exceptions. One was in a locked bedroom doing some last minute present wrapping because of the surprise guest. The other exception was Auntie who was in the hall next to the wall phone. She was practicing her butt kicking. She reminded Pete of a field goal kicker on the sidelines, who expects to be called in on the next play to attempt the game winning point.

Another group of young husbands of the daughters were discussing upcoming bowl games and making wagers. Young children were scurrying about, and breaking into first one group then another, jabbering nonsense and asking questions about Santa Claus. Occasionally one of the adults would issue the famous old threat about Santa only coming to good little girls and boys. Not the naughty ones that tied the cat's tail in a knot, jiggled the packages, ate too much candy, stood on the furniture, etc., etc.

In the center of the dining area was a large round oak table with several slats put in to extend its surface area and make it more oval than round. On it, was just about every kind of delicious food that one would find at a deli and a multitude of delicious desserts. Pete couldn't imagine anything grander. When Aunt Belle announced everything was ready they all lined up and went to the table. Each parent was responsible for their children.

While they were eating they noticed about 10 pickup trucks stop in front of the store. Soon there were about 30 Indians walking up to the house.

"I hope they are friendly Indians," Pete told Grace.

"They are. They are from the church over the hill and they have come to carol. They are from Barney's church." (She and her cousin Butch had nicknamed the Reverend Barnes "Barney" many years before.)

The carolers sang several songs, some in English and some in Navajo. When they were through, Bert and Belle offered them a choice of coffee or hot chocolate which they brought to them in paper cups and also some Christmas candies in little baggies which they took out to them on the porch with the help of several of the ladies. They did not come into the house (their choice) and were soon on their way to their next performance or serenade. For Pete, it was the highlight of the party.

After the eating was finished and the carolers had gone, Uncle Fezziwig told everyone to take a seat while he with the help from a few of the older kids started passing out the presents from under the tree. Outside of a department store, Pete had never seen so many gifts in one place. Except for the lack of a yule log, this Christmas was turning out to be everything Pete had dreamed or read about . . . and more. He had to sit on the floor next to Grace's feet because Auntie had plunked down on the sofa next to Grace.

Uncle Fezziwig, as Pete thought of him, stood up and recited a Christmas poem he must have memorized as a child. All Pete remembered were the words "Christmas in the land of the fir tree and pine. Everywhere, Everywhere, Christmas tonight."

Then the Uncle said, "Let the papers fly," and that they did. Everyone tore into the packages in front of them. There was no watching everyone open their presents individually and then thanking the giver. Pete couldn't believe the scene. He had never seen anything like it, even in movies or on television. Much to his surprise there was even presents with his name on them.

Those that lived in town were getting anxious to get safely home. Fortunately the snow had stopped falling. Some of the men went out to start their cars to let them warm up and sweep the snow off their vehicles. The temperature was in the single digits, and they still had 30 miles to go over snowy icy roads. The opening of the presents had been minutes of joyful chaos and Pete loved it. Everyone seemed grateful for what they received, none, more so, than him. When it was over, the town people left in a caravan of vehicles looking out for each other.

The five of them from the other side of the road stayed to help clean up before heading back across the street. While the women were working on the house, Pete and Sarge made several trips down to the other house carrying presents. Pete noticed that Auntie and Sarge kept sipping something out of a thermos that Sarge had brought back from the other house on one of the trips, and they seemed to be getting happier with each sip. When everything was shipshape they sat down and visited while waiting for a phone call telling them the others had made it safely to town. It came 56 minutes later. Sarge announced it was time for his platoon to head for the barracks.

Grace's mother led the parade followed by Pete and Grace and Sarge and Auntie. Pete and Grace were strolling contentedly through the cold night air listening to the snow crunch under their feet and marveling about how bright and shiny the stars were. They were holding hands, and wishing this night would never end when . . . WOOSH . . . a firm snowball socked Pete in the back of the head.

"Do yee strike your colors?" shouted the aunt jumping up and down with delight.

The war was on. They threw furiously at one another with only the mother not participating. She had continued walking down to the other house shaking her head. The battle was going pretty evenly with Grace and Auntie throwing at each other with few registered hits. Pete was getting a little the better of Sarge and registering a greater volume of hits. They had been throwing at each other's bodies below the shoulders. In desperation, Sarge packed one hard as he could and threw for Pete's head: a "hail" Mary to save the battle for his side. It caught Pete on the nose hard enough that his eyes started to water and he could hear a ringing in his head like the time the linebacker from Burbank had blindsided him. Sarge had done such a good job making the missile that it did not break. Pete scooped it up like a shortstop and threw it sidearm at Sarge's head as hard as he could. *Two could play that game, he* thought, without thinking.

In baseball they call it a wild pitch. The ball of snow sailed over Sarge headed for the large picture window from which Fezziwig and clan (those from Albuquerque who were spending the night) had been enjoying the show. Fezziwig saw it coming just seconds before it hit. A look of sheer terror crossed his usually jolly countenance. All the observers tried to beat a hasty retreat from the window before it got smashed into smithereens. Everybody's brain was working at warp speed while their bodies and the snowball were moving in slow motion. Fezziwig looked like his life had just flashed before him.

CRASH!

It hit so hard, Pete thought he saw shingles fall off the roof, but they were just icicles. Why it did not break the window can only be classified as a genuine Christmas miracle, only a few notches below virgin births, flying reindeers, and Santa Claus. It is possible that one of the thick icicles slowed the deadly missile just enough to save the window.

In a twinkling, they heard from the porch, "GO YOU DEVILS. PLY YOUR HOUSE DESTROYING HAVOC ON YOUR OWN SIDE OF THE ROAD."

Sarge had turned back towards the sound of his brother's voice. "Cease fire," he called out . . . too late. Two snowballs had already been launched. They both achieved their target arriving at the same time. The snow stuck to Sarge's chest and glasses. The aunt thought this was funny.

"Good shot, Gracie. Good shot, Snively," she shouted as she held her sides and laughed until tears ran down her cheeks. This gave Sarge the time to recover, and he did not appreciate this display of good sportsmanship from a member of his own team. He reached down and scooped up a large handful of snow, turned to the aunt standing next to him, and thrust it down the front of her dress.

Then he stepped back to admire his work and laughed, "HA HA." He might have got away with it if he had only given one "HA" and then run for his life, or no "HA'S" and run. But with the speed of a western gunfighter or Bruce Lee, Auntie screamed "SHIVER ME BOOBS" and kicked him in the shins, while filling her hand with a high-heel shoe from the bag she was carrying it in and bopped him along side of his neck. It made an interesting sound. Not as loud as a gun firing or a snowball hitting a big window, but loud enough to be heard from a distance. Pete named it the "WACK-BANG" when he filled out his journal that night.

Sarge dropped to the ground, out cold, like some who had been foolish enough to fight Joe Louis a second time. He lay there not moving. Pete tried to remember what he knew about the area where she had struck him. It contained the carotid artery and the vagus nerve. One carried blood to the brain and the other nerve impulses. A strike to either one could be dangerous.

Pete could not tell if Sarge was unconscious or dead. He thought probably the smart money was on "dead." The aunt was glaring at Pete with the "smoking" shoe still in her hand. "I didn't see a thing," Pete shouted. "I can't testify against you." He took a step back towards the gate and promised himself to be on the next bus north. His thoughts ran along the line of, *Legally, I could be considered an accessory? What if the family banded together and said I had done it. He took another step towards the gate.*

"Oh no you don't," shouted the uncle. "Don't go leaving any dead bodies in my yard."

That's your brother, Pete thought. *Could this be the same jovial man who was smiling and laughing and reciting "Everywhere, everywhere Christmas tonight and let the papers fly"?* This was a tough outfit. Too tough for him.

At that moment, Sarge groaned. It was the most beautiful groan Pete had ever heard. It meant Sarge was alive. "What happened?" Sarge asked.

Oh dear, he has a concussion and amnesia, Pete thought. *Why isn't he saying where am I? I thought you were supposed to say where am I when you regain consciousness after being knocked out.*

"You must have slipped," lied the aunt while trying to shake the snow out of the top of her dress. "Snively, get over here and help."

"NO. And the name is Wheatley."

"I mean over there. Help my brother-in-law up."

"YES," he shouted and breathed a sigh of relief happy not to be on the snow removal crew. Pete helped Sarge to his feet and asked if Sarge wanted to lean on him . . . or the name of a good lawyer. The old Marine declined both after warning Pete to be careful because it must be awfully slippery out. They continued towards the house across the street with the aunt in the lead followed by Pete and Grace and then Sarge. Fezziwig stayed on the porch until he was sure they were off his property.

When the mighty warriors got back to the house, the mother was already in her bedroom wrapping a few last minute presents and getting ready for bed. She had turned the radio on. One of the local radio stations was playing uninterrupted Christmas music, no commercials, just an occasional acknowledgement of which sponsor had given up their radio time. This was easier than continually changing records so the mother had switched to the radio.

The announcer had a peppy, happy voice and was a perfect complement to the music, both in what he played and what he said. The announcer was so good Pete wondered how a local station managed to get and keep him. Pete had become a big fan in just two days. Pete had first caught Sam on the radio doing a high school basketball game. He made it so interesting Pete stayed listening until the game was over. Pete had grown up in Southern California listening to Chick Hearn doing the Laker games and Vince Scully doing the Dodger games. They were acknowledged as the best in the country, and he thought Sam was as good as they were.

"I predict that before next year is out, that guy will be on one of the mega stations on one of the coasts or Chicago," Pete declared.

The mother who had stuck her head out of the bedroom to wish everyone a good night said, "I don't think so. He likes it here and loves the people."

"We'll see," Pete said.

"Yes, we'll see," she said as she pulled her head back, smiling, and closed the door to the bedroom.

"Snively," the aunt ordered, "Put another log on the fire. It is getting colder than a well digger's bottom or an aunt's tit." Then she hurried towards her bedroom to get out of her wet clothes.

Sarge was grumbling while rummaging around in the kitchen looking for the pill bottle with aspirins in it and not being very successful.

After poking the fire and adding several logs, Pete stepped back to admire his work. It suddenly dawned on him that he was standing under the mistletoe. At that same moment Grace came into the living room and made the same discovery.

"Pete, you are standing under the mistletoe," she whispered. This time it was Pete under the mistletoe and Grace stepping up. He spread his arms wide and she stepped into them like they had been doing it forever. "Do you want to see if you can get it right this time," she said with a twinkle in her eyes, beating him to the punch.

"Well if I must. I understand it is seven years bad luck if you don't kiss when you discover you're standing under the mistletoe."

Once again her nearness and the anticipation of a kiss was starting to block out the rest of the world. But the world came crashing back.

"In some cases, like right now, it is seven years bad luck if you do," said the aunt entering the room. "And besides you are confusing it with seven years bad luck is for breaking a mirror . . . or someone's front window."

For some reason his grandma's saying about "Smile, things could be worse" came to mind. He tried not to smile but was unsuccessful.

Things got worse. "Wipe that silly smile off your face. I've decided to sleep in the little room tonight. Snively, move my stuff to the little room off the dining area." This would put her door four steps from his instead of the length of the house away. "I'll wait in here by the fire while you move my bag and parrot."

CHAPTER 15

The Creatures Were Stirring

Grace said she would see him in the morning and headed off to her room. The silly smile was wiped.

Fortunately the parrot was still in the cage and easy to carry. Pete passed Sarge coming out of the kitchen. "Hey Sarge, someone put some mistletoe up in the living room, but I guess you're too old to do anything about that." The old boy bristled. When he entered the living room the only occupant was Auntie, and she was standing directly under the mistletoe with her back to him and her hands raised above her head. It looked to him like she was dancing to the music on the radio.

The ex-Marine charged. He'd show that young smart aleck that he was not over the hill. He wrapped his arms around the aunt and planted a kiss on her neck.

He should have known better or looked more carefully. The reason her hands were above her head was she had grabbed a poker from the fire place and was using it to try and knock the mistletoe down that Pete had put up there. The sequence went: GRAB-KISS-BONK- "Oh Snively, will you come and pick up my brother-in-law."

But Snively didn't come. He was in his bedroom with the door shut, looking for ways to make sure he wouldn't be murdered or bonked on the head in his sleep. He settled for sliding a heavy dresser halfway across the room and a short bookcase containing a full set of the Encyclopedia Britannica to where they were braced against the door. Then he shoved the bed against that.

The room was cold being deprived of the heat from the propane heater in the dining room. Pete fished around in his duffle bag for his long johns, ski gloves, thick socks, and knitted ski mask/hat. Then he sat down at the desk and started making entries in his journal that he had started on the bus. If he managed to survive the next few hours he was going to write a book about this experience. He caught a glimpse of himself in the mirror in his bright red flannels that had once been his fathers. He almost took them off. If his body was ever found he didn't want there to be pictures of him wearing those atrocious things. It would be embarrassing to his memory.

The first entry to the journal he had started on the bus was a rough map showing his travels so far starting at Fort Lewis. He wanted to tell the whole story, but he didn't remember much from his first drink until his father woke him up the next morning. He left the first five pages blank hoping the memory of what happened would come back to him. Starting with Page 6, he had no trouble filling in the pages. When he was caught up with the journal, he climbed into his cozy cocoon of blankets and quilts wearing an embarrassing conglomeration of clothes.

But he could not get to sleep. He lay there thinking about what an exciting, unbelievable adventure he was having. There was something about risking your life and surviving that put a person on an endorphin high. He recalled as a little boy jumping out of the top of a tree holding on to a rope attached to a larger tree and swinging out over a rock pile, a barbed wire fence and a neighbor's Doberman. Then there was the first time he rode the rollercoaster at Pacific Ocean Park; skiing the double diamonds at Telluride; skydiving using an old WWII' parachute that he had folded (packed) himself on a cold day in Fairbanks; climbing Wolverton Mountain; and riding in the car with Grandma driving.

He had never actually climbed Wolverton Mountain. It was a song about a man who loved a girl that lived on the mountain and her father would shoot anyone who came up on the mountain to court his daughter. That situation wasn't entirely different than the one he was in now with that bloody pirate stalking him at every turn.

Probably of all these adrenaline raisers, the grandma one was the scariest. She figured once she signaled, that gave her the right of way. She always used the arm signals because she could never remember which direction of the newfangled turn signals was for left and which was for right. There were no seatbelts in the 1939 Buick and any crash was sure to send them flying.

Pete was just getting relaxed and comfortable in the bed when he heard it. It was the sound of scurrying feet. There would be a scurrying of feet, then silence, then more scurrying. It had to be different members of the family sneaking presents under the tree and into the stockings that had been hung by the chimney with care.

That gave him a great idea. He called it Operation Semi-Santa Claus. Sarge would like that he thought. He would wait until 15 minutes passed without any noise. Then he would zoom (scurry) out of the room with the presents he had purchased, put them under the tree and be back in his room in under two minutes. At last the time had come. He crept out of bed, he slid the dresser and bookcase back far enough that he could open the door and slip out. He knew he could make it. He knew where every piece of furniture was which could act as an obstacle. He would be back in his room with the door closed before they could even get out of bed, if they heard him, which they wouldn't because he was quick and he was quiet. He mapped out the route in his head that he would take. It would avoid all obstacles.

He checked his watch. It was 0302. He scooped up the presents he had placed on the dresser with one arm. It was easy, they were all small and there were only four. He glanced at his watch again. He would time the operation. In his mind, the starting gun went off and he exploded out of the blocks. In his first two steps outside the room he hit something that wasn't supposed to be there and sent it flying. The house was filled with a horrible horrible noise. Somebody had put the parrot on a chair just outside his room. He grabbed the cage, set it back on the chair and was back in his room with the door closed and the bed, dresser and bookcase firmly up against it within two minutes. According to his watch, it was 0304. Fortunately the horrible horrible noise had covered up the sound of the dresser and bookcase being pushed towards the door.

It wasn't long before he could see a light was on in the next room from the gap under the door. It seems like everyone else was up and awake. He would have joined them but to do that he would have had to move the bed, dresser and bookcase to open the door wide enough for him to pass through. This was a noisy process and he didn't want to have to come up with a sociably acceptable reason for rearranging the furniture at three in the morning. He was able to pick up parts of the conversation. In his haste he failed to notice the door had not completely closed and there was a gap about one finger wide.

Aunt: "Where's Snively?"

Mother: "Mr. Wheatley is probably in bed asleep like the rest of us should be."

Grace: "Why was the parrot and his cage on a chair in the dining room, and why was he making that horrible noise?"

Sarge: "It looks like he probably fell off his perch, didn't recognize where he was, got scared and started . . ."

"Maybe he had a nightmare," interrupted the mother. "Whatever he was doing, I have no idea why he wasn't in the room with Auntie instead of on a chair in the middle of the dining room."

The aunt sounded like she was uncomfortable with the direction the conversation was taking and wanted to change it.

Aunt: "He was snoring and keeping me awake, so I moved him out of my room. Should we check on Snively? If he didn't hear all that noise he might be dead or the burglar."

Mother: "Wouldn't prove a thing. That noise was loud enough to wake the dead." Then she chuckled at her own witticism.

Sarge: "In the Marines you learn to sleep under all kinds of conditions and loud noises. I remember one night in Bougainville the sky was full of exploding . ."

Mother: "Hush. We've all heard that story two hundred times. Go to bed everybody. Go to sleep."

Everyone seemed happy to follow her instructions, including the parrot. It was now back on his perch in the cage in Auntie's room, probably wishing it was back in the jungle in Brazil. Pete was still in Fort Bedroom. He would get the presents under the tree in the morning, which he calculated would be another couple hours. He just knew he wouldn't be able to sleep a wink. He closed his eyes.

CHAPTER 16

Presents, Party, Prayer & Parting.

When Pete opened his eyes it was five hours later and light outside. He could smell coffee and bacon. He breathed a sigh of relief. The crazies and nose amputaters had not breached his security system. He got up and moved the furniture back in place. He had just finished and climbed back in bed when there came a loud knocking at the door followed by, "Eight Bells on the Forenoon Watch " Had to be Auntie. Where were his pants? They were across the room next to the dresser. Then he heard what sounded like someone trying to imitate revile.

"Good job, Malin," said the aunt.

Pete took off his long johns, then sweatpants and started moseying across the room to where his Levis lay on the floor.

From the other side of the door he heard, "If that doesn't get the little twit out of bed, I'll go in and rip the bloody covers off myself. In fact, READY OR NOT, HERE I COME," she shouted.

That did it. Pete leaped for and into his pants in a manner that would have done any fireman proud. He threw open the bedroom door and shouted.

"GOOD MORNING, EVERYBODY. MERRY CHRISTMAS! I guess I must have slept in."

"So did Rip Van Winkle," snorted the aunt. "Only not as long and when Rip got up, he put on shoes."

"Breakfast is ready," the mother called from the kitchen. "Grace is just finishing buttering the toast. We're having what we call Farmer's Breakfast. It is a mixture of scrambled eggs with hash brown potatoes, chopped bacon, cut-up onions, grated cheese, and then you season it with sour cream, garlic, and dill. It sounds scary, but is delicious. The toast has now been buttered and we have homemade strawberry jam that Gracie made the day she got back from school and peanut butter with nuts that Skippy made. To drink there is Orange Julius, coffee, and milk." She paused a moment while everyone sat down.

Pete reached for a piece of toast.

The aunt bopped him on the knuckles with her fork. "As soon as someone puts his shoes on, and we have the blessing we can start," added the Aunt wrinkling her nose at him. When Pete returned to the table and Grace had given the blessing, the mother said, "Shoo the flies off and take to it."

Pete looked around. He did not see any flies. Grace giggled, "That's just something Mama says."

It was the most delicious breakfast Pete could ever remember eating and everyone was in such a jolly good mood. He envied these crazy happy people. The only way it could have been better was if Auntie hadn't plunked herself down between Grace and him at the table and his toast reaching knuckles weren't sore.

When everyone had eaten their fill the mother announced it was time to go into the living room for the presents. The stockings that had been hung by the chimney with care were now resting on chairs and the sofa marking where that person was to sit. And miracle of miracle there was one with Pete's name on it **AND** it was on the couch next to one that had Grace's name. *Unbelievable. Auntie must be slipping,* he thought.

The aunt looked as surprised as Pete, but not as pleased. Someone had moved her stocking to the far side of the room after she had got up early and moved Pete's to the far side of the room. The aunt was trying to figure out who had sabotaged her. It could have been Grace, her mother, or Pete himself. She knew Sarge had no interest in the seating arrangements. She made one last feeble attempt. "My leg is really bothering me this morning. I need to be nearer to the fireplace. Snively, trade places with me."

Before he could move, the mother said, "Go put on your leg warmers, Little Sister." Pete caught a look pass between the aunt and the mother.

Once again the aunt backed down. "Never mind. It's feeling better."

And even more unbelievable were the amount of presents under the tree. The mother said the way we do the presents in this house is for the youngest adults to pass out the presents, and then we open them one at a time going around the room, starting with the youngest. This way everyone gets to see what everyone gets. There was a slight change in the process as Grace read the names and Pete delivered them to the spot where that person was sitting. When they had delivered all the presents Pete's pile was noticeably the smallest, but he was the unplanned for guest.

The mother announced they would start with Grace, then Pete, Malin, Auntie and her. Most of the items in the stockings looked like they had been purchased at the Five and Dime or the produce section of the Piggly Wiggly. The last item Pete pulled out of his stocking was a nice big orange about the size of a softball.

This Christmas was turning out to be everything Pete wanted it to be. These folks might be kooks, but they certainly had the spirit and knew how to celebrate Christmas. When all the presents were distributed they watched while first one person then another opened a single gift. After each unveiling there was cheering, congratulations and comments of appreciation by the recipient. That is until Grace opened one from Pete. It was The Canadian Airforce Exercise Book. Grace was speechless. What was Pete trying to say? She had given him a Bible because she thought that part of his life was lacking and because the Lord was so important to her.

"What the Hell," cried Sarge, "kind of Christmas present is that?"

"I . . . thought . . . she might enjoy life more if . . . she were in a little better physical condition. I exercise all the time." (He had noticed on a walk up to the campus one day from town that she was breathing hard and she needed to stop and rest several times. Grace was not, and never had been, interested in athletics. She even managed during her senior year in high school to work in the library during physical education period.)

"That makes sense," agreed Sarge, "in the Marines we exercised every day, and I felt great. I was in excellent physical condition."

"Oh rusty cannon balls," said the aunt in disgust.

"I'd sort of appreciate you leaving her *physical condition* the way it is," put in the mother.

"I second that," declared the aunt.

Grace's face turned red with embarrassment. "Oh look there's another book in the box too."

"Well, Romeo strikes again. What is it?" asked the aunt. "How to Sharpen a Chainsaw or Repair a Transmission?"

The group approved of the rest of his gifts: a book of Christmas pictures and one of poetry by Helen Steiner Rice. They showed thoughtfulness and caring, but in a safe category or area. They had been fearing something much more passionate, intimate, amorous, or romantic, like a ring . . . especially like a ring. The group wasn't ready to lose their only daughter or niece at 18 years old.

During the clean-up, Grace threw some of the wrappings in the fireplace and stepped back to watch them blaze. That put her under the mistletoe spot, just the excuse Pete needed. He leaped to his feet and started heading in her direction. "Look up," he said, pointing to the ceiling above her and then stopped dead in his tracks. It was as though he had run into a brick wall. The mistletoe was gone.

At that moment, a sinister voice behind him asked, "Lose something, Snively? Ha Ha Ha." She opened her hand to show him the sprig of mistletoe, then she closed it again.

Sarge's mother, who lived across the street with her second son's family, had four boys. To keep them all straight in his mind, Pete gave each one a nickname. With the exception of Sarge, he kept the nicknames to himself. The oldest had been a blacksmith and now lived in Wickenburg 340 miles away. Because of the storms he wouldn't be there this year. Pete named him Uncle Wickenburg. Then there was Uncle Fezziwig the Indian trader from across the street who reminded him of young Scrooge's jolly first boss most of the time. Next was the tall and impressive Uncle Bean; he owned a hardware store in town. He was the tallest at over 6' 3" and thin as a rail. He reminded Pete of a string bean which he shortened to "bean" to save a syllable. And finally there was Sarge who was in charge of the silversmiths at Tobe Turpen's. All the brothers and their families made an effort to get together on Christmas day for a Christmas dinner as long as their mother was still with them.

The people started arriving about two 'o'clock. When a family would arrive, the women would generally head for the kitchen bringing their contribution to the meal; the men would gather in the living room and divide into interest groups. The kids would scatter everywhere destroying everything in their path much like a battalion of army ants, and if any neighbors stopped by they would be invited to stay and partake. Pete suspected this was the neighbor's plan all along, despite their protests that they couldn't stay. *I guess it takes one to know one* he thought recalling all he had done to get to stay. It was a happy group of people. Pete had no idea how many had showed up, way more than he had fingers and toes. They all just seemed like happy country folks.

Pete loved them all, but was not too sure if any of them should be allowed out in polite or normal society. He was addressed in many ways depending on who had introduced him. And it was easy to tell by whom. He got to where he was answering to "Pete," "Mr. Wheatley," "Marine," "Post Toasties," and "Snively."

Suddenly the room got quiet. A tall man and woman had entered. It was The Reverend Barnes and his wife Penelope. Years before he had talked Fezziwig into donating part of his land for the church and parsonage over the hill. Fezziwig had even helped with the construction. He and The Reverend Barnes had become great friends.

At four, on the dot, everyone sat down at the main or satellite tables for the grand feast. There was a choice of every traditional Christmas food Pete had ever heard about except there was no greasy Christmas goose. There were even some choices he hadn't heard of. All over the room stomachs were growling in anticipation. They were waiting for the Reverend Barns to deliver the traditional Christmas Blessing, hoping he would not talk as long as he did the year before.

"DEAR LORD, Thank you for this bountiful feast which you have provided here for us on this the one thousand nine hundred and sixty-fourth anniversary of your son's birth. We have . . ."

At that moment the phone started ringing, and kept on ringing and ringing and ringing.

The Reverend Barns was a no nonsense type who put up with no interference while communicating with and for The Lord. He didn't miss a beat, but you could tell the ringing of the phone was starting to annoy him like gnats or mosquitos buzzing around his head. One of Fezziwig's daughters who claimed she could communicate with the spirit world told Pete later that Reverend Barns' aura was changing. He was starting to put out an aura like the ghost of things yet to come from Dickens Christmas Carol.

The Reverend Barns loved to give an elegant blessing, and on Christmas he was always good for at least thirty minutes.

The phone kept pace with him for the first five minutes before giving up. At Minute 12 it started ringing again and did not stop until minute 16. By that time, the blessing was becoming a little sarcastic. Pete could sense the underlying anger and Pete was reminded of famous unwavering people in literature like Simon Legree, Captain Ahab, and Dudley Whiplash.

"And thank you Lord for that persistent little piece of nuts and bolts invented by the GREAT Alexander Graham Bellbottom which allows us to communicate over vast distances and disturb people minding their own business . . . ."

Grace had attempted to slip from her seat and answer that persistent little piece of nuts and bolts or take it off the hook but was stopped by the great orator.

"Take your seat girl!" The voice could have been Moses scolding his followers. "Worship neither Golden Idols nor LITTLE Black Ringy Dingy Dingy Dingles!" The phone gave up and five minutes later . . . "Amen!"

The room was in shock. Some checked their watches. He had only gone 21 and a half minutes. Not a record. Not even average. Some congratulated him on his eloquence and told him the Lord would be pleased. One even wanted to discuss a few points he had made, but the majority just wanted to eat.

In a twinkling, everyone was merrily partaking of the traditional recipes of Christmas past and present. Pete was chewing contentedly on a juicy piece of Christmas ham and exchanging happy glances with Grace, and thinking how perfectly things had worked out for him, when the phone started ringing again. Grace's mother went to answer it. She returned in a moment. All eyes turned toward her as everyone wanted to know who had been instrumental in knocking ten minutes off the Christmas Blessing. (Did I mention that math was not . . .)

She pointed at Pete. "It's for you."

Pete flushed and choked on a piece of cornbread he had been enjoying. "It's probably my sainted mother," he said hurrying from the table and avoiding the Reverend Barns' glare. Pete should have kept his mouth closed.

Sarge looked thoughtful, "I wonder how much it cost to phone from Hawaii. Maybe they came home early," he said.

"Oh no, they're not in Hawaii. They're in Denver," Grace said innocently.

"Hmm," said Sarge. "The boy's got some 'splaining' to do."

"It didn't sound like no motha to me," said Donna. Quite a few at the table looked shocked. They had never heard the woman come so close to using an earthy expression. Donna looked embarrassed and tried to cover up. "Didn't sound like his Aunt Mary either."

"Who did it sound like?"Sarge asked.

"That Marian Monroe girl or the one who played Tammy in that movie." (Gracie had enjoyed the movie so much, she took her mother to see it.)

"Debbie Reynolds," said Grace.

"Marilyn, Marilyn Monroe," said Cousin Edward with a gleam in his eye. "She is a great actress and was a bosom buddy of the late president."

"I've heard of her. I think she has something to do with calendars," said his father.

Sarge had a puzzled look on his face. "She's like Tokyo Rose," said the mother to bring him back into the conversation.

"Count the silverware and if we have to shoot him, search his pockets first," said the aunt. "Don't want no holes in anything he stole."

When Pete heard the voice on the other end of the phone, he couldn't help himself. It was as though the last few days and the last trimester, had never happened. He was back under Mary's spell. She was like those hypnotist who can make a person drop into a trance and do silly things when they hear a certain word. He felt dizzy. Quickly he sat down on the nearest chair.

"Well Rover, I can't let you out of my sight for a moment, can I?"

"No . . . I mean yes . . . I mean . . . leave me alone . . . Please!"

"Can't. I guess it's about time you knew. You could be spoken for. I think this little charade has gone on just a little too long. I am leaving for Denver tomorrow to spend the rest of the vacation with the Wheatleys. I have already cleared it with your mother."

He was getting all he had been dreaming about since July when they first started spending time together. He had no idea that he **REALLY** had a chance with Mary. He believed she had just been toying with him, like a cat with a mouse, during the summer, amusing herself until the real players came back in the fall. He had to put a stop to it. He could slam the receiver down and then lift it off the hook so she couldn't phone back. He would tell the others that it was a telemarketer that wouldn't take "not interested" for an answer. But he didn't.

"You can't come. I didn't invite you."

"Your mother did. I'm coming."

"What if I don't go home? What if I stay down here?"

"I'll come down there and grab you by your pink little nose and drag you back."

Pete thought, *If my nose survives this Christmas, it will be a miracle.*

An idea occurred to Mary. "I could tell them that I was pregnant. Is that what you want to force me to do?"

"No!" (She wasn't playing fair, but she had won that battle.)

"I didn't think so. Merry Christmas, Wayward. See you in a couple of days. And Pete . . ." (He was stunned. This was the first time he could ever remember her using his real first name.)

"Yes."

"I'll have your babies." On that note she hung up before he could reply or catch his breath. He needed to sit down again for a minute. He just sat there in silence; in shock; almost comatose. He didn't want to love her. Sometimes he didn't even like her. He thought about the remaining two women in his life. Somehow he knew Sandy was no longer in the picture.

Grace was what he wanted in a women. She was good. She loved him, and since coming here he realized she had spirit, spunk, and was super fun to be with. At school he had taken her for granted because she was an underclassman, always agreed with him, and always did what he wanted.

On the other hand, there was Mary. She was fire, sparkle, and life itself. She got more out of everything for both herself and her companions than anyone.

But he had been happy here. Grace was practically perfect. He had felt so happy and comfortable with her, not to mention that magical moment under the mistletoe or the one back at Fort Lewis when she had loaned him the pencil. He had never had a moment that reached those heights with anyone, even Mary.

Why did Mary have to come back into his life? Should he stay or go? He had to admit the prospect of spending what was left of the vacation with the most popular girl on campus, was a dangled carrot hard to resist. He'd be a hero to the other fellows in the dorm. What was he to do? His decision of which way to go was perfectly balanced.

He got up and headed back to the dining room not sure what course of action he would take: stay or go.

When he went back into the dining room they were just finishing the desserts. Many were glaring at him. He could sense their hostility. *Where had that come from?* The delicate balance was fast shifting in favor of leaving and he didn't know why. He did not know that his lie about his parents had been exposed.

"Was it worth ruining a perfectly good sermon . . . uh . . . blessing," corrected The Reverend Barns. Several of the relatives assured The Reverend Barns the blessing hadn't been ruined. He smiled modestly.

"SHIVER ME TIMBERS," snorted Auntie. She was the only one there not worried about angering The Reverend Barns. "It was the best one you ever gave, by about 10 minutes." The modest smile left The Reverend Barn's face. "Now that I know what it takes," the aunt continued, "I may ringy dingy dingy you myself, next year or bring my bongos."

The Reverend Barns glared a look that would have turned a normal mortal into stone. But the Aunt just wrinkled her nose at him, and returned the glare. It was hard to tell whose was best. Pete interrupted the stand-off. The delicate balance of whether to go or stay had changed drastically. These people were nuts. He would head for Denver at the first opportunity.

Once again he made the vow to himself to quit lying after he lied his way out of this quagmire. At first he told them it was a personal matter and he didn't care to discuss it.

"Not good enough, Snively," challenged the aunt.

Pete tried again. "That was the lady from across the hall in my folk's apartment. She is the wife of the Honorable Reverend Dr. Steven Wayne Smith III of the Non-denominational Presbyterian Church of the Holy Ghost. She said my mother slipped on the ice in the parking lot, hit her head and injured her leg. She has minor memory loss and the doctors think it could help her get it back if she was surrounded by family. Especially after she had cut her vacation in Hawaii short to surprise her sons."

"OH BALLS," said the Aunt. "I don't believe a word of it." In that, she and The Reverend Barns were in agreement.

Everyone else was sympathetic.

"What in the blue Suzy kind of name is that for a church," grumbled the aunt.

"No such thing," declared The Reverend Barnes.

"I have to hurry home," Pete said. "If I can catch a ride with one of you good people when you go back to town, I will catch the first bus going north."

They were all good people and no one asked him anymore details, though some had stories about slipping on the ice and injuring themselves that they wanted to share with him. Pete tried not to look at Grace who sat down across from him as he ate some cherry pie with vanilla ice cream. When he did look he could see her eyes were moist, though there were no tears. She reminded him of a little girl that is trying hard to be brave and not cry.

The goodbyes with Sarge's family were a little strained and a complete reversal of the rest of his stay. He could tell they did not believe his story. He was like the boy in the books who had cried "wolf, wolf" once too often. He thanked them for a wonderful Christmas, and shook each one by the hand. The Mother looked at him disgustedly and said, "Mele Kalikimaka, Smucka." Sarge glared at him and said "Aloha, don't ever come back." The aunt was over the moon happy. She even gave him a quick hug, and whispered, "Wheatley, don't let the door hit you in the backside." She had a big grin on her face.

"Snively," he said. No one laughed, but the aunt smiled.

Guilt kept him from being able to judge Grace's reaction. She was such a fine person and great catch, he knew she would be scooped up quickly and he would soon be history in her life: ancient history, a bad memory. When it was her turn, she hung back and waved once. It was the same, permanent type of wave that Sandy had given him. Grace turned to go help her mother and others with the dishes. He returned the wave, but she wasn't looking. Five minutes later he had retrieved his duffle bag, and then climbed into Edward's truck and rode out of her life.

There were no more buses that day and Pete spent the night sleeping on a couch at Uncle Bean's. Early the next morning after a breakfast of bacon and eggs, Cousin Ed dropped him off at the tiny building serving as the bus depot. He would have preferred cereal, but for some reason The Bean would not allow milk products in his house.

They were very nice to him and Bean kept them entertained with stories of growing up on a trading post 25 years earlier and the trouble he got into with Fezziwig, Wickenburg, and Sarge.

CHAPTER 17

Mary & Mom

It was midafternoon when he pulled his car into the parking lot next to a 1950 Pontiac known far and wide as the Green Latrine; it was his brother's car. His brother had arrived the day before.

Pete had come to the conclusion that Mary would not really show up, but it didn't matter. Just being with his family, his sane family, was the important thing. The world he had left seemed almost unreal, like Oz, Narnia, or Tolkien's Middle Earth inhabited by hobbits, wizards, dwarfs and fairies. He had only seen one monster, and he kind of liked her in a way. Strangely enough on the drive up it was Grace he kept thinking about and not Mary. He was surprised by how often Grace came gliding into his mind. Time after time thoughts of her laughing, holding his hand, helping bring the tree in form the forest, or trying not to cry would take over his mind. Once, after one of these episodes, he nearly turned the car around, but Denver was two hours away and Gallup, where he was not sure of his reception was eight hours.

The Wheatley Christmas celebration was two days late, but they had waited for him and it was one of the happiest Christmases the family could remember since the boys started questioning the existence of Santa Claus. When something or someone is lost and then found, like the lost sheep in the Bible or the Prodigal son, they seem to magically increase in importance or worth.

Pete had decided and then reaffirmed on the long drive that he would try to be the perfect son. No matter what his father did or said, he would not rise to the bait. After Auntie, his dad would be a cinch, a pussy cat. But this pledge had not been necessary.

The father who had been expecting trouble, was relieved, and pleased at the change in his older son. By the time he went to bed that night, (a record breaking 2300) he realized both of his boys were becoming men, men he could be proud of and liked very much. And as for the drinking incident, he remembered a couple of times 30 years earlier when his parents had been ready to disown young George York Wheatley for very similar activities. Pete did not join the others in the drinking of alcohol. He had learned his lesson a week earlier. Party Pete would not be showing up.

As time went by, Pete realized he was where he belonged. The trip, the ranch, the girl, and the old fashioned Christmas were like a pleasant memory from an enjoyable book he had read somewhere, finished, and put back on the shelf for safe keeping. One he would treasure and return to in his mind from time to time..

The next morning the boys were up and off to the hills before the parents were out of bed. They had wanted to check out a ski resort that had opened in the last year called Vail. The father was the next up. He turned off the alarm clock and told his wife to stay in bed. He still felt stuffed from the day before and wanted to skip breakfast. He said he would take the bus to work. The bus stop was only a block away. He showered and went off to work.

It was almost nine before the mother forced herself out of bed. This was the first time in years she hadn't made her husband's breakfast when he was at home. "You must be getting old Jean," she told herself as she looked at her trim figure in the mirror. She went into the kitchen and sliced a pink grapefruit in half. On the refrigerator door was a note held on by a magnet that looked like a Monarch Butterfly.

> *Dear Mom,*
>
> *There is a slight chance a classmate of mine from back east might stop by trying to bum a place to stay and a ride back to school. I doubt it, but just in case, hide the silverware and the chocolate chip cookies.*
>
> *Pete*

The woman looked around the apartment and shook her head. What a mess. Should she clean it first or go to the grocery store and lay in a large supply of food? She had forgotten how much her sons could consume and how much they loved milk. She decided groceries first, cleaning second. She gave her head another shake. She couldn't remember her home **ever** looking this messy. It rivaled Pete's bedroom when he was in high school and they lived in La Crescenta, California.

She had just returned from shopping and was putting the last of the groceries away when there came a knock on the door followed by the ding dong of the doorbell. She sighed. "Now who can that be?"

Maybe it's Pete's friend the bum. If he had got here sooner I wouldn't have had to make four trips from the car with groceries. I hope he doesn't eat as much as Pete and Alan. She peered through the peep hole in the door. All she could see was the top of a head. It was either a short human or a tall fish. This peep hole never gave an accurate image of what or who was on the other side and made everybody look like a fish to her. Figuring she could hold her own against any short human or tall fish, but not positive, she grabbed her husband's putter that was leaning against the wall just to be safe. She hooked the security chain and opened the door as far as the chain would allow, hoping another one of those pesky sales ladies hadn't slipped into the building.

There stood one of the most beautiful girls she had ever seen: blond hair, terrific figure, immaculate complexion, marvelous smile, and wearing a stunning professional suit. She was carrying a small suitcase, probably containing her samples of whatever she was selling. She guessed it might be cosmetics.

"If you are using, whatever you're selling, I'll take all you have,"

The girl laughed. It was a pleasant sound. The mother wished she could think of something else to say to make her laugh again just to enjoy the sound one more time. "One moment please." She closed the door, unhooked the chain, and opened it again. "What can I do for you?"

"My name is Mary Louise. I talked to you on the phone the other day." She paused. "Are you on your way to the golf course? In case you haven't noticed, the ground is still covered with snow."

"No, this club is just to brain you if you try to force your way in."

The girl stepped back. "Mrs. Wheatley, don't you remember me? Didn't Pete tell you he invited me to visit?"

"No and no."

"I was here last summer. Peter gave me a ride from Durango."

"Your voice does sound familiar. Are you that scruffy looking girl with the wild hair that was wearing a tight sleeveless blouse and looking like something the cat dragged in?"

"That's me."

"Pete said you had been hiking and playing in the water when the wind came up."

"Guilty. We had been doing both. We also got in trouble with your husband for staying up too late, looking at pictures, and playing records."

"I remember. George and I were sorry about that, after you explained what you had been doing. Until then I didn't even know Pete was interested in girls. I can't remember him dating in high school and only a couple of times after that when he lived at home."

"Believe me, he is. And quite a few are interested right back. That is why I am here."

"Come in, please." Suddenly the woman realized how unpresentable the apartment was. It almost looked like there had been a frat. party there. "Wait!" She raised the golf club. "Stay out in the hall. This will only take . . . two days."

"What?"

The older woman shrugged and opened the door all the way. "Christmas came a little late this year. I went shopping this morning and haven't had a chance to restore the apartment. You must be the classmate who might be interested in bumming a ride back to school." She showed Mary the note.

The girl chuckled. "That looks like something he might write. Yes, I am the bum. By the way, where **do** you keep the silver and the chocolate chip cookies?" she said with a laugh.

"Hey, I still have this golf club. George and I like to practice our putting in here." She leaned the club against the wall in a corner.

The girl smiled her wonderful smile. "It looks like it was a marvelous Christmas. May I help you tidy up?"

"Is the pope a Catholic?" the mother responded.

Soon the two women were laughing, joking, and having a most wonderful time while they worked miracles on the apartment. Both were good workers, and before three o'clock, the apartment shined like a new penny.

Both were tired and went to their bedrooms for a nap: Mom to hers and Mary to the guest bedroom.

CHAPTER 18

Jeeves, Alan & Mary

Alan was the first to reach the apartment. He was exhausted after a long day on the ski hill and doing most of the driving. He could not believe the transformation of the apartment. He wondered if he was dreaming. He had actually been feeling guilty leaving it in the condition they had left it. "WOW! Mom you are a wonder," he called out.

Then Mary stepped out of his bedroom. "WOW! WOW! WOW!!!"

"Wow yourself," Mary said looking at the brother with interest. Alan was five inches shorter than Pete and built more solidly with an engaging smile and confident air. "I hope you don't mind, but your mother said I could use your bedroom."

"MY MOTHER . . . said what? The rules have certainly changed since I went off to college. Mind? No. In fact, I am going to nominate her for mother of the year. Maybe the century." Suddenly it dawned on him what **might** be happening.

"OOPS, I **bet** I'm in the wrong apartment. I'm sorry." He turned to go. "I **bet** I got off the elevator on the wrong floor," he mumbled more to himself than her. ***Bet****ter get out of here before I get arrested,* he thought. . . . ***BUT*** *. . . the key had worked. Maybe he had stumbled* *on a burglary in progress. He should get out and call the police. She could have an accomplice with a gun hiding somewhere in the apartment.*

"You do a lot of betting. Are you a professional gambler?" The girl asked.

"No."

"Good thing. You'd owe me a lot of money."

"Are you a robber?" Alan asked picking up the putter just in case she had an accomplice.

"No, I am a friend of your mother and brother. Is your name Alan and do you have a brother named Pete?"

"Yes. I mean no." (He decided he was dreaming or in a coma. Maybe his body was lying unconscious on the ski hill and he was hovering between life and death.) "There is one problem with this dream," he told her after deciding to play along with whatever was happening.

At that moment there came a banging at the door like someone kicking it with his foot. BANG-BANG-BANG "THAT, is the problem," he said walking to the door and opening it.

There stood Pete. He had lost a bet about who could get to the bottom of the hill first. The loser had to bring all the gear up to the fifth floor corner apartment from the car. The bet was Alan's idea and Pete had only agreed after getting Alan to give him a two minute head start.

Pete had two pair of boots hanging from his mouth by the laces and was cradling two sets of skis and poles in his arms. His plan had worked. He only had to make one trip. Where Alan had looked tired, Pete looked exhausted. Then he saw Mary. Clatter clatter clatter clatter clatter clatter clatter clatter went the four skis and four poles to the floor. Plop plop plop plop went the four boots, clang clang went his heart, and zing went his blood pressure.

Alan looked at his brother standing there dumbfounded amongst the mess and made a gesture towards the girl with his head. "DIBBS." Then he turned to face the girl. "This is the one problem I mentioned. Jeeves has been a loyal and faithful servant, and I know I should give him the glove and send him on his way, but I don't have the heart to. Perhaps we could name one of our kids after him if he would promise to go away and get out of my dream."

"Too Late. I saw her first," Pete said.

Alan turned back to the girl. "Don't be frightened, Miss. As I said, it is just my man Jeeves. However, I wouldn't get too near him. He is not a bad sort, but dangerously clumsy (he pointed to the ski equipment scattered on the hall floor as evidence) and he is a woman hating zealot," he continued. "He's not too bright either. Always trying to eat my ski boots. Thinks the laces are spaghetti and the boots are giant meatballs."

Mary smiled. "He looks a little bit like Igor." Pete smiled back. Alan had no idea what she was talking about.

At that moment the door across the hall opened. It was Sadie who had led the coalition to get them evicted after Pete's triumphal return from college a week earlier. The lady across the hall was **not** the wife of His Holiness the Honorable Reverend Dr. Steven Wayne Smith III of the Non-denominational Presbyterian Church of the Holy Ghost as Pete had told everyone back at the ranch at the last supper. Sadie turned and yelled to her husband who was watching the news on television. "ABNER, NOW THERE IS TWO OF THEM." She turned back and glared at Pete who was picking up the last of the mess and growled, "I trust there will be no middle of the night song fests, concerts and banging on doors." She waited for him to say something.

"There **"are"** two of them," he corrected her grammar. She slammed her door.

“She seems nice,” said Mary stepping closer to Pete. “I see you haven’t lost your unique way of charming women.”

"She's a sweetheart," Pete said. After a week with Auntie, Sadie did seem like a sweetheart by comparison. "I will have her eating out of my hand by Az...Labor Day." (He had been tempted to say "Aztec." He made a mental note to ask her about the ride from Durango to Albuquerque with Gorgeous George.)

Alan interrupted. “Like I was saying, Jeeves is a dangerously clumsy woman hating blighter, so please step back.”

Mary smiled. “I’m quite aware of Mr. Jeeves ‘andycaps. Allow me to introduce myself,” she curtsied. “I’m Mary (she pronounced it “May-ree) the upstairs maid. If Mr. Jeeves would like some elp with spaghetti, meatballs, stickies and wickets, I’ll be only too appy to oblige.”

The mother had come out of her bedroom and was standing back watching with a big smile on her face. She loved her two boys, but while they were growing up, she wished one of them had been a daughter. Maybe Mary could be that daughter. If Alan had been a girl, his name was going to be Susan. In those days, the early 40’s, they didn’t know the sex until the baby was actually dropped off by the stork. She had high hopes at the time because her mother had gone boy, girl, boy, girl, (Jim, Jean, Colin, & Betty) and George’s mother had gone boy, girl (George, and Mary).

That evening they all sat around visiting and had a wonderful time. The father had outdone himself again by staying up until nearly nine: 8:37 p.m. to be exact. By just being herself, Mary had the entire family eating out of her hand. Alan did his best to impress her, but it was obvious that Mr. Jeeves was the apple of her eye. It had only been a half effort, more honing a skill or taking on a challenge because his heart already belonged to a little girl from Portland he had met at college.

That night Pete and Alan lay in sleeping bags on the living room floor. Alan went right off to sleep, but Pete lay there staring at the ceiling and thinking about the girl one room away. So close, yet, so far away. He also thought about the quiet girl back at the ranch in New Mexico, and Sandy a true and good friend.

What a difference between Mary and Grace. He wished they were both, or even one of them, more like Sandy. He recalled how Sandy had left the group she was with to join him that last day at school, even though her current boyfriend was part of that group. She even suggested talking about the test, although she really didn't care to. Then when she had to leave, she had reached out her hand to his, gave it a gentle squeeze and wished him a Merry Christmas. He felt the emotion flowing from her touch and voice, even more now than then. His last sight of her was when she stopped at the door, turned back and slowly waved. That memory had been haunting him ever since. She had been a wonderful friend from his first trimester on. He had shared nearly all his thoughts and feelings with her. He drifted off to sleep with her last words to him playing in his mind: "MERRY CHRISTMAS, PIE." He dreamed about all three girls equally that night.

For the rest of the week, the three had a most wonderful time together. They were like the three musketeers. They spent days on the ski hill. Mary had never skied before, but she was a natural. She learned it faster than either boy had. And Alan had come in second in the downhill competition at Mt. Alyeska his first year in the 49th state, while Pete was still having trouble mastering the Bunny Hill at Arctic Bowl looking down on Anchorage and Cook Inlet from the Chugachs.

CHAPTER 19

Eric the Derrick

On the morning of the next to the last day of the year, Pete watched Mary ski in his direction and marveled at how well she was doing. They had been skiing together on easy hills while Alan was covering the rest of the mountain. She skied up to him gracefully, came to a perfect stop, showering him with snow, but then lost her balance and tumbled over and into him. They were like two dominos. The she domino crashed into the he domino and knocked him off his feet. They clung to each other and slid headfirst for nearly 30 feet before coming to rest, laughing all the way. She looked into his eyes, smiled, and kissed him lightly on the lips, right there in front of God and everybody. He could taste the Double Mint gum she was chewing. It seemed to fit in perfectly with the clean crispness of the mountain air. At that moment, Pete thought life was perfect.

Pete glanced at his watch. "Hey goofy, it's lunch time. We're supposed to meet Alan in the lodge." This was the day of the incident.

As usual, she attracted boys like a magnet. But they proved no problem, as she was able to rebuff them with such finesse, they did not know they had been put down. Then on this, their next to the last planned day of skiing, while they were in the lodge eating lunch, a very large ski instructor came out of the bar and tried to hit on her. She was standing in the cafeteria line, having gone back for a second carton of milk. He followed her back to the table where the brothers were just finishing.

Eric "The Derrick" Meany (as he had been nicknamed by the press) had been a local hero. In his playing days, he stood 6' 6" and weighed 278 pounds, all muscle. He had played for one of the Colorado Colleges all four years as a starter, and two years in the NFL as a linebacker. He was in his mid to late 40's. He was still big, tough, and handsome in a Charles Bronson sort of way. A back injury and two concussions had ended his playing career early. The worst concussion was caused by a blindside hit from a Chicago Bear and the back injury by a Ram. He had staggered out of a bar late one Saturday night and tried to cross the street to where he had parked. The driver of the Dodge did not see him until it was too late.

Eric came across as charming on television and was often used as a color man for football games and golf tournaments. He was a scratch golfer and always shot around par. His time was now mostly spent skiing in the winter and playing golf in the summer when he wasn't broadcasting sports or partying. He was a big favorite of the ladies. He enjoyed the nightlife, especially the tough bars where there would be a chance to get into a fight. He loved to fight and often started them. He would go into a honkytonk, look for the biggest guy and start insulting him. The opponent often ended up in one of the Denver hospitals and sometimes Eric did.

Mary sat down next to Pete and tried to ignore Eric's advances. But he kept on making one offer after another. He had been drinking his lunch for the last hour, but he was not drunk.

Alan looked at Pete and asked, "Is this who I think it is?" Pete nodded. He didn't speak. There was a big lump in his throat. This guy was a giant.

Alan said, "I read where he threw one of those wrestlers you see on television through the front window of a sports bar last year." Pete said he had read the same article too. His voice sounded an octave higher than normal.

"Pete, I don't think we can take him by ourselves," Alan said.

Why can't Alan shut up? Pete thought. Then he decided what the heck, que sera sera, what will be, will be.

He answered Alan, "Neither could the offensive line of the Los Angeles Rams, and the Marines are busy in Vietnam."

"Guess it's up to us," Alan said.

"Unfortunately I am going to have to let you handle this problem because I have picked up a splinter in my right index finger which is very painful and debilitating." Pete kicked Alan under the table. "But, I want you to know, there will be no charge for being one of your pallbearers. And if I stand on the right side of the coffin, I should be able to tough it out when we're expected to carry you to the limo and then to the grave site. "

"Bro, I have two splinters . . . One in each hand." He kicked Pete back. "Do you want me to go for help?"

No, but I wish the heck you would shut up, he thought. "We don't know anybody here. This is his turf. The whole dang state is his turf. Everybody likes their favorite bad boy."

"I won't let you down. I'll keep going until I find someone. Even if it is all the way back to Denver and hiding behind the couch or under Mom and Dad's bed."

Pete smiled a sickly smile. "I think today we may die."

Alan said, "I see no "**WE**" in this situation and **can** I have your collection of comic books?" The brothers were slowly starting to enjoy themselves. At least one of them was.

"You **may** not. And I want to go on record as stating I am very disappointed in your lack of support. And because of that, I intend to take the comics with me into the crematorium."

"**That,** is the most selfish thing I have heard in ages," Alan declared.

"I seem to remember someone calling "DIBBS" on the girl. She is your responsibility."

"I seem to remember someone saying, too bad, I called her first."

Fortunately, Eric was pretending to ignore the brothers as though they weren't even there. You had to be at least 6' 4" and weigh more than 250 for him to even pay attention to you as someone worthy of being put in the hospital.

Eric offered Mary an afternoon of free private lessons.

"Go ahead, Mary, if you want to. (*please)* You can learn more from a professional instructor in one day then I could teach you in a whole season," Pete said. He was thinking *that will give me a few more hours to live.*

"And you might just save our lives in the process," Alan added. "If he gets out of line, toss him a banana or some peanuts. You could be the next Jane Goodall. What she did for chimps and Tarzan did for apes, you could do for the Colorado Mountain Monkey."

"National Geographic could make you famous," put in Pete.

Eric was not enjoying this new table talk. "I think it's time for the Smothers Brothers to leave while they still have a full set of teeth in their mouths." (Tommy and Dickie, the Smothers Brothers, were a popular comedic and folk singing team at the time.)

"Yes," said Alan. "I agree. A full set of teeth is a good thing Tommy, let's go."

Pete didn't move. "How come I always have to be Tommy? I want to be the smart one."

"Then come with me while you can still smile, chew and breathe."

Pete looked at Mary. She nodded and said, "Go with your brother. I'd like an afternoon of free private ski lessons and you have been wanting to try some of the harder runs with your brother. I'll meet you down here when the lifts close."

Alan and Pete went out and put on their skis. The joy had gone out of the day for Pete. He felt like a child who had been humiliated by the school bully. Alan tried to cheer him up.

"Good move, Bro. Hated to sacrifice the girl, but war is Hell and there is always some collateral damage." Pete noticed that "Mary" had suddenly become "the girl."

However, Alan said, "I am sad to say, our family motto, *The Fighting Wheatleys*, may have taken some hits today, but at least we still have our arms, legs and teeth. What do you think about changing it to *The Loving Wheatleys*?"

"No, it sounds too much like something engraved on a tombstone, or something that should be followed by "Family Trust."

After a long silence Alan asked, "What are we going to tell Mom? I think she liked the girl."

"I'll tell Mom **you** sold Mary to some Mexican cartel or a band of Gypsies or pirates. Hmm, . . . *Pirates.*" Pete said it again out loud, then he started to smile.

Alan asked, "You are smiling. Why are you smiling? Is my zipper open? Is there peanut butter on my nose?"

"Probably both."

"Can you give me a hint?"

Pete just kept smiling and repeated the word "pirates."

"What are you going to do, send for Auntie and the parrot? I don't think they can get here by four when the lifts close." (Pete had told Alan about his week in New Mexico in great detail on their way to Vail the first day.)

"I've got a plan," Pete said. "And don't worry. That girl can handle any man alive, and he can do her skiing a lot of good. Besides he can't do anything to her on a crowded ski hill, and this is our next to the last day, so let's have fun." As they rode up the hill on the chair lift, Pete revealed his plan.

They made five runs and then went in search of Mary and Eric. They found them on a run named "Groovy." They hung back way up hill and watched. Mary's style had improved greatly under Goliath's instruction. Finally Mary and Eric stopped so she could rest a moment before tackling a more challenging part of the run. This is what Pete had been waiting for.

The next 100 yards was much steeper. They were stopped on the left edge of the run with their skis perpendicular to the fall line to keep from moving and they were facing across the hill. There was a space of about six feet between them and Pete skied down and stopped in between them. This annoyed Eric. Mary was highest on the hill, then came Pete and lowest was Eric.

"Hey Mary, you're skiing great," Pete said.

"Thank you. I have a great instructor. Thanks Eric."

"Good job, Eric," Pete complimented.

"Buzz off, Tommy," Eric ordered, implying Pete was the dumb Smothers.

"That's why I'm here. It's time for us to go. Are you ready to buzz off, Mary?" Pete asked.

Eric tapped Pete solidly on top of the head with his ski pole. "HELLO, is there anybody in there? There is something you don't seem to realize, **little** man."

"And what, pray tell is that?" Pete asked.

"She's with me now."

"BUMMER. Is this true, Mary? " Pete asked, turning from Eric and looking at Mary.

"Jackson, this ski lesson was your idea, not mine. If you are ready to leave, I am too."

When Pete had turned away from Eric to look at Mary, he lifted his ski just high enough to be free from the ground and let it follow his hips as he turned to face Mary. He kept his head up so as not to draw attention to the ski. When he turned back to face Eric, the ski came with all the centrifugal force and energy Pete could muster. Just at the moment of contact which came as a complete surprise to Eric, Pete shouted something. It wasn't Kiai but it was just as affective. When the ski connected with Eric's shin just barely below the knee, it felt to Pete like a perfect drive on the golf course or a homerun over the centerfield wall with room to spare. Eric let out a shout and bent over to grab his leg. This put him slightly off balance and the side of his neck in a reachable and unprotected spot which Pete's ski pole found.

Pete had heard the sound it made before . . . recently. In his journal he had called it something like, "WACK-BANG."

The giant didn't drop as fast as Sarge had. He more or less crumbled like a large building that is being demolished with explosives. He wilted to the ground and started sliding down the slope.

It was a while before he came to a stop. The contact with Eric's shin had been so powerful that Pete's safety bindings had released his boot. It was a matter of seconds to get hooked back up to his ski.

Mary looked at Pete in surprise. "I thought we were both going to have to fight him. Where did you learn that little trick?"

"Believe it or not, from a lady pirate."

"That might explain your war cry or whatever it's called," she said.

Pete had no idea what she was talking about. He quickly explained to Mary she needed to turn in her rental equipment and join him at the car in the parking lot as fast as she could. He told her he would report a fallen skier on Groovy to the ski patrol. He had his fingers crossed when he said it. And as everyone knows, it is okay to tell falsehoods if your fingers are crossed. He had learned that in the 4th grade. Then he said, "Exit, stage right," and they both shoved off.

Alan had been watching from 100 yards up-slope. He had been waiting as part of a backup plan. Pete called it Plan B. Alan thought they should make it Plan Z. That would give them 24 opportunities to come up with something better than this stupid plan which was for him to be Alan the human cannonball. He was to get up as much speed as he could and charge. Charge like the Light Brigade and crash into Eric. It wasn't much of a plan and it wasn't until after Pete left that Alan remembered the Brigade had a 40% casualty rate. There wasn't a happier person in the state of Colorado than Alan when Eric wilted toward the ground. Alan's role was now to check and see if Eric was still alive, and if he was, to help him. If he wasn't, to say a few words over him and get to the car as fast as possible.

Alan skied down to the big man. He checked his pulse; it was strong. He took off Eric's skies. He threw the left one out in the trees just in case Eric was in good enough shape to give chase when he came to. (It was found by a Boy Scout troop camping in the area the next summer.) Then he made Eric as comfortable as possible. Eric started groaning after a minute as he was regaining consciousness and his senses were coming back. He tried to stand up and as he did so he growled, "I'll get that little bastard and grind his bones to make my bread." (Alan wondered about the quote. Was Eric the terrible seeing the world through the eyes of a child? He had just quoted the giant from Jack 'n the Beanstalk, minus the "Fe-Fi-Fo-Fum." BUT, adding the word "bastard." Alan hadn't remembered the giant using profanity when his mother used to read the story to him.) A look of pain suddenly crossed Eric's face and he sat down quickly. "I think my leg is broken," he said to the Good Samaritan who had stopped to help him.

As Eric looked at Alan, recognition slowly crossed his face. This guy was more a bad Samaritan than a good one.

"I know you. You are one of the Smothers Brothers. You're Dickie, the smart one." He had never heard their real names. "You and Tommy are going to jail." Alan quickly stepped into his skis and shoved off. *Change of plans,* he thought. *I am not waiting for the ski patrol, and I have to get out of here.*

It was then that he noticed a skier lying in the snow wearing a pink outfit and taking pictures. What had she seen? The fact she had not skied over to help, led him to believe she had not interpreted his actions in a favorable light. He was glad the ski mask covered his face as he skied over to her and said, "I checked on the man. He's okay, but might have a broken leg. The man is a celebrity; it is Eric Meany. I am playing hooky from work today. I called in sick, so I have to get out of here. I could get fired if my boss sees my name or picture in the paper or on tv."

Then he pointed his skis straight down the hill and schussed for the bottom. He suddenly realized that the ski patrol would be carrying walkie-talkies and there wasn't a second to spare.

CHAPTER 20

On the Lamb & Pinkie

When he got to the parking lot, everything was ready for him. In two minutes they were driving out of the parking lot with Alan driving and Pete riding shotgun. Mary was lying down on the back floorboard under a blanket, so it would look like there were only two people in the car. This jived with the fact there were two sets of skis on the roof rack. The authorities and friends of Eric would be looking for two men and a girl. Not two men.

"This is his turf and his buddies will be looking for a girl and two brothers," Alan said. "He knows we're brothers. I figure we have 20 minutes before their posse is formed and organized." He rolled down the window and threw out the ski mask.

"Wasn't that a Christmas present from the folks?" Pete asked.

"Yes, but the lady in the pink outfit had several close-up pictures of me wearing it."

"Mom's gonna be pissed when I tell her you threw it out the window."

"Well, don't tell her."

"I took a vow to be completely honest with Mom and Dad."

"Well, don't forget to tell them the part about you hitting him with a ski when he wasn't looking and breaking his leg."

"Fortunately the vow doesn't go into effect until midnight tomorrow."

"I think you two are funnier accidentally than the Marx or the Smothers Brothers are on purpose," declared a voice from under a blanket on the backseat floorboard. "I told them we were heading west to Vail when I turned in my rentals. I was pretending to be the dizzy blond. Then I said, 'Oops, I wasn't supposed to tell anybody that.' They might look in that direction first. Is there anything else I can do?"

"Try to look ugly like someone Eric wouldn't be interested in," Pete said.

"Lots of luck on that one," Alan commented. "I think that would be impossible."

"I fooled your mother," Mary declared. "She didn't recognize me."

"Good. You do need to change your appearance," Pete persisted.

Mary undid her braids, mussed up her hair, and overdid all the makeup in her purse. She now resembled a hooker, more than the neat young college student who had been skiing with Eric that afternoon.

Alan got a glimpse of Mary before she lay back down on the seat. "Congratulations, you're an ugly success," he stated.

"The closer we get to Denver the safer we will be," Pete said. "Once we get passed Idaho Springs, I think we'll be safe and you can sit up."

"Okay, but if I see any police, I'm ducking down."

"Quack, quack," said Alan. Pete had the impression he was enjoying this.

They only saw one cop and he was busy giving someone in a yellow sports car a ticket.

During the ride home Pete warned them not to say anything about Eric when they got to the apartment, and they asked why.

"Mom is a fan of his. He works the golf tournaments for a local station. One time she went to one of the tournaments he was working just to see him in person. She spent the entire time in front of his booth where he was interviewing golfers, and she didn't see one minute of the tournament. She even got him to sign her program."

They agreed not to mention seeing him and figured that their little adventurous brush with fame and the law was over as they pulled into the apartment's underground parking lot. But it must have been a slow day for news because the Eric story was one of the featured stories on the evening news, complete with a fairly accurate, but not flattering artist's drawing of the fugitives from descriptions given by skiers who had seen them. "If I didn't know better, I would think it was you three said the mother. "The resemblance is remarkable."

Then she caught sight of Mary who was coming out of the bathroom. "Well, not you. You don't look anything like the girl they're looking for. What have you been doing, wrestling with windmills or alligators?" she asked looking at Mary's hair. Then she noticed the overuse of makeup and said, "you brazen hussy. Except for the hair, you look like the kind of girl I have always warned my boys about," she said jokingly.

One of the witnesses that was being interviewed was a lady in pink. *Oh No! We're toast,* Alan thought. Her name was Delores. She was in her late 60's, a couple of inches under five foot, retired, in good physical shape, a volunteer fire fighter who could barely see over the dashboard of the fire truck she drove, a leader in her church and quite opinionated. She had recognized the local celebrity moving in on the girl in the lodge and followed him and the girl taking pictures. She hoped to sell one or more to one of those papers like the Star, Enquirer, Sporting New, or Globe. Fortunately she had remained far enough back that the pictures weren't that sharp.

The television interviewer was a super pretty young man (almost cute) who wanted to show how smart and clever he was by finishing Pinky's sentences for her. Pete could tell she was becoming annoyed. It was a live broadcast so it had not been edited. It was also obvious because this was the station Eric worked for, that they were in his corner and interpreting and slanting everything in his favor.

Cutie Interviewer: "So this girl got his attention and lured him away from his friends where this gang of thugs mugged him breaking his leg and knocking him out. Do you think they were going to murder him until they saw you watching with your little camera?"

Pinky: **"LITTLE?** You condescending **dinky** donkey. Is there any reason your station couldn't send out one of the **big** real reporters? No. I didn't say anything like that. Eric spent the lunch hour in the bar and when he came out he spotted this gorgeous blond in line to pay for her milk. It looked like he was trying to hit on her, but she wasn't interested. He followed her to a table where two young men she was with were just finishing their lunch. They were half his size. I couldn't hear what was said, but the two men left and Eric sat down. Five minutes later they got up and left. I thought there might be a story here that I could sell, so I got out my **normal** size 35 millimeter camera and tracked them from a distance taking pictures. It just looked like she was taking a private lesson. At the time of the incident, they had stopped and rested for a minute. One of the men she had been with at lunch joined them and started talking to the girl. For no reason I could see, Eric bonked him on top of the head with his ski poles and the man whirled around and shouted one of those fighting things, and he hit Eric back with his ski pole. Eric collapsed to the ground and slid about 30 feet down the hill."

Cutie Interviewer: (Lowering his voice to seem more manly.) "He probably yelled "kiai." I myself am a brown belt and know something about the protocol."

Pinkie: "NO. It was like a pirate thing "Shiver Me . . ."

"Cutie Interviewer: (interrupting) "Timbers, Shiver me timbers. That's what pirates say."

Pinkie: "Grrr. I suppose now, Buttercup, you are going to tell us, you yourself were a pirate in the 2nd grade and know something about the protocol."

Cutie Interviewer: (taken aback) "I have never been a pirate."

Pinkie: "No? Well La Ti Dah. Me neither. But you **have** been a complete ass and still are. I'd say you are an expert in that protocol. Stop interrupting me and answering your own questions . . . wrongly, I might add."

The station broke for a commercial and Pete thought Cutie Interviewer was probably being taken to the woodshed and told to quit interrupting the lady. Pete felt the station would have to go back to the interview because those watching would want to know what the lady had seen and heard. Sure enough, they returned.

Cutie Interviewer: "If he didn't shout "kiai" then what did he shout?" he asked sarcastically. (Trying to take back control of the interview.)

Pinkie: "I'd rather not say. My parents could be watching from Heaven."

Cutie Interviewer: (This was his chance to show he could be a forceful newscaster.) "You are going to have to. The people have a right to know. What did he shout? "Shiver me . . . **WHAT**?" he said forcibly, almost yelling.

Pinkie: (Looking embarrassed.) "Sorry Mom and Dad. BOOBS! SHIVER ME BOOBS."

Cutie Interviewer: "Oh SHI---p." He caught himself just in time. He could see his career with the station going down the drain. "Do you think these three recognized a celebrity and decided to rob him, but when they spotted you, changed their minds?"

Pinkie: "No. The girl did not act like she was interested in anything other than ski lessons. The man was talking to the girl when Eric bonked him on top of the head. He retaliated. I have no idea why he shouted BOOBS, unless Eric had been getting too friendly with his girl or wife or sister on the chairlift. And I imagine it was rather annoying to have someone banging you on the head with his ski poles. Would you like me to demonstrate?"

Cutie Interviewer did not volunteer to take one for the team. "That won't be necessary," he said.

Pinkie continued her eye witness account.

"The third man came along after the couple had left. I'm not sure if he was the other friend of the girl or not. He was wearing a ski mask. He helped Eric and stayed with him until right before the ski patrol showed up. Then he took off like a bat out of Joplin. He yelled to me that he was playing hooky from work and didn't want his boss to come across his name or picture in the papers." (Cutie Interviewer kept trying to interrupt her, but she was on a roll and would not stop.)

Pinkie: "What I think happened was that creepo Eric was trying to hit on someone's wife; he has a reputation for doing that, and he got what he deserved. He picked the wrong man's lady this time. All the second man did was help Creepo. I don't know if he was the friend of the first man because he was wearing his ski mask. I don't know what he was thinking. It couldn't be robbery, he had plenty of time to do that if he wanted to. If you want my best guess, it is I don't know. My second best guess is I don't know. Would you like my third best guess?" (Cutie did not want her third best guess. He was thinking, *this is the eye witness from Hell and wishing he hadn't belittled her camera.*) "Your station should be ashamed of itself for hiring such a degenerate . . . "

The viewers were denied learning what kind of degenerate because the station suddenly went back to the studio and played a commercial for a toilet bowl cleaner. They did not resume the interview, apologizing and saying some gobble de gook about experiencing technical difficulties with their feed from the ski hill.

At the apartment, they switched to some of the other stations. One interviewed several witnesses who had seen the man they nicknamed "The Bonker" skiing with the woman in the morning, and several of them had seen all three eating in the cafeteria together. One even described witnessing Eric leaving the bar and moving in on them.

Back at the apartment the mother was irate. "How dare she," fumed the mother referring to Pinky. "Eric and Buttercup (not his real name) ought to sue her." One of the stations interviewed an officer of the law who asked to remain anonymous. The announcer said, "It was reported by a usually reliable source in the police department that their investigation was hampered by the fact Eric became irrational and kept insisting he had been attacked by the Smothers Brothers: Tommy and Dickie. The Smothers were currently performing in Vegas, 750 miles away."

The mother confided to the three that she had run into her friend Marian, the wife of a policeman down in the laundry room. Marian told her that the police had received a tip and were stopping cars at an undisclosed location between the scene of the attack and Vail. She said, "The police figure they are holed up somewhere and will make a break for Vail in the middle of the night. Apparently the blond female member of "the gang" had let their destination slip when she was turning in rental skis. The girl left a Chicago address when she rented the skis, and you know that is where those mafia's come from," the mother confided.

The three of them turned in early. They were exhausted from skiing and the brush with the law. They decided to play it safe and not go skiing the next day.

As he was lying in his sleeping bag that night on the living room floor, Pete reviewed the day. Basically he figured he was the only one in real trouble. He didn't think the others had broken any laws. How strange he thought. He had been happy, scared, unhappy and mad, but there was one emotion missing. He had not been jealous. He chalked it up to the idea that he might be maturing. As proof of that he hadn't asked his mother why Alan threw his expensive new ski hat out the car window . . . yet.

CHAPTER 21

Karen, Dad, Ice Cream & Cake

The phone rang at 0600 in the morning. Only the father was up and had been for two hours. He was working the morning crossword and drinking coffee. He answered it. The caller was someone called Karen inviting Pete to a party. She had seen a drawing of someone in the morning paper who reminded her of Pete, and she phoned to invite him to her New Year's Eve party. The story had something to do with an altercation on the ski hill.

"Yes," said the father, picking up the phone. He believed in getting down to business. He never answered with "hello."

"Hi. This is Karen. I'm phoning to invite Pete to my party tonight."

"Is it your birthday?" he asked her.

"No, not a birthday party."

"Will there be ice-cream and cake?"

"No."

"Then it can't be much of a party. What's the occasion? Did your dog have puppies?"

"**DUH!** It's New Year's. We'll be celebrating the New Year." (It was not a good idea to "Duh" the father if you wanted his cooperation.)

"Why would you want to do that? It looks like it's going to be a stinky year and last year was a terrible year." (He had lost his house in the Alaskan earthquake.) "Can we wear party hats and blow little tin horns or party blowers that unravel and making a horn like noise?"

"How old are you, six?" she asked.

"Fifty-four and I don't like your attitude," he said.

"Poor baby." She replied with a perfect imitation of a mother consoling an infant.

"Don't poor baby me if you want my cooperation? Pete's brother is here and some girl. May I invite them to come along too?"

"TOO? You're not invited and where do you get off inviting people to someone else's party?" (She did not give him a chance to respond.) "I didn't see your name on any guest list. You are not invited."

"Invited? Thank you, I'd love to come. What time does it start?"

"Eight thirty, but you're not invi . . . "

(He interrupted her.) "I can't make it."

"What a shame."

"Don't you want to know why?" he asked.

"No. Just knowing you won't be there is enough for me." (He must have thought *no* meant *yes* because he kept right on.)

"I go to bed at eight so I can get up early." (He had no idea his wife had accepted an invitation to join friends at the Petroleum Club.)

"I'll be sure to spread the word that you are not to be disturbed after eight p.m., your highness." (He thought she did not sound sincere.)

"That's very thoughtful of you." (His sincerity was about on the same level as hers.)

She gave him the phone number. He wrote 1-303-860-4753 on "Number 36 Across" because there were 11 free squares. The hint said, "Internal inspection." (I'll put the correct answer in the Ward—P.G.W.) On the margin of the page he scribbled, "Call Karen for a good time." Who said he didn't have a good sense of humor. He chuckled. Writing in the puzzle would mess with whoever had been messing with his puzzles that week. His normal routine was to complete half in the morning and half at night. But this week he'd come home and find someone using pen had tried to finish, screwed up and left him an impossible task.

Pete who was in his sleeping bag on the floor and pretending to still be asleep heard the whole conversation. He could hardly wait to tell Alan and Mary.

The mother was the next one to wake up. She was surprised to see her husband had already left, but she knew he was happiest at work. She was also surprised the kids didn't want to squeeze in one more day on the hill. The paper with Karen's note was clinging to the refrigerator with the aid of the monarch butterfly (magnet).

The three from the younger generation had decided it would be plum foolish to return to the scene of the incident or any other location where they were likely to be recognized. They decided this day was to be one of leisure and preparation for the trips back to college. They found the invite to Karen's party and turned it down for the same reason. They decided it would be fun to see the New Year in from the 10th floor where the pool was. It had a view on three sides where the glass went from floor to ceiling. At midnight, they would be watching fireworks from all over the Denver area.

The night before, the boys (as usual) spent the night on the floor in their sleeping bags. They visited until Alan fell asleep. Pete just lay there for an hour longer trying to go to sleep but his mind wanted to remain active and kept jumping from one memory to another.

One of the places his jumping mind landed was the ride home from the ski hill. Just thinking about it, gave him pause to wonder. About half way home Mary said she was super cold and started shaking. Pete climbed over the back of the seat and joined her under the blanket she had been hiding under earlier. They cuddled together and used each other's body heat to keep warm. It must have worked because when Alan pulled into the parking lot and turned around to look at them, they were both fast asleep.

CHAPTER 22

The Call; The Truth

It was 10:40 a.m. when the phone rang in the Denver apartment. The mother was in the laundry room waiting for the last of the clothes to come out of the drier. The boys were in the outdoor parking lot getting their cars ready for the trip back to school. Mary was in the kitchen preparing brunch. They had all skipped breakfast opting for sleep.

The week which had been so happy and full for Pete, had been lonely for Grace. She missed the young man terribly. Pete had burst in unexpectedly with the Christmas snow storms and disappeared just as suddenly, leaving a vacuum. She had hoped he would call when he reached Denver, nothing. All that week, she had stayed near the phone, hoping for a call. She wanted to phone him, but her mother insisted that nice young Christian ladies don't call young men.

Now was her chance. Her parents were out of the house. Her father was in the cutting room attached to the garage polishing some turquoise, and her Mom was helping in the trading post. She reasoned there would be nothing wrong with phoning and wishing him a Happy New Year. Even nice young Christian ladies would do that.

The phone was answered on the 4th ring. She thought she recognized the voice. "May I speak with Pete please?"

"Sorry, he isn't here right now. May I take a message?"

"Yes, tell him I did two push-ups this morning, and found his Bible."

"Who is this?" Mary asked. But she knew.

All the time she had been talking, Grace had been thinking that voice sounds familiar. It sounds like the girl who reports the campus news on a local radio station. The one all the boys were in love with according to Pete. Pete had told her that he had been friends with the girl during the summer and they had gone on hikes and swimming together. She, herself, had seen them walking together at the first of the fall trimester and remembered them as a couple from the first of her two days at A & W. She knew it was Mary Christmas, but she had to ask.

"Who is this?" Grace asked repeating Mary's question.

"My name is Mary (there was a long pause, then). . . Wheatley. Sorry, I am just getting used to saying that. May I take a message?"

"N, no thank you," she managed to get out. "I just wanted to wish him a Happy New Year . . . and it looks like it already is. Tell him good bye for me. I'm not going back next trimester. And tell him Grace wishes him well."

She gently placed the receiver on the hook and started walking slowly to her room but ended up running. She wished she would die. Her eyes had filled with tears, but she managed to control herself until she reached her bed. Then she flung herself on top of it and the dam burst. When her parents returned to the house for lunch, they found her crying uncontrollably with her face buried in her pillow.

While at the same time in Denver the boys were laughing and joking as they worked on their cars. A pleasant voice drifted down from the fifth floor balcony. "Hey, you greasy monkeys, come and get it."

When they arrived at the apartment, they were both oily and smelly from changing the oil and rotating the tires. "You can't eat with us until you no longer smell like pistons," the mother scolded using one of the words she remembered her brothers using when they were working on their cars as teenagers.

Pete agreed that Alan smelled, but said he smelled more like a crank . . . shaft.

Alan didn't know whether to comment on the "crank" or the "shaft" so he did neither. He suggested they go up to the top floor, shower, take a steam bath, and then eat out at the pool overlooking the city.

"Who is going to carry the lunch up to the 15th floor while the playboys are in the sauna?" asked the mother.

Alan smiled and tried to give her a hug. She ducked out of the way. "Not me, Mr. Grease. I have an appointment at the beauty parlor in half an hour. Your dad and I are going out tonight."

"Does he know it?" Alan asked.

She smiled, "Not yet."

"Are you going to Karen's party?" Pete asked trying to be funny. They all laughed. The father had phoned and explained the crossword puzzle with the phone number on the refrigerator door. "That would really blow Karen's mind if you showed up. You could shout HERE WE ARE! WE ARE THE WHEATLEYS. WHERE'S THE ICECREAM AND CHOCOLATE CAKE. I BROUGHT MY PERRY COMO RECORDS AND MONOPOLY GAME. Karen would shit."

"That would really be funny," Alan said backing up his brother.

"No it wouldn't," said the mother. "And if you think so, that proves the hospital gave us the wrong child, and your father can quit blaming me for your academic record, Peter. I am going to the beauty parlor in half an hour. Your father and I are going to the Petroleum Club with the Staffords tonight, and I want to look my best.

We went there last New Year's and had a great time. And I think I remember him saying, 'we should do this again next year.'"

"I'll do it," Mary said. "You two pop off to the shower and sauna, and I'll come up with the lunch after your mother leaves." They grabbed some clean clothes and their swimming suits.

They were swimming when Mary appeared with a large picnic basket full of goodies. The boys got out of the pool and went to the men's locker room where they had left the clean clothes. Mary had gone into the room next to the pool. It was an all-purpose room with tables where the bridge club met on Wednesday nights. There were some couches along the wall. The room could be reserved by the tenants but most of the time was available to any of the dwellers. Quite often several families could be using it simultaneously. Today, near the end of the holiday it was getting fully used.

They would not have the room to themselves. At one table were two kids playing *Go Fish*. There was a lady knitting in one of the chairs next to a window. Two teenagers, a boy and a girl, were using the ping pong table, but they were doing more flirting than pinging or ponging. Mary set up the lunch at a center table and had everything ready when they arrived. As they were eating, they kidded and joked with each other about everything from soup to nuts.

"By the way," Mary said to Pete, "one of your ex-girlfriends phoned to wish you a Happy New Year."

"Impossible, I don't have any other girlfriends in Denver. I don't have any other girlfriends."

"Glad to hear it, Jackson." She reached over and squeezed his hand.

Were it not for Alan, the conversation would have ended right there or switched to another subject, and the rest of Pete's life could have been entirely different.

"Did she leave a name? After meeting Mary, I have new respect for your choice in women," Alan joked.

"Well, it wasn't Jack La Lane or some fitness queen," said Mary. "She was proud of doing two push-ups and said she found your bible."

"Maybe its Mrs. Billy Graham," Alan volunteered.

Pete felt sick.

"Pete, what's wrong?" Alan said, "You look green, like my car. It isn't really Mrs. Graham, is it?"

Pete ignored his brother. He did feel ill. He remembered telling Grace he would call when he got to Denver, and how he would keep in touch. He was thinking about how he felt when Mary had done the same thing to him. He looked at Mary. "What did you tell her?"

"She asked who I was and I told her I was Mary . . . Wheatley."

"WHAT? WHY DID YOU SAY THAT? What did she say? What did her voice sound like?"

Mary's mood had sobered up nearly as quickly as Pete's. All the flippancy had gone out of her voice as she answered him, "The girl on the phone sounded sad, almost like her heart was breaking." Mary let that thought hang in the air for about half a minute, then asked, "Jackson, You are not stuck on this girl, are you?"

"Of course not." (He knew the second it was out of his mouth that it wasn't true, but he blustered on.) "But she is a fine and decent person and the last thing in the world I wanted to do was hurt her. I was going to break it to her gently when we were back at school."

Pete had lost his appetite. What he had already eaten seemed stuck in his throat. After a few uncomfortable minutes had gone by, he got to his feet, "If you'll excuse me a minute, I think I'll go down and phone her. I'll tell her . . . I'll tell her . . . I don't know what I'll tell her."

Pete walked over to the elevator. It was in service. Not wanting to wait for it, he headed for the stairs and started down taking two at a time. What must they be thinking of him down there in New Mexico? The last thing he had told them was he had to hurry home because of a personal matter. And now they heard he was married. They probably thought he had to get married. When he got to the apartment, he went straight to the phone in the living room and dialed the ranch. The phone rang four times before there was an answer. He recognized the mother's voice.

"Mrs. Cousins, may I speak to Grace please?"

"Grace is ill and can't come to the phone just now. May I take a message?"

"Yes, this is Pete. I have to speak to her. Tell her not to believe . . . "

The mother interrupted. "Pete, she won't talk to anyone. We have been trying to find out what's wrong. Her father is with her now. Sometimes she will talk to him when she won't talk to anyone else."

What was wrong? He had a pretty good idea of what was wrong. He liked both Grace's Mom and Dad and he loved Grace. He was in shock. That was the first time he had ever told himself that, or truly realized it. But it was true. He was in love with Grace.

Something else dawned on him. He had never told himself that he was in love with Mary. He might have used the word, but he really meant "infatuated," "gaga," "pie eyed," "smitten," "besotted," "twitter pated," "longing for," "hankering for," "mad about," etc., etc., but not "LOVE."

Grace's mother interrupted his thoughts. "I'm going to check on her. I'll tell her you are on the phone. Do you want to hang on?"

"Yes!" (*Wild horses couldn't pull me away from this phone*, he thought. Then he realized they probably could. Horses were pretty strong. What was happening to his mind?) "Thank you. I'd appreciate it very much."

The mother's voice had sounded kind.

It was five minutes before the mother came back on the line. This time her voice sounded different. It sounded more like her sister's (Auntie) and it sounded angry. "Grace doesn't want to talk to you, **BUT** her father does." Then Sarge's voice came roaring over the phone, sounding more like Pete's old drill instructor than any voice he had heard since boot camp.

"Listen, you miserable little piss ant. Vermin crawl the face of the earth which I would rather associate with than you. Grace will not be going back to Fort Lewis, and if I ever see you again around here, I will put a load of buckshot right where it will do the most good." Then he slammed the phone down.

Pete sat there stunned for five minutes just staring at the phone. Why did he feel so low? Everything was working out for him. He had been wanting Mary since the middle of the summer. Now everything was working out. He had been dreading breaking the news to Grace. That was no longer a problem. He worried about having to face Grace on campus. That was no longer a problem. Mary liked him, and he had everything he had been dreaming about. Why did he feel so sad?

He took the elevator to the 10th floor. He needed to be with his brother and his girl. For some reason all the good news had taken a lot out of him. He wasn't as happy as he thought he would be. Maybe he had a bit of a guilty conscience. He wondered what college Grace would transfer to and what kind of lucky person would take his place with her. It was all the snow's fault he decided on the ride up in the elevator.

The elevator stopped on the 10th floor and he got out and went to the rec. room. Alan and Mary were not at the table where he had left them. He looked around the room. Everything was pretty much the same. The teenagers were no longer playing Ping-Pong and there was a couple in the darkest corner making out. *Lot more fun than Ping Pong*, he thought. He started looking for them. He did not want to be alone. He checked all the rooms on that floor: gym, steam room, pool, etc. Nothing. They were gone. He wondered if they had gone down to the apartment on the 5th floor. They could have taken the steps like he had. He went to the elevator and pushed the down button. While he was waiting for it he took one last look in the rec. room. Nothing. But there was something about that room which was bugging him.

He closed the door and went to wait for the elevator. It arrived at the same time he did. He got in, pushed the five button, and it started down. He tried to recall what he had seen that had bugged him. Then it struck him. On the floor, next to the couple in the dark corner who were making out, was a picnic basket. It looked like his mother's picnic basket.

He did not get off at the 5th floor. He pushed the button for the top floor.

This time when he went into the rec. room he walked right over to the couple. "Well well Miss Roverette," he said to Mary, "I can't let you out of my sight for a moment, can I? They write country songs about this kind of thing. With my own brother!"

"BUSTED?" said Mary.

"Dear John," said Alan.

"Yes. Dear John sung by Ferlin Husky and Jean Shepherd comes to mind."

"We were testing you," said Mary.

"Did I pass?"

"Failed miserably," said Mary.

"It won't be his first time," quipped little brother.

"You should have been angry. Maybe even thrown or kicked something," continued Mary. "How would you feel if it had been Grace taking advantage of your absence with your brother?"

Pete did not speak. He could not imagine anything so terrible. Grace would never do anything like that to him. She loved him. What would he do? He thought about it for a minute. He would probably just leave, like Grace was doing.

Mary kept looking at him. "I'm waiting for an answer."

Pete shrugged.

"You love her, don't you?" Mary pressed.

For a moment, nothing. Then a slight nod.

"I was afraid of that. I became suspicious when you let me ski with Eric the Terrible. I was starting to get the feeling that all wasn't as it should be. Then I became almost certain when you got so upset about the phone call from New Mexico. I asked your brother to help me perform this little experiment."

"No sacrifice too great for my favorite brother." Alan smiled weakly.

"When we get back to school, I'll stay in the background and let you attempt to win her back with that pathetic charm of yours."

(On one of the nights they had gone to a special little theater which showed old time movies. One of the shorts they had seen was a Laurel and Hardy.)

Looking at Mary, Pete attempted to imitate Oliver Hardy, "Well Stanley, this is another fine kettle of fish you've gotten me into. The aunt will probably attack me with some kind of weapon; the parrot will probably snap off my noble sniffer, and the father intends to shoot me. He, in fact, said he would put a load of buckshot where it would do me the most good. The fair damsel doesn't want to ever see me again, and she is not returning to school."

There was a short pause before Mary spoke. "Well Jackson, NO PROBLEM. You have to go back to the ranch and win out. Whip the Pa. Whip the Aunt. Whip the parrot. Charm the mom. Sweep the lady away in your arms. I have confidence in you. I know it can be done. I think I saw John Wayne do it in a movie."

"I know it can be done. Eddy Arnold did it on a record called The Tennessee Stud," Alan added.

"God Bless John Wayne," Mary quoted from something she had heard, and then to be fair she added, "and Eddie Arnold too." Alan was not sure she knew who Eddie Arnold was.

"John whipped some girl's aunt?" Pete asked unbelievingly.

"W-e-l-l, (Mary dragged it out) maybe there wasn't any aunt."

"I thought so, and I bet there wasn't any attack parrot named Nose Snipper either."

"Maybe not, but there were some vultures and a lot of Indians."

"Oh joy. I forgot about the lot of Indians. There is bunches of them. I could end up getting scalped or burned at the stake. They love and protect the Cousins family."

"There's no other way. You'll have to go back," Mary declared.

"All right. I'll go down there on Spring Break. That should give them time to cool off and for me to come up with a . . . strategy."

"You mean a lie," Alan volunteered

"**Tonight!**" declared Mary forcibly.

"TONIGHT? WHOA, NELLIE. He wasn't kidding when he said he'd shoot me where it would do the most good. I'm man enough and mature enough to give him some time to cool down and reconsider. Haven't you heard about 'Haste makes waste?"

Mary pointed at his mouth. "Stick a sock in it, Junior. All you have to do is put a pillow in your trousers."

"I hardly think that will provide ample protection against a shotgun, and besides, what makes you think that is where it will do the most good?"

"Don't tempt me, Jack." Pete started to speak but she cut him off. "Hush. **We** are practically packed. If we hurry, we can be on the road within the hour."

"I don't even have a horse. Eddie Arnold had a horse."

"Forget the Tennessee Stud, you **are** the COLORADO STUD."

"I don't want to be the Colorado Stud, it's too close to New Mexico. Why can't I be the California Stud or the Hawaiian Stud, or the Chinese . . . (He stopped mid-sentence.) **WE**, did you say **WE**? Are you coming?"

She nodded.

"Fine. You take care of whipping the aunt and protecting my" (she interrupted his soliloquy).

"I'll share the driving chores with you as far as Albuquerque, but then you are on your own, Colorado. Betty invited me to her New Year's Eve party when it looked like I would be flying back to Albuquerque and riding to school in her car."

"Are they going to have ice-cream and cake?" Alan asked. Nobody laughed.

"It seems to me like you're taking my loss rather lightly," Pete ventured.

Mary turned away so she would not have to look him in the eyes. "Jackson, you were starting to bore me. Now let's get cracking."

They were gone within 50 minutes, leaving Alan to make the excuses.

CHAPTER 23

Good-byes

The eight hour trip to Albuquerque was uneventful except for the fact they both let their guard down. No longer the gentle fencing of male and female trying to impress each other. Gone was the joking; left, were two friends who cared and wanted what was best for each other, and knew the time for parting was rapidly drawing near.

It was eleven thirty when the car reached the outskirts of the Duke City. Mary was driving; she had been there at the start of the Christmas vacation and had no trouble finding Betty's house which was only five minutes from the interstate. It was a large two story house with a fleet of cars in front of it. The house was lit up like a Christmas tree, and the noise (music) was deafening. Despite the gaiety of the scene, Pete felt depressed as Mary parked the car as close to Betty's house as she could get: almost across the street because she was able to squeeze the tiny car into a space too small for normal size cars. It fit in the space with 12 inches to spare.

"Jeeves, my luggage," she said as she leaped from the car and flipped him the keys. Her voice didn't sound quite natural. She ran on ahead.

Betty and Mary met Pete at the door. Betty pointed to a guest room at the top of the stairs and he started up followed by Mary. He pushed open the door and flipped on the light. Then he walked across the room and set the luggage next to the bed. He turned to face her for what he thought was the last time. The moment had come to say good-bye, but he could not find the words. Somehow, he felt he would never see her again if he said them. Down below they could hear the party goers counting off the last thirty seconds of the year.

Slowly, as though being drawn by a gentle but powerful magnet, they came together. He looked down into her upturned face.

"Happy New Year, Wayward," she said softly. They held on to each other long after the New Year's kiss. Longer than any of the couples at the party, knowing that when the embrace ended, so would something that had been very special to both of them.

Finally, it was Mary who took the initiative. She pushed back gently. He did not resist. "Well Jackson, I think you better trot along. You still have three hours and a lot of whipping to do."

He stepped back with a hurt look on his face. "Aren't you even going to walk me to the car . . . or get it out of where you managed to park it?"

"I think not. I am going to shower, change into my red dress, and then go down and liven up Betty's party. It is supposed to go until four, then some of us will head out to Denny's for an early breakfast. If you are still here trying to get your car out, you can come with us."

"God Bless," he managed to say through a husky voice. For some reason that reminded him of the way Red Skelton used to sign off his television show. "See you at school."

"Maybe not. **I** am thinking about joining the Peace Corps and **you** might not make it through the next 24 hours."

"Bye," he said, then turned and walked out of the room. When he reached the top of the stairs, he stopped and looked back. The door to the room was still open, and she was holding up her red dress examining it for wrinkles as though he had never existed. She looked up and saw him watching her, smiled, gave him a big wink, and then walked over and closed the door. "Time to change into Little Red," she said as the door was closing.

As he walked down the stairs, he saw a pair of eyes watching him. It was George, the campus lover. Pete wanted to go over and punch him in the face. He was still unhappy about the "eating out of my hand by Aztec comment. As he got closer he noticed a horrible looking deep scratch on George's face. He did not look quite as handsome as before. Also, his right hand was wrapped in gauze. Pete wondered if it was covering teeth marks. *Good for you, Mary,* he thought. Just then a pillow hit him in the back of the head. Mary was at the top of the stairs.

"You can put that where it will do the most good." Then she turned and went back into her room.

"She also bites," George said.

"Happy New Years, George." Pete patted him on the shoulder. He wondered if he had saved Mary from Eric or Eric from Mary.

When he got outside, he stopped under a street light and looked back and up at the window, hoping for a last look, wishing that she had at least cared enough to watch him go, but the room was already dark. He stood looking up at the window for about thirty seconds, brushed something from the corner of his eye, and gave a sad little wave of farewell. It was like the one Sandy had given him. *I bet Sandy was trying to tell me that she was going to marry Gene,* he smiled as he turned and walked slowly to his car. The car did not have power steering and it took him a while—almost five minutes--to wiggle it out of the parking space. *That girl could really parallel park,* he thought. *She must be a magician.*

The dark room hadn't been empty. A girl stood in the shadows and watched the lone figure through tear filled eyes. When he stopped and looked back, she felt her heart had stopped. For a full thirty seconds, she shared an agony equal to his. Was he going to march back into the house and carry her away? She held her breath.

His painful wave of farewell was returned in kind, and she touched her fingers to her lips and blew him a kiss, a kiss good bye that he could neither see nor feel. She smiled at his pitiful attempts to get out of the parking spot. *What a clown,* she thought, *they ought to revoke his license*. Finally sad eyes watched the little car manage to get free and disappear into the night. She continued watching long after it was out of sight.

Instead of going down to the party, she lay down on the bed and stared in the direction of the ceiling, reflecting on her life and life in general. It wasn't long before Betty came into the room looking for her and flicked on the light.

"Hey, thought you were coming down."

"I think not. I'm kind of tired and in a blue mood."

"What's wrong?"

"I'm thinking of taking a trimester off."

"What are you going to do?" Betty asked.

"I've been giving lots of thought to the Peace Corps."

"That's cool." Betty gave it the two minutes she thought such a life changing decision deserved then got back to a more important topic. "Are you sure you don't want to come down, several people asked about who the girl was that had come in right before midnight."

Mary smiled. "You know it's funny. A little while ago I told Pete I was going down to liven up your party. But it doesn't seem to need any help."

"If you can't help it, perhaps it can help you. That's one of the purposes of a party," Betty volunteered.

A smile crossed her face as though she were remembering something pleasant. "Is there going to be ice cream and cake?"

Betty looked stunned. "No."

"Then it can't be much of a party."

Mary told Betty about the phone call between Karen, who they both knew and didn't care for, and Pete's dad. Pete had heard it while lying in the sleeping bag and told Mary about it. Both girls laughed. The atmosphere in the room had brightened considerably, thanks to Pete's dad. She hoped he was having a good time at the Petroleum Club.

"You're right," said Mary grabbing her make-up, red dress and heading for the bathroom. "I'll be down in fifteen minutes." She paused and called out catching Betty at the top of the stairs getting ready to go down. "Betty, who were the boys that expressed interest in who I was?"

"How do you know they were boys?" Betty called back.

Mary just laughed. "They always are. If anyone asks my name, tell them it's Happy New Year." Mary had that wonderful ability to compartmentalize like doctors do. Doctors can't bring the problems of the hospital home to their families. Mary believed when one door closes another one opens. The Pete door was closed and a new one was just about to open all the way. In fact, it had been more than slightly ajar for quite a while in the form of the one Pete called the Mystery Man and she called James.

(I'd like to think if God had been watching, he would have smiled and declared, "Merry Mary is back. Go Girl. Happy New Year!")

CHAPTER 24

Hellos

Pete did not have any trouble staying awake. He didn't want anything to interfere with his thoughts, so he left the radio off. For the first half of the trip he thought about the girl he was leaving and during the second half he thought about the girl he was heading towards. Mary's influence seemed to grow weaker with every mile. It almost scared him when he realized how easy it might have been for her to prolong the break. He was grateful to her for making it so easy without being unkind. He imagined she was probably planning her next adventure already, and he was grateful to have been part of one of her past ones.

The last half of the trip was divided between thoughts of love for Grace and concern about surviving her unusual family. He knew he had to stand up to them, but gently, without anyone getting hurt. How was he going to manage it?

The trip had taken a little longer than usual because the police were out in force, and he even went through two traffic stops where the police were looking for drunk drivers. After all, it was New Year's Night and the men in blue were trying to save lives. At 4:00 a.m. he was on the hill overlooking the little valley. He turned off his headlights and coasted down the hill stopping in front of the stone wall surrounding the house. He decided the best plan would be to wait until they got up. He got out his Arctic sleeping bag and found a place behind the stone wall where he wouldn't be seen. He was sure he wouldn't sleep a wink. He was wrong. His forty winks turned out to be eighty.

The sun was well up the next morning when he was awakened by the sound of voices nearby. He unzipped the top of the sleeping bag and stuck his head out. He cautiously peered over the wall. Sarge and the aunt were standing next to his car. The mother was down on one knee letting the air out of his right rear tire.

"We owe him one," she told the others. "Actually we owe him two. These tires are much smaller than ours." She moved on to the left rear tire.

"What do you mean," asked Sarge.

"Remember that flat tire we had right before Christmas? The one Doc's service station could find no reason for?"

He nodded.

"Perry saw him let the air out of that tire."

"Revenge," cried Sarge.

"With interest," said the mother as she finished flattening the second tire.

"Compound Interest," cried the aunt as she depressed the valve stem on the right front tire.

Pete would have stood up and shouted like Uncle Fezziwig might have, "Stop you devils. Ply your tire destroying havoc on your own chitty chitty bang bangs, but he noticed Sarge was carrying a shotgun in his right hand, so he was as quiet as a little mouse. "Sure is a funny looking car," Sarge remarked looking at the little Nash Metropolitan.

"Looks like a pregnant roller-skate," said the aunt.

"It looks lopsided with three flat tires. Terrible tilt," said the mother.

"I'll fix that," declared the aunt. She depressed the valve stem on the remaining tire. There was about thirty seconds of a hissing sound and then the little car was perfectly level. "How do you think it looks now?" the mother asked.

"Derelict," the aunt replied. "We should be able to claim it according to the rules of salvage."

"Scuttled but balanced," said Sarge. "Too bad we can't get at the spare."

"Perhaps a better word would be abandoned," expressed the mother. "I wonder where he is." The tone of her voice sounded like a mother playing Peek a Boo or Hide and Seek with a little baby. She could just as well have been saying, "I wonder where Peter is hiding?" When that game is played, the adult usually knows where the baby is. That did not bode well for Pete.

At that moment, the cold morning air caused Pete to sneeze.

"What's that?" said Sarge.

"Polecat," said the aunt.

"Sounds dangerous," said Sarge.

"Shoot it. Shoot it," cried the aunt. "The sound came from behind that wall."

Sarge winked at the ladies and fired the gun straight up in the air. Almost immediately a stick with a little white hanky was raised and waved. Pete had come prepared to negotiate under a flag of truce.

"What's that?" said Sarge.

"Looks like a hanky on a stick," said the mom.

"Maybe it's a panky," said the aunt remembering her poem.

"Anybody need to blow their nose?" asked Sarge.

"Take no prisoners. Off with his nose. Give him another broadside," shouted Guess Who.

Pete looked up and around for an avenue of escape. He remembered a famous saying, "He who fights and runs away, lives to fight another day. . . or was it lives to run away another day." Another drawback to that saying was you had to fight first." He suddenly found himself staring into the face of Sarge who was looking over the wall.

"Howdy Boy. I thought I kind of discouraged you from coming back. You sure look silly with that pillow sticking out of your trousers." Something didn't jive. There was no pillow sticking out of his trousers and he was still 80% in the sleeping bag. Somehow they were aware of his secret plans made at a final strategy meeting with his two most trusted and loyal lieutenants: Alan and Mary. There must be a spy or a mole on his team.

"Sir, Mr. Cousins, there has been a wee misunderstanding, and I have driven 800 miles since yesterday afternoon to clear it up."

"No need for that, Son. Your YOUNG Aunt Mary phoned us from Denny's last night, actually early this morning and explained everything. We were just funning with you. Grace is in the house waiting. The rest of us are going across the street for an hour. Got to admire your gumption coming back unarmed. Too bad about the tires. There's an old bicycle pump in the garage. I'm not sure if it still works, but you're welcome to give it a try. That will give you some good exercise. In fact, it will give you a whole passel of good exercise. I wonder if the Canadian Royal Airforce knows about the bicycle pump exercise. It would definitely give you some of that air-oh-robics I keep hearing about." Pete couldn't tell if he was trying to be funny or was serious.

The mother came up to him. "We hoped Gracie wouldn't become serious about a young man so soon, but all we really want is her happiness. And I've never seen her happier, or sadder than she's been this Christmas. Happy when you're here, sad when you're not." She turned to follow her husband who was waiting for her by the store.

That just left Auntie. Why had the saner members of the family deserted him and left him to face her alone? He sighed. Might as well get it over with. She was now standing in front of the entrance to the house, blocking his path. While he had been talking to the others, she had moved to block the entrance to the house. She stood her ground, with her hands on her hips, glaring at him. Pete stuck out his hand, "Truce," he said in a voice higher than usual. He felt tingling in his shin and was prepared to block any moves towards his carotid artery or vagus nerve: favorite targets of hers.

She handed him a piece of paper she had clipped from one of those sporting papers they sell at the grocery store. It showed a long distance shot of Eric lying in the snow. He had a goofy looking grin on his face. The caption read, "SHIVERING HIS BOOBS."

"Never did like that bum," she said. Pete smiled and thought, *I hope Pinky got a good price for the picture.* The aunt continued, "I believe I said, when Malin attacked me, that my boobs were shivering, not 'Shiver Me Boobs.' It makes me sound like a blooming pirate." Pete was not about to contest her recollection although he knew what he had heard that night. He wasn't sure what he shouted on the ski hill. He was pretty nervous.

She stuck out her hand to shake his. Her grip was firm, but she did not squeeze. He felt something being slipped into the palm of his hand. He looked down; he was holding two objects and it was then he knew everything would be all right, at least for a few minutes. The aunt winked at him and then hurried after the other two with that unusual gait of hers. This time it reminded him of Chester on the Gun Smoke television show. Somehow it seemed friendlier than when she was Long John Silver, but he couldn't tell you how it was different.

He looked at his hand. There in his palm lay a cracker for Nose Snapper and the missing sprig of mistletoe.

When he reached Grace in the kitchen, they hugged, and held on to each other for what seemed like a happy eternity. She had been watching the proceedings through the kitchen window. Then he showed her the mistletoe and said, "Let's put this back where it belongs. She didn't speak but followed him to the living room with a smile on her face and a twinkle in her eyes, those sparkly eyes. She didn't have to help him put it back. She had already gone out and picked another sprig and put it up.

"Why you sneaky . . . " She stopped him with a kiss. They walked over to and under the new mistletoe. They tested it out. It worked as well as the old one, maybe better.

Pete took the cracker to Snapper who was in his cage in the aunt's room. Before he could give it to him, the parrot said,

SHIVER ME TIMBERS
AND BLOW ME DOWN
I GUESS HE'S BACK
PETER THE CLOWN

Pete withheld the treat and worked with the bird until it would say.

LOONY, LOONY
AS A BAT
AUNTIE, AUNTIE IS
GETTING FAT

(Historians claim this was the first volley in what became known in the family as the Thirty Years War.)

CHAPTER 25

Christmas Present: A.D. 2021.

I remember sitting in front of the fire on the couch with Grace that night back in '65 after the old folks (30 years younger than I am now) had gone to bed. I remember wondering what the future would bring. Turns out it was ten times better than I could possibly have imagined.

It seems like I blinked and 60 happy, adventurous, wonderful years, that I'd like to tell you about sometime, flew by at the speed of warp. Maybe not quite warp speed which the computer said is 299,792 kilometers per second (670,615,495.85 miles per hour.)

Did I ever mention that math is not . . . **NO!** No more lies. I have a confession to make. I . . . (In case you didn't notice) am not quite as good at math as I led you to believe. In fact I hate math. BOO MATH. YOUR MOTHER WEARS COMBAT BOOTS AND EATS LIVER. Ahh! That felt good.

Grace and I are even more in love now than we were then. If you ever come for a visit, watch where you are walking. You might just step on a great grandchild or two. Cousin's Valley is filling up with family. Thanks for letting me tell my tale.

MERRY MERRY MERRY CHRISTMAS ! ! !

(Not as clever, but I like it better.)

All for now, **Snively out.**

P.S. It's me again, Margaret. As long as we started this fairy tale with "Once upon a time," let's end with,

"AND THEY ALL LIVED HAPPILY EVER AFTER."

Peter Grant Wheatley was born in Miss Frelse's Maternity Home: 1939 in Bakersfield, California. He was not anxious to leave the womb, earning him the nickname "Peter the Procrastinator" and making an enemy of his mother during the mere eighteen hour struggle. After the doctor had had his shot at Pete's rear, she declared it was her turn. She had to be restrained by several nurses.

His writing career started in elementary school where he earned the attention of adults with an award winning essay: "The Reson Peter Wazn't in Scul Yeasterday." "He waz sick. Sined by my mom"

In Yucca Valley as an adult, Pete edited the popular "Desert Wind." His work has been featured in the international "American Square Dance Magazine." For over 30 years his column was the most popular in the state magazine: "The Southwest Dancer."

Mr. Wheatley's working career started at the age of six selling the Sunday Los Angeles Times from his wagon. In high school he worked after school as a cleanup person in a bakery, a caddy, and a fast food cook. He has also been a bus driver, truck driver, driller's assistant, rough neck, geophone placement engineer, cook, and crew on an LST, dormitory proctor, U.S. Marine Reserve, school teacher and Indian trader. Other than his inability to hold a job he is known for his sense of humor.

Mr. Wheatley has been in love with and married to the same woman for 56 years.

Things happen to Mr. Wheatley and he has the ability to write about them in a humorous manner. His wife thinks he's funny, so does his cousin Susie. So you should buy his book. They both can't be wrong.

www.ingramcontent.com/pod-product-compliance
Lightning Source LLC
Chambersburg PA
CBHW072017210726
48294CB00012B/729

* 9 7 8 1 7 3 7 6 7 9 5 0 9 *